Readers love the Enhanced World
series by VICTORIA SUE

Beneath This Mask

"Victoria Sue has quickly turned into one of my favorite authors. This series is filed with action, a very good plotline, lots of hurt/comfort and pretty sweet romances."

—Gay Book Reviews

Who We Truly Are

"It's no secret that I had a book crush on *Five Minutes Longer* and I can wholeheartedly fess up that the crush only intensified. I'm madly in love with Talon and Finn…"

—Dirty Books Obsession

"The deepening relationship between Talon and Finn is adorable to watch and the plot was gripping enough to keep me turning the pages."

—Sinfully: Gay Romance Book Reviews

"This was another great addition to the Enhanced universe."

—Scattered Thoughts and Rogue Words

By Victoria Sue

ENHANCED WORLD
Five Minutes Longer
Who We Truly Are
Beneath This Mask

Published by Dreamspinner Press
www.dreamspinnerpress.com

FIVE MINUTES LONGER

Victoria Sue

DREAMSPINNER
PRESS

Published by
DREAMSPINNER PRESS

5032 Capital Circle SW, Suite 2, PMB# 279,
Tallahassee, FL 32305-7886 USA
www.dreamspinnerpress.com

This is a work of fiction. Names, characters, places, and incidents either are the product of author imagination or are used fictitiously, and any resemblance to actual persons, living or dead, business establishments, events, or locales is entirely coincidental.

Five Minutes Longer
© 2016, 2019 Victoria Sue.

Cover Art
© 2016 AngstyG.
www.angstyg.com
Cover content is for illustrative purposes only and any person depicted on the cover is a model.

Mass Market Paperback ISBN: 978-1-64108-080-4
Trade Paperback ISBN: 978-1-63477-915-9
Digital ISBN: 978-1-63477-916-6
Library of Congress Control Number: 2016913762
Mass Market Paperback published April 2019
v. 1.0

Printed in the United States of America
∞
This paper meets the requirements of
ANSI/NISO Z39.48-1992 (Permanence of Paper).

To all the group members of Victoria's Secrets for your unfailing
support and sexy pictures!

"Heroes may not be braver than anyone else. They're just braver five minutes longer."

—Ronald Reagan

Chapter One

FINN MAYER was so excited, his hands shook as he tried to open the official-looking letter. This was what he'd always wanted. This was what he had dreamed about every day. This was why he did six long years at college while slogging his ass for minimum wage. *Regretfully we have to inform you....* The rest of the words blurred as his heart plummeted. He held the letter out so he didn't get tears on it and blinked furiously. It wasn't possible. He'd convinced himself it would be a conditional offer of acceptance, which was almost a guarantee. He'd just had to get through the poly, the personal interviews when they called him back, and references. What had happened? What had he done wrong?

The screen door slammed, and Finn stuffed the letter in his pocket quickly before his older brother, Deke, saw it.

Deke stood in the doorway, absently scratching his crotch. He was thirty-seven but looked a good ten years older. His balding sandy-brown hair was going gray at the temples. His double chin burst from his collared shirt, just like his beer gut spilled over his wrinkled suit pants. Finn was too distracted to even crinkle his nose in disgust.

The screen door slammed again, and his mom's voice piped up. "Finn, did you start supper?"

"Yeah, Finn," parroted Deke. "Did you start supper?"

Finn ducked his head and brushed past Deke into the kitchen. He knew Deke wouldn't get into anything with him while his mom was there. Not that he was convinced she would care if he did. "I just got in, Mom. I'll start now," Finn said woodenly. He needed to think, but he couldn't disappear until they were eating.

His mom narrowed her eyes and followed Finn with her gaze as he opened the cupboard and took out a bag of potatoes. "Finlay," she sighed disapprovingly. "You know your brother works incredibly long hours to support this family. It isn't much to ask for a little help around here while he's providing a roof over all our heads."

Finn didn't reply and quickly started peeling potatoes. The "incredibly long hours" were a joke. Deke took twice as long to do anything because he was too lazy. Finn knew he and his other two cronies—Albert Crawford, the bank manager, and Desmond Attiker, the local deputy sheriff—could always be found in Alma's Café on Main Street, having at least a two-hour lunch every day. It was pointless to argue anyway, and his mom knew full well half of Finn's wages also went to pay for the upkeep of the so-called roof. The only thing that had stopped him from moving out years ago was the fact that he wanted Deke not to make waves with his application when the FBI did the family interviews, and even the rent Deke charged him was cheaper than getting his own place.

What had he done wrong? He knew he wouldn't have failed the poly. His boring existence contained no secrets to keep. Well, maybe one, but Finn was so far in the closet, he was almost able to pretend it wasn't real.

And Deke would never think Finn had a chance of getting accepted into the FBI, so he wouldn't have bothered trying to sabotage it by giving him a crappy reference.

Finn fisted his hands, the peeler cutting into his palm. It was impossible. They'd made a mistake. Deke couldn't have been right, not now, not after all this time.

He'd laughed hysterically when Finn told him the reason he wasn't joining him at the insurance company Deke owned, as his mom and brother expected, was because he needed to attend college full-time. Deke had insisted college was a complete waste of time and Finn just needed to join the real world, but Finn could think of no greater torment than working with Deke for the rest of what he knew would be a miserable life. There were only so many online courses he could cope with for another reason, which meant he had to be physically present in class at least three days a week. The entry requirements for the FBI were tough, and as law and order, languages, and computer sciences were all impossible for him, the only other recommended professional field they would take from was accounting.

Finn had stacked shelves at the local Z-Mart since he was thirteen. Mr. Jacobson was blind, and Finn had discovered accidentally that he was being robbed by his CPA. Finn had been asked to copy some papers for Mr. Jacobson, and Finn, quick with numbers, had noticed the discrepancy straight away. Mr. Jacobson was eternally grateful, and Finn had taken over his bookkeeping when he was seventeen, then studied it at college. In return Mr. Jacobson had exaggerated his professional ability on his references.

Mr. Jacobson had recently accepted an offer for his two stores and had told Finn he was retiring. The thought that he had a prospective FBI agent stacking shelves for him for years had always tickled the old man, and he'd been happy to help.

Finn could feel the letter rustle in his pocket as he moved to fill the pan with water. *Ten years.* Ten years since his school had two agents come and talk to their class as part of a college awareness scheme. Cookeville High School, Iowa, had a really low rate of seniors going to college, and the new principal had tried to change all that by bringing in what he thought might be tempting job opportunities.

It worked with Finn. At fourteen he was hanging with an increasingly wilder crowd. His reading challenges just about turned him off school. He was lucky, really. Were it any major city, his crowd would already be doing drugs and probably stealing. It was only the lack of opportunity that kept his nose clean up to that day. He walked out of that lecture theater completely changed.

He wasn't stupid, though. His dad was the only one he told, and his dad promised not to mention it.

His dad. The knife trembled in his hands as he chopped the potatoes. Three years didn't dim the memory of him coming home one day to find his dad had finally lost his battle with depression and blown the back of his head off with his old service revolver. Another souvenir he got from the Vietnam War.

He never forgave his mom for her part in it. Every day she was out on one of her committees or seeing her friends. Her hair done, her nails carefully manicured. The cab fares because she never learned to drive and wasn't willing to. It never occurred to her to get a job, to help his dad when he needed a newer power chair. The endless arguments Finn could hear because his bedroom was right next to theirs. How, if his mom could drive, they could start going out together.

He never forgot the last one, though. When his dad quietly asked if the reason they never went out together anywhere was because she was ashamed of being seen with a cripple, as he bitterly called himself.

Finn had held his breath as he lay in his dark room, staring up at the ceiling, waiting for the denial that never came from his mom's lips. The next day he came home early from college because a tutor was sick and found his dad. The powder burns around his mouth, the blood, and brains all over the wall behind him.

Finn nearly threw the peeler in the sink. His mom got out the store-bought pie she purchased that morning. He laughed giddily. He could go rob a bank, take drugs, *have sex....*

Tears sprung to his eyes, and he blinked rapidly so his mom wouldn't notice. No one knew he was gay.

No one. Not the FBI because he'd read on an inter-
net forum that, while they didn't discriminate, it could
sometimes be the difference between being accepted
or not. Apparently it was something guys could be
blackmailed over. So he played the game. Took a girl
to prom. Had occasional college dates. Nothing serious. No one knew he'd never slept with a guy. No one
knew he'd never actually had sex with a girl either.
He had plenty of jerking-off material in his bedroom
and made sure he had enough copies of female tits in
case Deke ever came snooping. His favorites he could
pass off as sports magazines. He never even dared get
a porn subscription. He was pathetic.

Finn dried his hands and mumbled to his mom
about not being hungry. He was going to start right now.
He was going to get a decent job, move to a big city, and
subscribe to the most expensive porn site he could find.

"Des Attiker told me he had one of those weirdos
in lockup today," Deke said as he passed.

His mom made a sympathetic noise.

"Should have 'em put down at birth." Deke took
a swig out of the beer bottle he was holding. "There's
actually some talk about them being allowed in law
enforcement."

His mom followed Deke into the lounge. "What,
actually to become cops, you mean?"

"Yeah, Des says they're lazy bastards and he'll
never accept one working for him."

Finn tried to tune him out. Deke was like 50 percent of the human population: completely against the
enhanced humans being trusted to do any sort of government work whatsoever. Finn never usually rose to
anything he said, but keeping the peace didn't matter

anymore. He didn't need to shut up and take whatever crap came out of Deke's mouth. Finn was going to shoot him down when his mom spoke up and silenced him.

"You remember Adam, Finlay? If you ask me, his poor mother should have disowned him years ago for all the trouble he brought their poor family." His mom clucked unsympathetically.

Finn's feet froze just as he was about to disappear into his room. "Adam? Adam Mackenzie?" Finn added for clarification, but he knew it wasn't necessary. He knew exactly who his mom meant.

Finn and Adam had been best friends all through elementary school. They pored over the old car magazines Adam's brother got. They played on the same soccer team. Finn found math easy and helped Adam, and Adam explained his English questions to Finn when the words never seemed to be in the right order on the page. He also read to Finn when Finn struggled to do it himself.

Then he went to Adam's house one morning, as he always did to catch the bus together, and heard hysterical screaming before he was halfway up the path. Adam's big sister opened the door, crying, and said Adam was sick and wouldn't be going to school that day. Finn bit his lip in worry. It sounded like something awful was happening inside, and he wanted to make sure Adam was okay. But at eleven years old, there wasn't much he could do, so he spent a miserable day at school and then rushed back to Adam's as soon as he jumped off the school bus and his feet hit the pavement.

Finn arrived to find an ambulance and two black cars parked outside. His heart nearly bounced out of his chest, and he dropped his schoolbag and ran down the path just as the door opened.

Finn screeched to a halt and stared in horror as Adam was led outside with his hands tied. Special zip ties, the sort Finn knew were used on the enhanced because some of them could do clever things with locks and metal. He knew that because Deke's friend Des had just gotten a job at the sheriff's office and told him how they were taught to use them on the vermin, which Deke had thought funny. Finn didn't understand then who Deke meant by vermin, but everything was crystal clear now, and he spent the next thirteen years remembering that moment.

Adam was crying hysterically and pulling against the two cops leading him away. He was in such a state that he never even saw Finn, and after the cops unsuccessfully tried to make Adam walk, one of them just picked him up, and Finn saw his face and finally understood.

The small jagged mark under his left eye was livid on his skin. That was when Finn started crying as well, because he knew Adam would never be back at school and he'd just lost his best friend.

Finn never saw Adam again. Adam's family moved away shortly after. Finn's mom said they couldn't deal with the stigma, the shame.

"I heard he might get locked up for good, finally. New York. They'll throw away the key. Good riddance, I say."

Finn rounded on his mom in fury. "Good riddance? He was a child when they took him away. Eleven fucking years old and sent to live in a prison for doing nothing wrong other than waking up one

morning with a mark on his face. How would you feel
if it had been Deke or me? Would you have called the
cops on one of us?" It wasn't compulsory. The police only ever got involved if the child's abilities were
deemed dangerous and the parents couldn't cope.

His mom started spluttering about Adam turning
out no good, in and out of prison for petty crimes after
he aged out of the foster system, and how his mom
was a saint for still going to visit him.

The horror of his mom's words finally sank in.
"You told me you didn't know where they'd moved to.
How do you know his mom is so upset?" Finn pressed
his lips together in anger as his mom reddened slightly. "You knew," he accused. "All these years you've
known where they lived."

He could have gone. Maybe found out where
Adam was. Told his best friend a small scar made absolutely no difference to him. That he was important
to Finn, even if he was no longer important to anyone
else.

"How could you? All those years I begged you
to try to find out." Finn swallowed the bitter taste of
betrayal.

"You don't want to go near any of their sort,"
Deke said, unimpressed and uncaring. "They might
infect you, give you something."

"Infect me?" Finn repeated incredulously. "It's a
genetic condition, not a fucking disease," he shouted.
"You really are as fucking stupid as you look."

Deke opened his mouth, but his mom beat him to
it. "Finlay Mayer, I won't have such disgusting language in this house. While your brother is providing a

roof over your head out of the goodness of his heart, you will show him proper respect."

Finn laughed shortly. That was it. The only upside of the fuckup his life had become. He could leave. He was finally free. He didn't have to worry about any interviews anymore or swallow Deke's daily insults and goading. He didn't even bother to respond to his mom. He just walked toward his room to pack his stuff.

He could feel his phone vibrating in his pocket as he headed to his room and absently answered it. He wasn't really listening to the man on the other end of the call; he was too busy seeing Adam's face in the same nightmare he'd had for thirteen long years.

FINN WAS exhausted. Two days later he was still reeling from the telephone call that threw all his plans for porn sites out the window. Apparently they had made a *mistake*, and should he want to discuss a possible future with the FBI, he should be present at this meeting. He also should tell no one except his next of kin, which was all kinds of weird. He had absolutely no fucking idea why the hell he was currently standing outside the FBI field offices in Tampa, Florida. Since when did new FBI recruits get trained in field offices?

He even challenged the agent he spoke to on the phone, not trusting Deke to have found out and somehow set the whole thing up as an elaborate joke. Agent Gregory, Assistant Special Agent in Charge, as he had introduced himself, just sounded amused and told him to call back on the telephone number he was sending to his phone. After Finn was directed back to the same agent after calling a very official-sounding main switchboard, Finn's apologies were cut off with another laugh, and he was told being cautious was a good attribute to have in a trainee.

His second connecting flight from Des Moines was grounded due to "technical difficulties," which meant he was on standby for over eleven hours because it was spring break, and they wanted him to go to one of the busiest tourist areas in the entire Western Hemisphere.

He left home before either his mom or brother woke up and decided to leave a note just saying he was going to do some traveling. He wouldn't give either of them a chance to jinx this until he found out exactly what *this* was.

Which was why, after over twenty-four hours, he was standing there, sweating in what felt like hundred-degree heat in a very rumpled suit and tie. It was his only suit, the one he got for his dad's funeral. He had no idea what to wear, but the agents he met all through the interview process were dressed in suits, so he copied them.

Finn stared at the huge building in front of him. It looked new. At least four stories high and next to one of the many Florida lakes. The access from the road was dominated by a big gatehouse with guards stopping every vehicle that tried to enter. Finn heaved his bag, which hadn't seemed that heavy yesterday when he started carrying it, but now felt like there was an elephant nesting in there. He blew a breath out and wished he hadn't finished his last bottle of water in the cab. He walked toward the guard, who carried a very respectable-looking MP5 slung over one shoulder. He put his bag down and introduced himself and tried to explain why he was there.

Finn was completely convinced he sounded more and more suspicious until he mentioned Agent Gregory's name and the guard checked the list of expected visitors and immediately waved him forward. Another guy in a suit, looking a lot cooler than Finn, met him at the door.

"Hi, I'm Agent Fielding—Drew Fielding." He seemed pleasant, with reddish brown hair and brown eyes. Clean-shaven and "buttoned up," as his brother would have said—not always a compliment, coming from Deke. Finn grimaced at his sweaty palms and resisted the urge to wipe his hand down the front of his pants before they shook. Agent Fielding didn't seem to notice anything, though, and led Finn through a door past a large reception desk. He waved at a couple of doors as they went past. "I'll give you the proper tour after you've spoken to Agent Gregory."

And eight hours sleep, a shower, and a gallon of water.

Finn licked his dry lips. He debated whether to ask why he was here and not at Quantico, then thought discretion might be in order and he should wait until he saw A-SAC Gregory. Agent Fielding took a turn to the right and started up some steps—some very narrow back stairs he thought no visitors were ever likely to see. In fact, Finn was convinced they were the step version of the service elevator. It was getting weirder and weirder, and he was getting hotter and hotter, despite considering himself physically fit and despite the air blasting out. At least there was no way he was going to take his jacket off, even if it was appropriate. His shirt would be soaked through.

Agent Fielding stopped at what seemed to be the fourth floor, and they entered a plain unmarked door into a small, unmanned reception area. Just a few chairs and a vending machine graced the lobby. Agent Fielding waved toward a chair. "Take a seat."

Finn swallowed and looked at the vending machine. "Do you mind?"

Agent Fielding followed his gaze. "Sure, sorry. I should have asked."

Finn put his hand in his pocket for some change, but Agent Fielding continued. "It's free. It's just a good way of keeping it cold." He smiled and disappeared through another door.

Finn eagerly pressed the button on the machine, and it dropped a bottle of water. He'd gotten the cap unscrewed before he sat, and half the contents drunk before he stretched his legs out. He could feel the water cooling his throat. He stared around him. Not what he imagined a field office would look like. He expected it to be busier somehow. If it weren't for the official phone call he'd made, he would still suspect this was all an elaborate hoax. Finn finished his water and looked again at the closed door Agent Fielding had disappeared through.

He sighed heavily and rubbed a hand over his tired eyes. He was never able to sleep when he was traveling. Not that he'd done much except by car. He'd flown more in the last twenty-four hours than he had in his life. Finn stifled a yawn and got to his feet stiffly. If he wasn't careful, he'd be asleep.

"And what use do you think he's going to be?"

Finn turned and faced the closed door the angry voice could be heard from. Finn's heart sank. He hoped to God they weren't talking about him. A quieter voice he couldn't make out responded briefly. It sounded like a third voice joined in.

Finn was wondering whether to risk sitting down again when the door burst open and Agent Fielding stormed out. Without so much as a look in Finn's direction, he disappeared through the door to the stairs they had come up. Finn swallowed. Now what had he done?

An older man appeared at the doorway. Finn would put him in his fifties, at a guess. About the same height as his own five foot ten. Quite a stocky build, brown eyes, hair graying at the temples. The same ubiquitous suit. He put out a hand to Finn and flashed a tight smile. "Mr. Mayer? Good to meet you, and I'm sorry you have had such a trying journey. Agent Gregory."

Finn stepped forward in relief and shook Agent Gregory's hand firmly. "Pleased to meet you, sir," Finn responded.

Gregory waved Finn in front of him. "Come in, take a seat. There's someone I want you to meet."

Finn walked in, sat, and looked up, a pleasant smile fixed on his face. Two seconds later the smile went, and Finn could barely hear Gregory's words over the pounding of his heart.

A man lounged in the corner of the room. Finn wasn't sure exactly if "man" described the giant he faced. Certainly the office chair, substantial enough for Finn, looked like dollhouse furniture because of the guy who was sitting on it. Pale blond hair was tied back in a leather thong at his nape. He had on a suit, but this one was obviously tailor-made. No suit off the rack would fit the most powerful shoulders Finn had ever seen, and that's when, as far as Finn was concerned, the shit really hit the fan. He couldn't even swallow. He never registered the piercing blue eyes that stared in challenge. He barely noticed the stubble surrounding his jaw or the tightly pressed full lips.

All he'd heard about enhanced humans came flooding back into his mind. The height. The build. The—as if to confirm Finn's thoughts, the man turned to his right—*birthmark*. The small mark under his eye that looked like a lightning bolt.

He fixed his blue eyes on Finn, and Finn felt completely pinned. His arms grew heavy. His legs felt like lead. He strained to inflate his chest to pull oxygen in. Sweat broke out on Finn's brow; he couldn't breathe.

"That's enough, Talon. Dammit," Gregory cursed, and in an instant, the weight crushing him lifted, and Finn took a gasp of oxygen. Then another.

"You see?" The huge man—Talon—lurched to his feet, and Finn couldn't help but wince.

"And how is that test at all fair?" Gregory spluttered. "No regular human can withstand you—you know that."

Finn had had enough. He got shakily to his feet. "Can someone tell me just what the hell is going on?" he demanded.

"You just proved what I have been saying for the last thirty minutes," Talon said in disgust. "That enhanced don't partner with regulars."

Finn looked in astonishment at Gregory.

Gregory sighed. "Finlay Mayer—" He gestured over to Talon. "—meet Talon Valdez. Your new partner."

Finn gazed in horror at Talon. Everything he had spent the last ten years working for had just come crashing down around his ears.

Chapter Two

"JUST WHAT exactly did you think was going to happen here?" Talon lifted a sardonic eyebrow.

"Talon," Gregory said in a warning voice.

"No." Talon looked Finn up and down. "He deserves to know why he's here."

Gregory subsided, and Finn looked back at Talon.

"Why am I here? Why am I here instead of Quantico?"

"Because you're too dumb for Quantico," Talon snapped.

"W-What?" Finn turned to Gregory. He could feel the angry, embarrassed flush work up his face.

Talon sneered. "You were a B-average student, and your physical merits barely made up for it. Your references were mediocre at best." He leaned over Finn threateningly. "The hiring rate in the FBI is over sixty-eight to one. In what alternate universe did you honestly think you would get in the FBI?"

Finn leaned back and stared up at Talon, deliberately fixing a bored look on his face. "Well… you should know."

Finn honestly thought the guy was going to explode.

"Sit down," Gregory barked. "Talon, that's an order."

Talon whirled around, but Finn had had enough. "If you've finished with me?" He left off the honorific *sir*. "I realize there's obviously been a mistake." He bent and picked up his bag. "I'll be out of your way."

"Sit down, dammit," Gregory fumed.

Talon stalked to the door. "You know where to find me." He turned and gave Finn another pitying look and said, "I don't do babysitting. When you find a real agent, give me a call."

Finn's jaw dropped as Talon swept out.

"I'm sorry. Finn, is it?" Gregory asked quietly.

Finn acknowledged his nickname mutely.

"Sit, please. That wasn't how I wanted you to find out our plans. I'm afraid Talon has a very short temper."

"I didn't know enhanced humans had started working for the FBI," Finn said, curiosity getting the better of him and his temper dissipating.

Gregory sighed. "Not officially. Not yet. The pilot scheme is underway to introduce them in gradually, and Talon's training has been conducted away from the regular channels because of it. They are to be teamed with regular humans, as we both know there are some places enhanced humans are not only unwelcome, but actually barred."

Finn nodded. The government made it compulsory that they were allowed in all public and government-owned areas. Unfortunately private businesses and homeowners were still under no such obligation. Finn supposed it wasn't fair. He just hadn't really thought about it. "But surely the FBI would be allowed anywhere?"

"Ever heard of the phrase 'hearts and minds'?" Gregory sighed.

So that's it, thought Finn. They wanted to persuade the public, not force them.

"I suppose he had a fair point," Finn acknowledged. He'd just scraped by his courses. He struggled with the tests, and despite the hours of work he put in, he'd never managed better than a B average.

To be honest he had a feeling his English teacher maintained his B because he was diligent in everything—never a late mark, never a missed assignment. Diligent, and possibly she even took pity on him a little. She even urged him to get tested for dyslexia, which completely freaked him out and had him begging her not to write that in his record anywhere. He knew the FBI had no official policy that would discriminate against anyone, but Talon was right. Even in the years immediately after 9/11, they only hired just over two thousand new agents out of a hundred and fifty thousand applicants. He was convinced a diagnosis of dyslexia would have put paid to his dreams in the FBI straightaway, even if his coping mechanisms usually only failed now when he was really tired or stressed. They simply had too many perfect candidates to take a chance on him.

Finn sighed. "So what am I doing here?"

Gregory leaned back. "I will overlook your tone because I am aware that you have gone a long time without sleep and you have had a confusing two days."

Finn swallowed his pride. "My apologies, sir."

Gregory nodded in acknowledgment. "Succinctly, Talon was in a lot of ways correct. Your B average would never normally get you into Quantico, and while you had glowing reports from your tutors despite your grades, your brother, in particular, was less than complimentary."

Finn fumed. He knew it. Why the hell the FBI had to insist on family references was completely beyond him.

"He went as far as to indicate that you were lazy and unsuited in his opinion for a job in law enforcement of any kind."

Finn fisted his hands. He would kill him.

"However, you should know that we received a letter—or rather, one of our agents who wishes to remain nameless received a letter." Gregory's face softened. "From your father."

"W-What?" Finn exclaimed. Then he hurriedly tagged on, "Sir."

"Three years ago. I believe it was written the day before his death. The agent in question had been instructed to keep it should you apply for the FBI."

Finn swallowed and stared unseeing at the floor. That was the last time they spoke about his dream of becoming an agent—the last time they'd spoken at all.

"The agent your father wrote to served with him in Vietnam. Normally that sort of thing won't make any difference at all, and your dad actually didn't ask for any special favors. He just said to disregard any reference your brother made concerning his opinions on your suitability." Gregory leaned forward and laid his forearms on the desk.

"But even if you decided to give me a chance and ignore what my brother said, that still doesn't explain why I'm here and not at Quantico," Finn argued.

"Because we want to keep this quiet for the time being. Your physical training will take place both in the gym downstairs, which will be closed for your private use, and in various locations around the city. Normal agent training is nearly eight hundred intense hours of academics, firearms, case studies, and operational skills. Skills that include everything from behavioral science to safe-driving techniques."

Finn knew all that. He'd read and memorized every bit of every training document he was able to get his hands on.

"You, however, will miss all that," Gregory said with a hint of disbelief. "Your training will be completely private and will last only four weeks. You will then take part in some joint operations with experienced agents for a period of three to four months. If you prove that the partnership—hell, the whole idea, even—is worth the gamble, then a whole new unit will be set up and staffed with equal members of regular and enhanced, and you will then receive your full FBI training." Gregory paused. "But we have a lot of people to convince before then."

Finn shook his head. He was beyond tired and not completely sure he understood everything being said to him. "So, sir, what you're saying is, we're basically guinea pigs?"

Gregory laughed shortly. "Essentially, yes."

"That still doesn't explain why you wanted me. Setting aside the request to ignore the bad reference, why, if this is so important, do you not want someone already trained?"

"Because Talon has had three partners already trained. The longest any of them lasted was six days," Gregory said dryly. "Our final option is getting someone he can train himself. However, we are so far behind schedule that you are the last chance to make this work. I should also warn you that he is a complete bastard to work with and has a chip on his shoulder the size of the Empire State Building."

Finn chewed his lip. It had been a disaster since he walked into the office. Talon had taken nearly an instant dislike to him.

"What are you thinking?" Gregory asked.

"Respectfully, sir? That I'm completely screwed. Talon made it clear he's not interested in working with a *B average*." Finn used his fingers as quotation marks.

"And how do you feel?"

"That I have a hell of a lot to prove, sir." Finn looked up and noticed Agent Gregory's smile.

Agent Gregory laughed. "Forgive me. I was reacting to you not saying your biggest problem would be in working with an enhanced."

Finn shrugged. "It makes no difference to me, sir. I just want a fair shot." He knew the papers were full of whatever dirty laundry they could get, but it never bothered him.

"I will try to keep it quiet for as long as I can, but even my superiors are agreed we won't be able to keep this under wraps once you are out in the public eye."

Finn thought furiously. "Sir, even wanting someone untrained still doesn't explain your willingness to take a chance on me."

Gregory's lips thinned. "We wanted someone who would be eager to meet the challenges of the irregular entry system."

Finn parted his lips soundlessly, and his heart thudded. They wanted someone who wouldn't ask questions. They wanted someone who was so desperate, they would accept everything. They wanted someone who knew this was his only chance.

He stared back, trying to communicate silently his understanding to something he knew Gregory would never publicly admit to.

"Am I allowed to know Talon's specialty?" Finn asked.

All the enhanced were different. They all had different abilities, and some had more than one. Abilities were discovered as they transformed—one child had burned his house to the ground in complete panic after waking up with the mark. Others didn't come to light until years after. Some of the abilities just weren't something any adolescent would normally do, and there still weren't that many of them. In fact, at one point, one of the papers had suggested there were barely enough of them countrywide to fill a maximum security prison. It had been a veiled suggestion as well as a comment. That much Finn knew.

"Talon demonstrated his ability for you," Gregory said, seeming relieved at Finn's acceptance. "I think I'll let him discuss it with you further." He stood and offered his hand. "Welcome to the FBI, Finn."

Finn shook his hand and marveled at Agent Gregory's informality. Whatever he'd just agreed to was certainly different. He picked up his bag. Now where the hell did he go?

Gregory opened a drawer in his desk and took out a brown envelope. "This contains your car keys, directions both to where you are staying and back here, and also directions to our outside training facility. And a cell phone that you will use exclusively during your training, programmed with all the numbers you will need. Unfortunately your delayed flight means you and Talon will both be here at noon tomorrow for initial assessments. You have medicals to pass first, and a physical test, and the usual ton of paperwork."

Finn sighed silently. He thought he'd done all that.

"Go out of the door at the side of the vending machine and you'll be facing an elevator. Take it to the lower floor, where you will find the parking lot to your right. Please don't discuss anything we have talked about with anyone. Don't forget you had to sign a nondisclosure agreement at your last interview."

Finn gave an exhausted smile and carried the envelope and his bag to the elevator. When the doors opened, he walked in, pressed the bottom button, and dropped his bag with a thud. He'd never been so tired in his life. He hoped like hell the hotel or whatever wasn't far. He wasn't even sure he should be driving. He opened the envelope and took out some keys. They had an alarm fob on them, so he supposed he'd just have to press it to see which car was his.

The elevator dinged, and Finn picked his bag up, took a thankful step out into the parking garage, and looked up at a shout.

Shit.

Six big guys all wearing ski masks were beating the crap out of someone with baseball bats. The man lay on the floor, curled in a fetal position. For a second Finn froze, not believing what he was seeing, and then the guy on the ground moved, and Finn stumbled in shock.

It was Talon.

"Hey!" Finn shouted. Not for one moment did he think it wasn't a good idea until they all turned at his shout. Then he gulped. Talon was huge, and they had just taken him down. What the hell were they going to do to him? For a moment he contemplated taking a step back before the elevator doors shut behind him. They were too far away to get to him in time. He could go get reinforcements or something.

Then indignation took over. They were beating his supposed new partner, and he wasn't going to walk out on him.

"I'm Agent Mayer," Finn shouted. "You are all on camera. The parking garage will be surrounded by agents within seconds, and they"—he eyed the closest man in disgust—"won't be carrying baseball bats." Shit, he didn't even have a gun, but the implication and the authority in his voice were clear.

The first man laughed but turned to the others.

The smallest one at the back grunted. "Let's get out of here."

The first one turned back to Talon and gave him a vicious kick in the ribs. "We don't want your sort here," he spat and ran out after the others.

Finn had a split second of satisfaction, and then he heard Talon groan quietly on the floor. "Talon," Finn said, dropping to his knees. Talon was blinking groggily, so Finn put a hand on his arm. "Stay still. I'm going to get an ambulance." He fished his cell phone out of his pocket and looked up. Did they even have cameras? Surely they did. Maybe the ambulance was already on its way.

"No." Talon's voice came out croaky. "You can't call anyone."

Finn bit his lip. "They have to treat you," he said tactfully in case that was what Talon was worried about. He knew all hospitals now had to accept enhanced as patients.

"No. Just help me get up."

Finn sighed and tried to plant his legs firmly as Talon heaved himself up, almost using Finn as a crutch. He gasped as Talon threw an arm around his neck. He weighed a ton.

"Keys are in my pocket."

Finn shoved his hand awkwardly into Talon's pants pocket and blinked as his fingers brushed something else. Fuck, the man was huge everywhere.

"Don't get any fucking ideas," Talon growled.

And straight, thought Finn in resignation. Not that he was interested in his ungrateful ass. The size of him just briefly distracted him, was all.

"You should be so lucky," Finn snapped in annoyance, and his heart gave a jolt as Talon laughed abruptly. He'd been beaten up by six men with baseball bats, could hardly walk, must be in unimaginable pain, and he'd just laughed. *He shut up quickly, though*, thought Finn with some satisfaction. *It must hurt to laugh.* Not that he deserved the mess someone had made of him, but still.

Finn pointed the key fob desperately in the general direction of all the cars and hoped. He didn't know how far he could actually get with Talon. Finn wasn't completely sure he could even make it to the line of cars. He praised every god he'd ever heard of when he saw the lights of a truck just a few steps away turn on, and he half carried, half dragged Talon toward it. He barely registered the size of it until he got Talon leaned up against it. "You're gonna have to get in," he gasped. There was no way he was going to get him up there. Finn would need a stepladder.

He opened the door, and Talon gave the truck and Finn a bleak look, and with another grunt, he put his boot on the wheel and pulled himself in. Finn slammed the door in annoyance and ran back for his bag. He walked around to the driver's side and looked in desperation at the height of the wheel, then opened the door. He looked around, noticed a small cutout step on the side of the truck, awkwardly stuck the toe of his shoe in there, and reached up to grab the seat that was higher than his waist.

His eyes darted upward when instead of the edge of the seat, his hand met warm skin. Talon leaned over, and without any effort, soon had Finn inside.

"You're gonna have to tell me where we're going," Finn said as he started the truck.

Talon barely opened a swollen eye and pressed two buttons on the dashboard. "GPS. When you get to the gates, press the bottom one."

Finn stared at him. Blood was seeping from the cut above his right eye, and his left eye was completely closed. Finn was convinced at least one of his cheekbones was broken, and Talon poked masochistically at his split lip. Finn lowered his gaze and cataloged the rest of him. Talon had a patch of blood on his left sleeve. He was favoring his right arm, and to be completely honest, Finn thought he should get it X-rayed. He couldn't see the rest of him because he was still in his suit.

Finn started the truck in resignation.

TALON STARED down at the sleeping young man. He was too damn good-looking for his own good, for starters. He'd noticed his dark green eyes last night when he first looked at him in Tony Gregory's office. That was before they widened with shock when he saw Talon's mark. He didn't want to wait around to see the look of shock turn to one of disgust—or worse, pity.

He wasn't sure which was harder growing up: the looks of fear on people's faces or the do-gooders who decided he was mentally subnormal and always talked really slowly and carefully to him.

Finn moaned and moved restlessly. Talon stood there, leaning casually against his spare bedroom door, sipping his coffee. The other full mug of coffee sat steaming next to the bed. Finn's nostrils had flared a couple of seconds ago as the coffee aroma settled in the room. Talon took another sip and winced as the hot liquid stung his cut lip. He flexed his sore arm carefully, thankful it was only Finn who was having physical tests today and not him.

At some point around 5:00 a.m., when Talon woke to find Finn completely passed out in the chair next to the bed, he had stared in astonishment. Not only had Finn interrupted his beating without taking one look and getting back in the elevator, but he'd also challenged six armed men. Either he was one of the bravest men Talon had ever met, or he was incredibly stupid. Talon was leaning toward the incredibly stupid.

Gregory told him that Finn had been awake for nearly thirty-six hours by the time he arrived in Tampa, but the guy had absolutely no situational awareness. He never stirred once when Talon lifted him out of the chair and tucked him into his spare bed. Talon would have to get him cured of that straightaway.

Talon smiled sardonically to himself. At around the same time as he carried Finn to bed, he'd decided Finn deserved a fair shot, and he wasn't sure who would be the most surprised when Finn woke and he told him that.

A fair shot at getting into Quantico, he hurriedly corrected himself. He still hadn't changed his mind about working with regular humans.

Talon wiped the smile off his face as Finn stirred and blinked sleepily. "Coffee's there," he said mildly, somewhat satisfied as Finn started a little and opened his eyes wider to look at him. The green in his eyes was as dark as he remembered.

Finn stared at him, clearly not knowing what to say, reached for the coffee, and then took a sip without looking. "Eww," he said, looking at his cup as if Talon had given him dishwater or something.

"Don't like coffee?" Talon drawled, not really giving a rat's ass.

"Have you got any cream or sugar?" Finn asked hesitantly.

"No," Talon said shortly, trying not to roll his eyes. He waved to the door next to the window. "Shower's in there. I got your bag from the truck. We leave in thirty minutes."

Finn blinked again and stared at Talon. "Are you all right?" he blurted.

Talon paused just as he was pushing himself off the wall to go back to the kitchen. The question threw him. "I'll live," he answered and shut the door behind him as he walked out, probably a little harder than he intended.

He walked into his small kitchen and drained his coffee. He'd already called Gregory, and they found the cameras in the parking garage had been tampered with, which meant inside access. Gregory was uncomfortable, but it was clear he thought what Talon already knew. The guys who beat him up were cops. Cops or agents. The field office shared the same secured parking as the local sheriff, and a lot of them were friends. He wasn't surprised. He'd been exposed to that sort of hate and discrimination since he was twelve. It shouldn't shock him anymore.

Gregory didn't even bother asking if Talon was going for treatment somewhere. He knew better. His rapid healing ability was one of the few benefits of being an enhanced. His bones could still break, and it wasn't some amazing shit that could heal in a few hours or anything. He'd broken his tibia once and his arm twice, maybe a few ribs when he was sparring with Vance, another enhanced. Those bones completely healed in less than three weeks, and the injuries he got last night would barely put a dent in his stride.

He wasn't stupid, though. He knew it would have gotten a lot worse if Finn hadn't intervened. Talon was angrier at himself than he was at the goons with the bats. He'd been careless. He was furious at the FBI for foisting off some substandard schoolboy on him and wasn't concentrating when he stepped out of the elevator. The first blow was to the back of the head, and that was the only reason they got the drop on him.

He heard the shower stop and grunted. Finn, at least, took his instructions to hurry up seriously.

Five minutes later Finn appeared in the kitchen wearing nothing but a pair of boxer shorts and his towel draped over his shoulders. He was carrying his rumpled suit jacket. "Have you got anything I can clean this with?"

Talon blinked and had to unglue his tongue from the roof of his mouth. He stared at Finn's chest. Solid muscles but slim. The guy looked in reasonably good shape. *Fuck.* His life would get immensely more complicated if he was attracted to Finn. Talon shifted his weight from one foot to the other and took another gulp of his second cup. He forced himself to look at the jacket. He could see the blood stains—his blood—on the sleeve.

Finn looked up at him, obviously wondering if he was being ignored. An angry flush crept up his neck. "Never mind," he said in resignation and turned to go.

Talon reached out and caught his shoulder. Finn stiffened, and Talon dropped his hand. "We'll drop it off to get cleaned on the way in. It's Saturday. Wear jeans."

Finn turned around suspiciously and eyed Talon's own denim. Then he shrugged.

They both heard Finn's stomach rumble in the quiet kitchen, and Talon watched in fascination as Finn's face turned pink. "We'll get some breakfast on the way," he said as Finn disappeared back into the bedroom.

Talon swore again to himself. Finn was greener than his yard. He hadn't shown any sense thinking he could take six assailants on. A stranger just touched his shoulder, and he didn't object. He let someone carry him to bed without waking up, and he blushed. Real, honest-to-God blushed. Like some teenage girl. He also didn't come up to Talon's shoulder, and the sight of him walking around in his boxers made Talon want to pick him up and take him back to bed, or the shower, or any available surface that was convenient to bend him over.

Talon was so screwed.

Chapter Three

FINN WAS such a complete dork. Talon had looked the most receptive since they'd met, so when Finn had the chance to ask all sorts of cool questions about the team, what did he have to go and say? He asked him about fucking laundry. Finn threw his jacket on the bed and pulled in a ragged breath. He was only going to get one shot at this—one shot to prove himself worthy of the FBI—and he wasn't stupid. He knew damn well if this "experiment" didn't work, they wouldn't give him a chance with the regular FBI. Both Talon and Agent Gregory made that very clear. The FBI didn't take B averages. If this didn't work, he'd be back in Cookeville faster than he could say "Quantico."

He actually couldn't believe Talon was walking around and drinking coffee. He wondered if the enhanced had super healing abilities and knew a lot of them were wary of going to a hospital. Even in the last few years when treatment was made mandatory, there were still some places that were complete dicks to them. The enhanced couldn't get insurance of any sort. He could kind of understand an insurance company not wanting to touch people who could jump buildings and set things on fire, but unscrupulous hospitals used that excuse not to treat until the government once again stepped in and instigated a mandatory duty of care.

After he found out about Adam, Finn had read everything he could get his hands on about the enhanced. Not that there was much. Plenty of official statements citing they were as much US citizens as anyone, though that was only in recent years. But every time an enhanced so much as breathed in the wrong way, the papers would blow everything out of proportion. The media's favorite was the story of one guy who electrocuted someone, then successfully escaped during the trial by setting a charge so high, half the courthouse blew off. That was in the early days, though. Any time an enhanced was said to be causing a problem, the special units would roll out. They didn't have ordinary bullets; they had powerful sedatives that could be fired from anything as small as a 9mm Luger to something as large as a rocket launcher to take out a large group.

He knew all this because firepower had become his favorite subject since he decided to join the FBI. It was even something his dad had helped him with. They spent hours poring over pictures in *Guns & Ammo*. One of his dad's buddies used to send him a bunch of back copies every so often. Finn knew his dad wasn't interested, said the 'Nam War cured him of any attraction to guns, so Finn knew he did it for him.

He never even got to go to a firing range. The only local one was run by a friend of Deke's, and there was no way he was going there. So he waited. He knew everything about guns. He could strip, clean, and reload in seconds. Or at least he could in his imagination.

His dad never even told him he still had his old service weapon.

Finn pulled his jeans on sharply. He didn't need that image in his head today. He took a look around the room and thought about last night. He was so worried the big lump was gonna die on him or something, he never made any attempt to get back to the field office and get his assigned car.

He kept Talon awake long enough to get him some painkillers and water from the kitchen. Then Talon shucked off his pants and jacket and crashed on the bed. Finn even dared wake him up three times, which he knew he was supposed to do for a head injury. The last time Talon quietly informed him that if he woke him up one more time, Finn would be the one with the sore head.

He finally fell asleep in the chair around 4:00 a.m. To be honest, after nearly forty-eight hours of little or no sleep, he couldn't believe he lasted that long. And much to his embarrassment, he was obviously carried to bed sometime later. He never remembered undressing, but he woke up this morning just in his Superman boxers, and he wanted to die. The front showed Christopher Reeve pumping his fist with the caption "Up, up, and away." He'd headed out of the house so quick, he just grabbed what was clean and decided to travel in those. His grown-up underwear he was saving for all the medicals. Fuck, he hoped he undressed himself. The thought of Talon seeing them made him want to crawl into a hole and die.

"You ready?"

The growl made Finn jump, but he grabbed his keys, wallet, and the security tag from the brown envelope and turned around. He nodded and took a step forward, then stopped in surprise when Talon didn't move.

"Look," Talon said. "I don't apologize for not wanting to babysit a wannabe fed, but you could have cut and run last night…. You didn't, so." He shrugged and took a step away from the door so Finn could move.

"You're welcome," Finn called out to Talon's retreating back. Finn grinned when he paused for a millisecond but didn't acknowledge his words.

One point to Finn. He smiled wryly. He had a feeling he wasn't going to win many of them.

In the daylight, the step to fit his toe in to climb in Talon's truck wasn't so daunting. It was the passenger side, of course, but at least Talon didn't need to hoist him up like some child. They drove in silence for about a mile while Finn struggled to come up with an intelligent question that might not be shot down.

"You know, someone had to put out the cameras in the parking garage last night."

Talon grunted again in response. "Ya think?" he said, and Finn had to bite off a huge sigh. It was good while it lasted, he supposed.

He didn't attempt to say anything else, but in five minutes, they had pulled up outside of Betty's Diner.

Finn's belly rumbled again, which earned him another sardonic look. He climbed out as gracefully as he could before Talon had a chance to come around, and inhaled appreciatively as a customer opened the door to exit. The place smelled delicious. Finn had barely eaten in the past two days, and he was starving. He wanted to rub his hands in glee as they walked in.

He didn't, of course.

Finn looked around. The place seemed popular, and an older gray-haired woman looked up from the cash register as they walked in. Her face broke out into a huge smile, and she stepped around to greet Talon.

"Where have you been? You haven't been to see me in three days." Finn watched in astonishment as the pint-sized lady battered Talon on the arm. "Are you eating properly?" She squinted up at him and then seemed to notice Finn stood behind Talon. "You've brought a friend?" she asked, astonished, and Finn nearly laughed. Her blatant surprise at the thought of Talon actually having friends mirrored Finn's own opinion. He hadn't exactly demonstrated many social skills since they'd met.

Finn stepped forward before Talon had a chance to say anything. "Hi, my name's Finn, and I'm starving." He grinned. It sounded like an announcement at an AA meeting. *It's been three days since my last meal.*

The lady completely ignored Finn's outstretched hand and pulled him to her. "Nonsense," she said firmly as Finn was squashed rather alarmingly against a very ample bosom. He inhaled quickly. She smelled of cinnamon and baked yummy stuff.

Finn's belly growled again.

"Oh, you poor thing," the woman exclaimed. "I'm Betty, surprisingly enough." She waved at the sign. "Go and sit yourself down."

Finn followed Talon to the end booth, and Talon slid in decisively. Finn was quick enough to notice that he'd walked past two empty ones until he got to where he could put his back to the wall and see everyone who walked in. It seemed instinctive. Maybe in a few weeks, he'd be doing things like that too.

For the first time since yesterday, Finn allowed himself to get a little excited. He was in the FBI—*almost*. He was out from under Deke's eagle eye, and he was about to get fed. Finn loved food. Any kind, really. In fact, he wasn't entirely sure he'd ever met a meal he didn't like. He scanned the menu eagerly as Betty brought coffee to the table.

She chuckled as she saw Finn's rapt concentration. "I'll leave you boys a minute to decide." She went to pour a few more refills.

Finn absently reached over for the basket with the sugars and creamer, dumped four creamers and two sugars in his coffee, stirred, and took a cautious sip. He was very interested in the breakfast platter, which seemed to just about include every breakfast food known to man, and he looked up as a sudden awful thought occurred to him, only to find Talon looking at him in astonishment.

"How the fuck do you possibly stay in shape, drinking like that?"

Finn blinked at Talon's question. *He thinks I'm in shape?* A warm feeling settled in his belly, and it had nothing to do with the mouthful of creamy goodness he'd just inhaled. He ignored Talon's question, assuming it was rhetorical. "How soon will we be doing any fitness tests this morning?" He would cry if he had to settle for whole wheat toast.

Talon grinned. "You can eat. It's paperwork and medical first."

Finn didn't reply. He got too lost in the smile. Talon's face completely changed when he smiled. He almost seemed... *normal*. And that wasn't any sort of a jab at his enhanced status. It was more an acknowledgment he wasn't a complete asshole every minute of the day.

Betty appeared and beamed at them both. "What ya havin', boys?"

Talon smoothly asked for a large breakfast platter with sunny-side up eggs and bacon.

Finn, utterly relieved, asked for exactly the same and picked up his coffee.

Betty paused. "You want *exactly* the same?" She looked at Finn, and he glanced at Talon, who had quirked his eyebrow in a silent challenge.

Finn raised his chin. "Yes, please." Fuck, if it included a side of fried eyeballs, he'd be on the next plane out. "So paperwork on a Saturday?" It was all Finn could think of to start any sort of a conversation.

Talon raised his eyebrow higher. "The agency isn't Monday to Friday, nine to five. If you want that, you're in the wrong place."

Finn put his cup down sharply. He hadn't meant that. Talon had to know he hadn't meant that. "I—" When he saw the humor on Talon's face, Finn bit off the angry retort, both due to the surprise that it was there and from the knowledge Talon was just yanking his chain.

"So why do you want to join the FBI?" Talon took a sip of his black coffee.

Finn was ready for this. He had a whole speech planned that he'd trotted out at interviews. He could even quote the latest terror and violent crime stats he cleverly worked into his answer. But as he opened his mouth, it suddenly clicked that Talon was putting out feelers. If they were going to be friends, giving him a BS line wouldn't win him any more points.

"Some agents came to talk at our school when I was fourteen. Nowheresville, Iowa, didn't have a high college uptake for seniors. In fact, the graduation rate wasn't all that good either." Finn picked nervously at the napkin. He could feel the icy-blue eyes bearing down on him. "Anyway, something they said just kinda clicked with me. I kept my nose clean, graduated. Got my degree." He grinned. "I even worked as a bookkeeper part-time." Finn looked up, hoping to see another smile, but Talon's face was unsurprised.

Of course.

"You know all this," Finn said accusingly. He had no doubt Talon had seen his file.

"I knew about the job and the college," Talon conceded. "I've seen your grades and your references. I didn't know what made you want to join." He hesitated. "I guess it was hard to study while you were working a job."

Finn fumed. He knew in Talon's half-assed way, he was trying to offer some justification to explain his average grades when he was so determined and had wanted to join the FBI since he was fourteen. Finn lowered his head. There was no way Talon would ever find out how he struggled with reading occasionally. It wasn't that hard anymore, and audio was a godsend. He learned a few tricks to adapt and could usually correctly anticipate the words even if he couldn't always make them out.

Betty arrived, and Finn looked up thankfully. She was carrying such a huge tray of food, Finn thought they would both be lucky to get through it. Then he gaped as he saw the teenager standing behind her with more stuff.

Talon chuckled again. "Stop teasing him, Betty."

Betty grinned and waved the teenager to the next table.

Finn let out a low breath and swallowed. There was still more food on there than he'd eat in two days. Eggs, bacon, sausage patties, mushrooms, grits, and toast on one plate, and a huge fluffy stack of pancakes on another. And it wasn't just the variety; it was the quantity. He wouldn't need a box—he would need a tow truck.

"I only eat this on a Saturday, but she does the best omelet I've ever eaten as well."

Finn nodded in amazement. *I mean, yeah—who'd wanna cook?*

He gave up gracefully when he was just over halfway through. He could have pushed on, but he didn't think a food coma was a good idea for his first day.

Talon waved his money away when Finn got out his wallet after Betty cleared their table. He reluctantly refused a box, as he didn't want to look like some kid going in with his school lunch on his first day either.

Talon didn't say a word, just allowed Betty to try to wrap her arms around him as he stood up to leave. Betty waved them both off with an admonishment to stay safe.

Just as they cleared the last booth, heading for the exit, Finn clearly heard the words, "I ain't coming here again. No idea they let that sort in here." The older woman who said it dropped her fork in disgust. "Don't eat it, Barney," she said to the guy seated opposite her, who Finn assumed was her husband. "You don't know what you might catch."

Finn inhaled a sharp breath and stared at Talon's retreating back. He hadn't paused, but he must have heard what she said. Finn deliberately looked the woman up and down. Her pink blouse stretched over her ample belly, and her many chins wobbled as she spoke.

He stopped and deliberately leaned over. "That's probably just as well, madam," he said quietly. "You could always try the egg-white omelet and low-fat vegetable smoothie. My colleague, as you can see, wouldn't touch either of those. He doesn't need to diet."

Finn heard the indignant gasp as he walked away without saying another word. He looked up as Talon stood in the doorway with a puzzled look on his face. He probably heard Finn be rude to a member of the public. Another reason he wouldn't make the four weeks.

TALON HEARD what the woman said, but it didn't bother him. It was barely a blip on his radar. He'd heard far worse over the years, said by people who could actually physically hurt him, and he didn't care what some random customer said.

What he was struggling with was the quiet response he heard from Finn. Not only did Finn stick up for him in the sarcastic way he appreciated, but he did it not expecting to be heard. He wasn't doing it for show or to gain ground with Talon, and it kind of knocked him off balance a little.

"Is that usual?"

Finn's question brought him out of his thoughts as he automatically showed his pass at the barrier.

"I've seen plenty of photos of field offices and obviously been for the interviews. I've never seen one with a barrier."

Talon waved at the guard as they were shown through. "No," he said bluntly. "That's for us." He didn't offer any further explanation. The thought that enhanced were less trustworthy even if they wore a badge burned something deep in his gut. Talon ground his teeth and kept the sigh silent.

For the first time, he might actually regret the situation when his prospective new partner failed because Talon knew with what he was about to be put through, the kid would run home screaming to his mommy. He was right when he told Finn the morning was for medical and paperwork. It was what he set up for the afternoon that would finally convince Gregory the unit should be for enhanced only.

Chapter Four

FINN FOLLOWED Talon up what he now termed the "back stairs." He still hadn't seen what the rest of the building looked like yet, and it didn't seem like Talon was interested in stopping now. He led them into the same reception area as yesterday, still unmanned, but through the third door this time. There was no sound from Gregory's office, so Finn had no idea if he was working or not.

Finn stopped in astonishment as they walked into what looked like a mini hospital. There were three treatment tables and all sorts of equipment dotted around the walls. Some he recognized, obviously, like the basic blood pressure cuffs, but some computerized terminals looked like they belonged on a spaceship.

"Doc?" Talon grunted as they walked in.

A young woman sat in front of a computer screen. Finn guessed her to be around thirty years old, with dark brown hair and green eyes. Slim, pretty, and professional in her white coat. She turned around as soon as they entered and stood, smiling. "Agent Valdez. And this must be Mr. Mayer." She looked at Finn pleasantly. "I'm Dr. Natalie Edwards."

Finn put his hand out automatically. "Nice to meet you." He returned the smile, but her attention was already back on Talon. *Not that I blame her*, he thought with resignation, and he proceeded to watch her flirt for a couple of minutes, though she got absolutely no reaction whatsoever from Talon.

"Doc's just going to go over your results. I'll be back for you in a little while." And Talon disappeared through the door they'd entered in.

Finn was immediately given a small plastic jar and directed to the bathroom. "Monthly drug testing is compulsory." Dr. Edwards smiled again.

It turned out Finn didn't have to have much of a medical because his last one was recent enough. Dr. Edwards basically went through his general health profile and confirmed some personal details, had a quick listen to his chest, and hooked him up to a monitor. She drew what seemed to Finn as an enormous amount of blood and split it into four vials, and asked a ton of medical questions about his family.

She looked up as Talon let himself back in the room after an hour. Finn was just buttoning his shirt. "He's all yours, Agent Valdez," she said cheerfully, and Finn thanked her and followed Talon.

"Come on. Paperwork. You get to sit on your ass for another hour." Talon led Finn back to the elevator and pressed for level two.

Finn still hadn't thought of an intelligent response by the time the elevator doors opened again, and he stepped out into what seemed like a corridor.

Agent Gregory was just coming out of an office two doors down. He looked up and smiled. "Finn, good morning. Are you ready to meet your teammates?"

Finn's jaw dropped. *Teammates?* He thought it was just him and Talon. He glanced over at Talon in confusion and took in Talon's stony face.

Gregory sighed. "Talon, you were supposed to go over the background of the unit this morning."

"There wasn't time. He needed feeding."

Finn rounded on Talon as the injustice registered. "You ate more than I did," he blurted, feeling like a child.

Talon raised an eyebrow and smiled. "Too easy. *Way* too easy. You're not gonna last two minutes in there."

"Talon," Gregory almost growled, and Talon shrugged.

Finn took a slow breath and stared at the plain door Gregory had indicated, his good mood and excitement quickly evaporating.

"Come on, then. They're all waiting," Gregory said, pushing the door open.

Talon waved Finn through in front of him, and Finn followed Agent Gregory, wondering if the gates of hell were this hard to walk through.

Probably not.

Finn stood uncertainly as the four giants who were seated around a large conference table all turned toward him, four livid scars under their left eye and every one of them staring at Finn with a mixture of distrust and contempt.

Crap. He looked at Talon uncertainly, but Talon just walked around the opposite side of the table and sat.

"Sit down, Finn, and I'll do introductions," Gregory said.

As Finn dove into the nearest seat, a low voice drawled, "Yeah, Finn. What's your name and where do you come from?"

Finn flushed as the snickers rose around the table.

"That's enough," Gregory snapped, and everyone subsided. "I have as little choice in this as any of you."

The silence around the room was deafening, and Finn stared at Gregory openmouthed. Fucking A. His boss—the one guy he was convinced yesterday was on his side—just admitted to the room that he'd been forced into having Finn here. It was like high school all over again.

Finn pressed his lips together and glanced back down. Four weeks. He'd get out of here in four weeks, and then he'd go and see about starting the rest of his life. He had a brand-new degree he could take out for a spin, and just because he wouldn't make the cut for the FBI didn't mean he couldn't see what the rest of the Sunshine State had to offer. If he got desperate, he'd go check out Disney or something.

He suddenly looked up as he heard his own voice echo around the room. He stared in shocked silence at the TV in front of them.

"Last night's assailants had forgotten about the backup feed. There were no recordings in real time, but the engineer found this while he was doing repairs."

Finn cringed as he heard himself announce his agent status to the guys with the baseball bats, expecting to be shot down or ridiculed by one of Talon's team. He didn't even dare take his face from the screen to check their reactions.

"Not like you to let someone get the drop on you, Talon."

Finn stared in amazement. He heard the teasing in the voice, but it wasn't directed at him. He met the eyes of the speaker. Another blond-haired giant, but Finn had to school his features carefully not to appear shocked. The entire left side of his face was covered in ugly scars, even twisting his mouth a little, but his mark was still livid on his skin.

The man stood and offered his hand to Finn. "That took some guts, kid." He gestured to the screen with his chin, and Finn returned the handshake cautiously, his own hand completely disappearing in the massive grip. "The name's Gael Peterson." He nodded around the room. "Sawyer Rollins, Vance Connelly, and the grumpy one in the corner is Eli Stuart."

Most of the agents stood to shake Finn's hand, some pressing a little too hard, but Finn was determined to hide when it hurt. Sawyer and Eli were both what he would have called tall-for-a-human size, neither as large as Talon. Sawyer's green eyes flickered over him expressionlessly, but he did at least extend his hand, unlike Eli. Finn held his own out to Eli, but he never even looked in his direction, so Finn dropped it awkwardly.

"Welcome to the crazy house." Vance pumped Finn's hand enthusiastically. Finn tried not to gape at the sheer size of him. He was the biggest individual Finn had ever seen.

Gregory cleared his throat, and Finn sat quickly. They all looked at the screen. "No IDs possible, unfortunately," Gregory added.

"Like we need them?" Gael said, the sarcasm in his voice again apparent. "Look at their feet."

Finn glanced at where the vid had paused. It showed Finn taking a threatening step toward the group as the first guy turned and planted a boot in Talon's ribs. They were all wearing nondescript jeans, but Finn blinked at the matching black-shined dress shoes. "They're cops," he blurted and looked at Talon in horror. Cops. "Why would they do that?" he asked, then cringed, forgetting his determination to stay quiet.

"You been living under a rock the past twenty years, kid?" Sawyer stood and walked to the coffee machine.

Finn opened his mouth and shut it just as quickly.

Talon spoke up. "What Sawyer means is, there are just as many law enforcement professionals who don't want us on this side of the fence as there are criminals."

Finn nodded. "That makes sense, I suppose. You could all beat their asses and look cool doing it."

Gael spluttered after taking a mouthful of coffee. A couple of them grinned. Talon just raised an eyebrow.

Finn focused his attention back on Gregory, quietly pleased with himself.

"If it helps," Vance spoke softly, "the first guy is a native Floridian. Definitely Tampa. The second one I would say Atlanta."

Finn looked in surprise. He hadn't thought about an accent particularly. It must be one of Vance's abilities.

Gregory nodded and turned off the screen. "To summarize, you've all met Finn. We have four weeks to prove this can work. I expect your cooperation and your assistance, but that starts tomorrow. Finn has some short profile tests to sit this morning, and later you will all be in the gym." Gregory smiled and walked out as a few of the others got up. One or two murmured something pleasant to Finn, but he didn't hear anything after the word "test."

His heart pounded, and his earlier breakfast suddenly threatened to make an appearance. Fuck. What if he messed up? How important was this test? Was it written, or maybe physical? He swallowed.

"S'up, kid?" Talon stood, frowning at him.

Finn licked his lips. "What, umm, sort of test is it?"

Talon shrugged. "Basic behavioral insight, so they can see what you might spot automatically. Or more importantly what assumptions you have that you have to unlearn fast." He looked assessingly at Finn. "It's no big deal. I think you just read the questions and pick an answer. It's timed, but it's not like you get graded or anything."

Finn felt sick. It was timed. He'd expected there to be tests at Quantico, but not on his first day, and not when every single person on his team wanted him to fail.

"You okay, kid?"

Finn looked up at Talon, who was looking puzzled, and gulped. He needed to calm down. "Yeah."

"Good. Come on. Let's get this over with, then." Talon led him into yet another room and gestured to a chair next to a desk.

Finn could already feel his palms sweating and his heart pounding, and he tried to breathe slowly. He'd done all sorts of breathing exercises to prepare for his SATs and one of his interviews. He knew to start with the questions that had the most points attached. When he was younger, he made the mistake of always starting at the beginning, and because it took him longer to read the questions, he always ran out of time. It just seemed harder now that he knew the stakes and knew everyone wanted him to fail.

Talon didn't seem to notice his anxiety, however, and picked up a folder from the table and dropped it on the desk. "There's actually no right or wrong answers. We just need to get a feel for your thought process. So we know your starting point. Don't forget we're condensing eight hundred hours of training into four weeks." Talon shrugged. "Some of the things I may ask you to do will seem difficult to understand."

Finn looked blankly at the folder. Of course there were right and wrong answers. Even he wasn't stupid enough to believe this wasn't something else he could fail at.

TALON SAT back down and rubbed his face, trying not to hiss when he caught his lip. He didn't know how he felt, and it was confusing the hell out of him. He was always convinced having enhanced and regular humans working together wasn't a good idea. The basic tenet of his team was trust. Knowing each of his guys had his back and wouldn't hesitate to pull the trigger to save his life. His first trainee didn't even make it through the test Finn was currently looking at. Fifteen questions, all designed to see if the trainee would fail to respond as quickly if the victim was regular or enhanced, and not just that straightforward. Sometimes candidates would try to go the other way, be too preferential for enhanced to try to win favors.

That scenario didn't cut it with any of his team either. None of the questions used the words "regular" or "enhanced." The clues were more subtle, and someone a lot cleverer than Talon had put the questions together. He glanced at the clock. Twenty minutes for the first round of ten questions. Five pretty simple ones, and five that required a little more thought. Then there were some basic math problems as well.

He stood and wandered over to where Finn was sitting, then stopped in surprise. Finn was looking at the last page. Had he finished it already? Talon narrowed his eyes as he looked at Finn. His hand shook as he turned a page, and Finn hadn't so much as picked up his pen. What was it? Nerves? Was that the reason Finn hadn't done so well on his exams in college?

Talon absently filed the thought away. It wasn't his business, and he wasn't here to babysit someone he wanted out anyway. Served him right if he did fail the test. Talon leaned back against the wall and stared at the ceiling. He smiled a little as he remembered the vid with Finn's voice declaring he was a federal agent. Even if he wanted him gone, he could grudgingly admit the kid had balls.

Talon glanced over at Finn again and was suddenly struck by the mask of desperation on his face. What the fuck was wrong with him? He knew he could read. There was no way he would have gotten through high school without that, and Finn had a fucking degree. Talon blinked. He'd read the glowing reports from his

tutors. Finn's dedication. His single-mindedness, almost. What he told him in the café. Why would someone put himself through all that and not study his ass
off 24-7 to make sure his grades were good?

Unless there was another reason.

Talon stood. "How are you getting on? Halfway
through," he added in case Finn just needed a kick up
the ass to get started. He'd also seen some trainees
overthink things to the point that it nearly paralyzed
them. No decision because they were frightened of
not making the right one. That was sometimes even
worse. Being an agent meant split-second choices.
Talon looked at the clock. Eight minutes left. Eight
minutes and Finn would be gone, and they wouldn't
even need all the scenarios the team would put on for
him this afternoon. Eight minutes and the brass might
concede to what he'd been telling them for months—
that the unit should be enhanced only.

He glanced over to see what Finn was writing
and frowned. Absolutely nothing. Talon took a step
and fisted his hands. *Don't fucking ask, Talon,* he told
himself sternly. Then the defiant voice of Finn challenging the bastards who attacked him yesterday came
into his head, and he sighed. What the hell? He could
ask, right?

Talon sat on the desk and picked up the paper.
"Your pen not working, kid?"

Finn pushed himself upright. "I'll go." He lowered his eyes, but not before Talon saw the frustration
and disgust darkening them. He looked at the question
that had gotten Finn so worked up. It was a scenario
that subtly lead the trainee to favor the enhanced over

the human. Not because it was the right thing to do for the situation, but to weed out reverse favoritism.

Talon read the question out loud and lowered the paper. "Why are you having problems with that?"

Finn jutted his chin out. "I'm not," he said, and he reeled off the best answer.

Talon narrowed his eyes. "Then why didn't you put that down?"

Finn shrugged.

Talon took a breath as a thought filtered into his mind. "What about this one?" He read off the next question, and Finn answered it promptly and correctly. Talon nodded to the typed instruction fixed to the bottom of the portable scanner cart. "What does that say?"

Finn looked over, and a dull flush crept over his cheeks. "I can read," he ground out.

"What does it say?" Talon repeated. "Count to ten in your head and then tell me."

Finn blinked at him, puzzled.

"Take three deep breaths first," Talon instructed.

Finn did as he was asked and then calmly read, "Please put the power cable away after use."

Talon scowled. "Why the fuck did you not tell any of us you are dyslexic?"

Finn scowled. "I'm not." He turned to the door.

Talon nodded. "Let me guess. You anticipate. You find some fonts much easier to read. That's why your coursework was so much better than your written tests."

Finn stood still, feet planted, hands shoved in his pants pockets. He didn't turn around.

"Text to speech? It's an allowed resource," Talon continued.

Finn turned slowly. "How—how do you know all that?"

Talon debated for about ten seconds. He didn't share, ever. "Because my little brother's dyslexic. And when I say little, I mean by one year. He's currently a prosecutor in the Washington DA's office. A successful prosecutor," he added.

Talon picked up the test and started reading the questions. Finn rattled off most of the answers, and by the time they were halfway through the last section, he was writing his own.

"You're actually better than Sam," Talon said. "He wouldn't be able to work out the last question even with his breathing techniques."

Finn looked up, and Talon's belly squeezed a little at his eagerness. "It only bothers me when I'm timed or under pressure most of the time now. Even then I can anticipate the simple stuff. We had an old computer in the library at college that had a darker screen than the rest. Everyone hated it, but it was the easiest one for me."

Talon nodded. "It helped Sam if we overlaid the screen with a blue tint." He sighed. "I don't get how I missed your diagnosis, though. I read your file and…." Understanding slammed into Talon. "You've never been diagnosed, have you?" He shook his head. Of all the stupid, irresponsible….

Finn's smile faded.

"You could easily have put your teammates' lives at risk by not declaring this," Talon ground out. It was incredibly selfish, and as far as Talon was concerned, the last nail in the coffin.

"I thought once I got into Quantico, I could find someone to talk to about it," Finn mumbled, and Talon opened his mouth to rain down a world of hurt on Finn.

Then he stopped. Because the fact that Finn wasn't at Quantico wasn't his fault. He would have had twenty weeks to sort it out. It wasn't Finn's fault they only had four.

Fuck.

This was his excuse. This was exactly what he had wanted. The perfect reason to get rid of the regular human and push for a solo team of enhanced. Finn was handing him the reason on a plate.

Sam's face swam into his head. How Talon found him in their tree house, crying his eyes out because some dick of a kid called him a retard because he couldn't read when it was his turn at school. But Sam had their family behind him. He had a huge support network, and what did Finn have? His brother sounded like a complete lazy asshole. His mom, on the surface, not too bad, but at the same time, if she'd let Finn go through school without getting any help....

And his dad. His dad who came home from Vietnam in a wheelchair and finally blew his brains out. And Finn found him.

Talon grimaced. He'd give him a week.

Chapter Five

TALON SHOVED yet another bottle of water in Finn's hands, and Finn quirked his lips. "This is your secret ploy, isn't it? You need me to fail the physical tests because I'm going to be holed up in the bathroom?"

Talon grunted. "You have some basic stuff to go through next. A video, some history of the enhanced."

Finn looked up as Agent Fielding let himself into the room and smiled at him.

"I'll catch up with you later," Talon said before retreating.

"So I hear you had some excitement last night?" Drew said, looking eager.

"It wasn't exciting at the time," Finn countered mildly as Drew grinned. "What are we doing now?"

"You're going to watch a boring-ass video." Drew thumped him on the arm.

Finn followed Drew back to the room they were in earlier, when he met the team, and decided to risk a few questions. "I hadn't realized you already had enhanced working for the FBI."

Drew gestured for him to take a seat. "It's new. We've got five of them at the moment. Talon, Vance, Sawyer, Eli, and Gael."

"And they've all been through Quantico?" Finn asked in disbelief.

"Hell no." Drew shook his head. "Everyone needs this kept quiet. They've all had training at our outside facility over the last few months, and Talon's the leader because of his brothers. He also has a background in private security."

"His brothers?" Talon said one was a prosecutor, but that wouldn't get him any preferential treatment, surely.

Drew sighed a little and sat down. "Confidential?"

"Of course," Finn responded, a little worried about what he might be agreeing to.

"Talon comes from an influential family. Four brothers altogether, and one sister. One of them is an agent, and two work for the DA's office in Washington. Hell, even his sister is married to an attorney." Drew lowered his voice. "Talon's the only one who's enhanced."

"Wow!" Finn murmured appreciatively. He would love to have come from a big family. Sheer statistical chance would have meant he'd have had at least one brother he would get along with out of four.

"I know. Crap, isn't it?"

Finn looked up from the blank TV screen. "Crap?"

"Yeah, I mean, can you imagine having all that to live up to?" Drew shuddered. "Makes me glad to be an only child."

Finn stayed quiet, not wanting to openly disagree with the first guy who had tried to be friendly. "So Talon's got a security background?" he asked casually. He didn't want Drew to have any inkling that he had any interest other than simple curiosity.

"Yep," Drew said succinctly. "I'm sorry you drew the short straw on that one, although all of them are pretty much badasses."

"I would imagine some sort of trained background's good, though?" Finn said tentatively, not really understanding why Drew didn't seem to be a fan.

Drew raised his eyebrows. "Oh yeah. Working with people who already know a zillion ways to kill you, and that's even before their abilities are included?"

Finn shifted uncomfortably, and then a shiver ran down his neck and he turned around quickly. The room was empty, and he scanned the corners for obvious cameras. It was as if someone had been watching him. Though just because he couldn't see the cameras didn't mean they weren't there.

He decided to change the subject. "So what's the video, then?"

"Boring crap about how the FBI was set up." Drew sighed. "I'm going to get a coffee. Seen it a million times. Do you want one?"

Finn shook his head and turned around as the TV came on. He heard the door close behind Drew and then shivered slightly and whipped his head around. The room was still empty. It was Drew's fault; he must have gotten him spooked. Finn settled in to watch the video as J. Edgar Hoover's face came on.

TALON LOOKED up as Sawyer appeared next to him and Gael. Gael jumped and cursed, but Talon knew Sawyer was there. The slight blurring around the edges of a notice about the fire evacuation procedure clued him in to his presence. "Well?"

"Drew's currently giving the kid the 101 about the team. Your name was mentioned."

Talon didn't move. He was expecting it. "He knows about Sam already."

Sawyer raised his eyebrows, but he made no comment.

"We still all on the same page here, Talon?" Gael asked.

Talon glanced at him. "Meaning?"

"Meaning do you still want rid of him? Meaning you still want the group enhanced only?" Gael nodded at Sawyer. "If anyone knew the shit that Sawyer can do, they'd have him strapped to a gurney and wheeled into a lab faster than you can say 'experiment.' You know that."

He did. No one, not even Gregory, knew about Sawyer. For all intents and purposes, Sawyer's ability was metalworking, and he didn't mean sharpening knives or making fancy statues. Sawyer could deconstruct any metal and render it useless. When Talon first met Sawyer at the gun range, some probie swung his gun around carelessly as he walked in. The gun immediately dropped to pieces in the guy's hands. Talon had Sawyer signed up and on his team three days later.

Talon glanced in concern as Sawyer sagged a little by the door. "You didn't have to do that." He knew it took it out of him.

Sawyer shrugged and sat down. "I'll be interested to see his situational awareness skills later."

Talon groaned. "He doesn't have any."

"I think you're wrong, boss," Sawyer said. "He couldn't see me, but there was something telling him someone was behind him. It's the first time I've noticed that in any regular."

"That's impossible," Talon scoffed. "Finn never even woke up when I carried him to bed." He winced as the silence in the room thickened as his team took in the implication. "It was after the attack in the parking garage. The kid insisted on waking me every hour to do dumb head-injury checks. I woke up to take a piss around five, and he was passed out in the chair. I just took him to bed because I felt a little sorry for him. It's not his fault he's being set up to fail." Talon glanced when Sawyer gave a low whistle. *Shit.* "I took him to bed on his own, Sawyer. *And left him there.* You know what I mean."

"So let's review the evidence," Gael drawled and started counting off on his fingers. "He's had a spectacular first day so far. Whatever spin you put on it, he saved your butt in the garage. The only red flags he's showing are his dick for a brother—" Gael ignored the slight stiffening from Sawyer at that word. "—and his crappy test results."

"He's dyslexic," Talon said immediately. "Seems to manage except when he's tired or stressed."

Gael grinned. "Find that out while you were putting him to bed?"

"Well, that's it, then," Sawyer interrupted. "He won't have passed the initial written assessments you just gave him. So how come he's still here?"

Talon had the grace to look a little uncomfortable. He shrugged. "I read them. It's only the same as text to speech. That's approved, and he aced the math questions."

"How is that possible if he can't read properly?" Sawyer asked doubtfully.

"Different brain strategy," Talon explained.

"Which brings me back to my original question. Are you sure?" Gael asked slowly, and Sawyer frowned.

"Of course he's sure," Sawyer snapped and looked at Talon for confirmation.

Talon sighed. "You're right. I do owe him for the garage. Do I think he'd make it on the team—no. Do I think regulars partnering with enhanced is a good idea—no."

"But?" Gael asked.

"I'm gonna give him a week and see if my brother can pull any strings to get him into Quantico. If we throw him out now, he won't get another chance."

Sawyer didn't say another word, and Gael just grinned. "So we can still have fun with our new toy this afternoon?"

"Yeah," Talon sighed. "But for fuck's sake, don't break him."

TALON WATCHED carefully as Drew brought Finn out to the mats. They were going to see what his hand-to-hand combat was like first. They had to start with a human, and Drew was one of the agents Gregory trusted around the enhanced.

They both had protective headgear on. Talon did his best not to stare at the lithe little body that followed Drew out, remembering how it felt in his arms the night before. Talon had tried to shake Finn awake at first when he came back from the bathroom, completely stunned he was still there. He looked like shit. Talon could see the dark shadows under his eyes, and his own blood stained Finn's pants and his shirt. The jacket had been discarded.

In the end, Talon just picked him up. Then what did the kid do? Instead of lying there while Talon took him to his spare room, he moaned softly and curled up in Talon's arms, burrowing his head in the crook of his neck. Talon had nearly groaned right back and had hurriedly laid him down on the bed. Finn had let out a deep sigh, and Talon just stood and stared and thought about how uncomfortable he looked. With resignation he'd undone Finn's pants and slid them off his hips. He'd chuckled softly when he'd seen the Superman shorts. He would bet money Finn had never wanted another living soul to see those.

Talon had covered him up and taken a determined step back as Finn had rolled on his side. He wasn't about to go there. He couldn't ever go there. Talon had been able to get his rocks off when he wanted to. Surprisingly, for all that regulars seemed to be scared of the enhanced, there were always plenty of willing bodies ready to get a thrill out of a hookup. It was a bit like the thrill of extreme sports, and for some reason, it had bragging rights attached as well. He supposed it was because they were convinced an enhanced could and would lose control in the middle of sex.

Talon fisted his hands. Not gonna happen. Talon would never lose control ever again.

"So I want you to do whatever you can to pin each other to the mats for five seconds," Talon said. "You are not here to kill each other. I am mainly concerned with what Finn uses for avoidance and defense. The other members of the team will be jumping in the ring at certain times, but they will not execute any moves. Their presence is simply to distract, and they won't show any favoritism."

Drew nodded once. He knew the drill.

Finn glanced at Talon, and Drew took full advantage. In one move he shoved Finn to send him off balance, side-stepped, and brought the flat of his hand to connect with Finn's nose. Everyone winced as Finn hit the deck. Talon's fingers itched as Finn howled and brought both hands up to his face. Talon raised his hand, and Drew immediately stopped. Drew had properly held back, actually. Finn's nose would hurt like fuck, but Drew could have easily knocked him out.

Talon opened his mouth to explain to Finn that in a fight, there would be no referees around to tell him when to start, when Drew took a step forward and extended his arm to help Finn up. Before anyone could blink, Drew was on his back, staring up at the ceiling. Finn had waited until he came in close and then used his own foot in a sideways swipe to take Drew's legs from under him.

Gael laughed out loud, and even Talon had to hold back a smirk. Finn was still holding his nose. "Gael, get Finn some ice."

Sawyer snorted. "Yeah, can't have pretty boy getting a black eye."

Finn lowered a bloody hand and glowered.

Drew got to his feet, grinning. "Sorry, man. I didn't mean to bust your nose."

Finn ignored them both and walked off the mats, heading for the restrooms.

Talon sighed and held his hand out for the ice as Gael came running back. Gael dumped the bag in his hand with a smirk, and Talon followed in the direction Finn had gone.

Talon pushed the door open a few seconds after Finn disappeared through it. Finn was wetting some paper towels in the sink. Talon pulled out the chair. "Sit."

"I can wipe my own fucking nose," Finn said, except the anger didn't really cut it because "nose" sounded like "dose."

Talon struggled not to laugh. On second look there was barely any blood. He doubted if it would even merit a black eye tomorrow. "I'm sorry. Did you want me to tell Drew to go easy on you?" Talon asked pointedly and got a glower for his efforts. He sighed. "Whatever happened yesterday doesn't mean I can show you any favors."

"Did I ask for any?" Finn rounded on him indignantly. "Don't you think I don't know you're just waiting for an excuse to get rid of me?" He turned back and washed his hands.

Suddenly the door banged open. It was Gael. "Talon, we've got a situation with an enhanced. They want us to try to get there before they send in the cops."

Talon took a step and turned to Finn. "You're done for the day. Go get your car and situate yourself. I'll drop your bag off later."

DREW CAME jogging in as Talon and Gael left. He looked sheepishly at Finn. "We just got finished for the day, huh?"

Finn nodded and pressed his nose gently. It didn't really hurt. Drew looked apologetic, and Finn laughed. "I'm just messing with you."

"You got the drop on me, though," Drew pointed out.

"Where are they going, and how come you're not going?"

"I'm not part of their team, officially. I was just brought in to spar with you. I work out of here, so Gregory kind of co-opted me for the project. They just got a call about some kid who's gone nuts at school." Drew shrugged.

Finn followed Drew as they walked back to the locker room.

Drew got changed quickly. "I'm going to go straight home and do some cardio. Then I'll get showered. What are you doing tonight?"

Finn laughed. "I don't even know where I'm living yet."

Drew brightened. "Oh, I do. You've got an apartment in the same community as me. Gregory has got six of them on hold for the project. How about you follow me home, and I'll show you around? You've got a bucar, right?"

Finn blinked at him.

"A bureau vehicle," Drew explained. "Normally agents only get to use them for work, but you have the authority to use it as a sole vehicle for all your training."

Which is just as well, Finn thought dryly. He didn't have another car. Finn nodded at Drew, though. Might as well. Not like he was doing anything else.

Chapter Six

FINN WHISTLED quietly to himself in awe as the barrier lifted at the entrance to the apartment complex. Drew had shown him the code for the gate and the barrier and even preprogrammed the address into the GPS in case they got separated. Finn had found the map in the brown envelope, but he let Drew fuss.

He pulled up into the bay next to Drew's and got out. The complex was beautiful. There was a huge central pool area complete with Jacuzzi and fitness room. Three identical apartment buildings surrounded the pool, with plenty of parking at the rear of each one. It was like he was on vacation, and he suddenly itched to get in the water.

"Totally cool, huh?" Drew grinned at Finn's reaction. "Your home for at least four weeks." He looked down as Finn shut the door of the small rental compact he'd been given. "No bag?"

Finn shook his head. "All my things are in Talon's truck."

"Well, that doesn't matter. We're about the same size." He looked at Finn assessingly, and Finn stared back in confusion.

"I'm sure I'll be able to get them off Talon later."

Drew waved his hand. "Sorry, I forgot. We thought we'd go out tonight. Nothing fancy, and I know you have training, but there are a few agents who live nearby. I kind of arranged for us to meet them later. Thought you'd like to get to know some people of normal size." Drew smirked. "And none of your team live here." He walked to the closest building. "Up here. Building B. You're on the second floor. Apartment 214. The kitchen is stocked, and my number is preprogrammed into your cell. I thought we'd meet the guys around six thirty—get some wings or something. I'll pick you up." Drew showed him how to slide his card into the building door. "I'm in building A, apartment 310. If you want to go for a walk around to see the place, just give me a call."

"To be honest I'm kind of wiped out," Finn answered apologetically. "But I'll see you later?" He turned and headed into the cool building. He didn't bother with the elevator, as he really needed to start thinking about his fitness. He ran at home and considered himself in reasonable shape, but he had a feeling the bar had just been raised considerably higher. He was still smarting over making a fool of himself in the gym. He'd gotten back at Drew, but he'd looked stupid in the first place.

Finn unlocked his apartment door and stepped in, and his mouth dropped in amazement. It was perfect.

A tiny kitchen to the left widened into a much bigger living area, complete with couch and TV. He crossed the room eagerly as he spotted the sliding doors. *Fuck me*—he even had a damn balcony with a view of the pool.

He turned and headed back to the kitchen and walked through another door. A bedroom and a fairly decent-sized bathroom. He grinned. Decent-sized? Listen to him. The bathroom at Deke's was smaller than this, and they'd had to share, and this was way nicer.

Finn took one look at the bed and ran and jumped on it. He stretched out and stared at the ceiling. Whatever happened at the end of four weeks, there was no way he was ever going back to Cookeville. He was here to stay.

FINN LOOKED around the numerous scattered tables outside the bar and knocked back his Bud Light. It seemed to be a thing in Florida, where there were more tables outside the bar than in it. All the tables had huge Hawaiianesque straw umbrellas that looked like two scarecrows had just died on them.

He looked at the group seated around the table. Drew, four guys, and two women. The loudest one was currently regaling them with a story about bugs, and he didn't mean listening devices. Apparently this guy, Eric, was a deputy sheriff, and they'd been called out to a reported home invasion. Except when they got there, it wasn't anything on two legs doing the invading, but three large palmetto bugs that crawled out when the lady was moving furniture. The lady had screamed and called 911.

Finn joined in the laughter around the table when Eric added that she wanted SWAT called in, and the only way they managed to get her off the dressing table she'd climbed on was by pointing out the critters could actually fly. Apparently she screamed so loud, a second patrol car was dispatched because the neighbors reported her being attacked by the police.

Finn was glad he picked out some sunglasses in the airport because everybody was wearing them, and not because they looked like some bad commercial for a *Men in Black* movie. The Florida sun was so bright, everyone actually needed them. It also meant he could surreptitiously study everyone from behind them.

Eric was definitely the loudest of the group, and it was a toss-up whether the shades were needed for the sun or the god-awful Hawaiian shirt he was wearing.

His partner, Angela, had come along, a soft-spoken woman Finn guessed was in her late forties and around ten years older than Eric. They seemed to make it work, though, because Eric was quite tender toward her, and Finn wondered if they had more than a working partnership.

Drew spent most of the time talking to the other guys: Matt Harker, Dennis Painter, and Emilio Harve. They said they worked out of the Tampa field office, so Finn assumed they were agents, but he wasn't going to ask outright at the bar. Matt had reddish brown hair and white skin that one wouldn't think had ever seen a Florida summer. He seemed pleasant enough. Dennis—the oldest of the three—reminded Finn a little of Deke, unfortunately, and his coloring was the opposite of Matt's. His skin looked like it had been baked by the sun. In fact, the bread Finn liked wasn't as toasted. Emilio, Black-Hispanic in coloring, barely said one word. Neither Matt nor Emilio said much, just listened to Drew and Dennis. Finn couldn't hear what Drew was saying in hushed tones over Eric, but Drew and Dennis each glanced at Finn twice, so he guessed he was the topic of conversation.

The last of the group was a woman called Hannah Bishop. She had just quit her job in a bank, and after a two-week vacation, was flying to Quantico for the latest intake. Apparently she'd known Drew since they were kids. Finn tried not to feel envious.

"You know, I can't decide whether I'm jealous or plain relieved it's not me," Hannah said, smiling.

Finn put his Bud down. He wasn't sure what to say. It couldn't be discussed, and certainly not in a bar. Gregory was very insistent on that. He eyed Drew to see if he had heard what Hannah had said because only he or Drew could have told anyone about it, but Drew was still talking in whispers to the other guys.

Angela leaned forward a little when Finn didn't immediately reply. "I mean, everyone's seen them on TV, but I can't believe they're actually going to be allowed to be agents."

Finn grimaced. They were already fucking agents. He kept his mouth closed, though. He wasn't about to be drawn into a conversation about something he shouldn't be talking about.

He was saved from any reply when Drew stood and offered to get the third round, but both Emilio and Matt stood and gave their apologies. Angela murmured something quietly to Eric, and they stood.

Drew raised his eyebrows. "One more?" He looked at Finn, and Finn nodded. He wanted the chance to talk to Drew, but he wasn't saying anything in front of Hannah.

Hannah must have sensed his reticence, because she also stood. "I've actually got a ton of packing to do, and I'll be away all next week visiting Mom."

Drew walked toward her, and they hugged. "Say hi to your mom for me. I'll try and be up for Thanksgiving."

Finn smiled pleasantly as she left and waited while the server put down three more bottles. He'd hoped Dennis was also leaving, but it didn't look like it. Finn glanced around. There was a ball game on TV near the bar, and most people were over there. He wouldn't be heard.

"So who did you piss off in a former life, huh?" Dennis drawled and took a swig from his fresh bottle.

Finn smiled politely, assuming the question was rhetorical.

"He actually didn't do too bad for his first day," Drew said, also smiling.

Dennis grunted and looked around. He leaned forward a little, not easy because of the bulk around his middle. Finn absently wondered if the guy was an agent, because he knew there were fitness standards, and Dennis didn't look like he could chase after a suspect anytime soon. "You take it from me, son. Go get yourself another job," Dennis said.

Finn didn't reply. He had no clue what to say.

Drew shifted in his chair a little. "Go easy on him."

Dennis tipped the bottle back and drained it in one go, then stood. "Just telling it like it is. See you Monday, I expect."

Finn nodded politely and watched as Dennis stumbled a little as he walked away.

Drew sighed. "It's okay. His sister's picking him up."

"Is he an agent?" Finn asked quietly.

Drew shook his head. "No, he works in white-collar as a computer analyst. Insurance fraud, that sort of thing. Sorry if he's a bit negative."

Finn shrugged.

"So what did you think of your first day, then?" Drew grinned, changing the subject.

Finn shook his head. "Unbelievable. I actually can't believe I'm here." He considered a question he'd been dying to ask. "You work with the team quite a bit. It isn't something you've ever wanted for yourself?"

Drew took a swig from his bottle, and Finn got the impression he was thinking about his answer. "To be honest, yeah. I haven't applied, though."

"Mind me asking why not?"

Drew took another swig of his bottle.

"I know I'm being set up to fail," Finn said. "I know full well the only reason I'm here is because the agency wouldn't take me normally. I'm dispensable." He grinned to soften the words. He didn't want Drew feeling guilty by shooting down his dreams.

Drew sighed. "Caught that, did you?"

Finn smiled, but he couldn't help the twist he felt in his gut at having it confirmed. Seemed like everyone knew. "But you're already a trained agent. The failure of this team isn't going to impact on your career, surely?" He was convinced there was something Drew wasn't saying. "Tell me about the others who didn't make it."

Drew looked up, startled, and Finn's stomach took a quick dive. That was it. His innocent question to keep Drew talking had hit on something. He waited patiently.

Drew started. "You're the fourth that I know of."

"All already agents?"

"Yeah. One of them—Hillier—was a close-combat specialist, and even he couldn't put Vance down. That's his ability, Vance."

"Close combat?" Finn queried.

"No, incredible strength. Think Superman-type shit."

Finn blinked. *Wow.* "To be honest I kind of thought most of the abilities were exaggerated on TV. I mean, how come they're not set on world domination or some such shit?" He was joking, but he shut up when Drew didn't laugh. Okay, so he was officially getting a little more freaked out.

"Because there's not enough of them, and so far the incidence seems to be confined to the US." Drew played with the label on the bottle. "What do you know?"

"The first kids were born in the seventies. There's been no cause identified. Suspicions vary from everything from genetics to pesticides," Finn replied promptly. "There have been some major crimes reported. There was one guy who raided banks…. Something to do with being able to crack computer codes. Another who seemed to be able to do something with explosives. But there hasn't been anything major since the task forces were implemented."

"All that is true, and because the circumstances were very isolated, no major panic has happened. The government has never tried to initiate any sort of testing without consent, despite the law affecting the deceased."

Finn nodded. They passed a law ten years ago stating any enhanced would be subject to special post-mortems. There were a few religious groups that made a fuss, but Finn was surprised at how little people seemed to be disturbed.

"I don't think I would get into trouble telling you this, but we've had at least fifteen years with the rate of transformation being very low. You know transformation...."

"Yeah, yeah," Finn quickly agreed. That was when the enhanced first developed their abilities and the mark on their face, usually around adolescence.

"And you know the enhanced are sterile?"

Finn swallowed. He'd heard that on the news. Actually he heard some religious nut saying it was God's wrath, punishing the abominations so no one else had to suffer.

"Thing is, when they found that out, it was as if people weren't worried anymore. Aliens or super beings weren't going to take over the world." Drew chuckled. "I think that's why we've never had a mass panic on our hands or anything."

"But you've got some super beings," Finn argued.

"Yeah, and no other law enforcement agency will touch them. Gregory thinks that's very shortsighted."

He has a point, thought Finn. "I guess a lot of the abilities are being kept out of the news. What you said about Vance, for instance. First I've heard about anything like that." And the thing Talon did in Gregory's office, which was downright scary.

"Yes, the government has been downplaying things for years."

"So why did none of the trainees work out?" Finn finished his beer and waited to see if he was going to get an answer.

"Two failed the standard questions on the first day." Drew grinned. "At least I know you passed those."

Finn hesitated. "You do?" He cleared his throat.

"Yeah. You wouldn't still be here. Seriously, they didn't tell you? That sucks." Drew finished his beer also and stood. "The third one had a massive argument with Talon and quit. Said he wasn't working with murdering freaks."

"Wow," Finn said. "And the fourth one? You said there were four."

"I didn't tell you." Drew almost glared at Finn.

"Okay." Finn's heart sped up a little.

"I'm not sure exactly, but I think Eli lost control."

"What happened?"

Drew shrugged. "Look, it's not for me to say. I wasn't there. All I know is that Michaelson was carried out of the gym on a stretcher with severe burns and never came back to work." He grabbed his car keys off the table. "Six weeks ago."

Chapter Seven

DREW PULLED his car up to his building this time. "I'd offer a ride tomorrow, but it's my day off."

Finn smiled and thanked him for the beer and the ride.

"Do you want to borrow some jeans?"

Finn shook his head. "Nah, there's a washer and dryer in there. I'll manage."

He slid the plastic entry card to open the door to his block and headed up the stairs. So Drew wasn't as confident as he seemed at first, then? He wondered what Eli had done that caused the burns. Finn had only seen him at the meeting with Gregory and the rest of the team, and Eli hadn't even glanced his way when the introductions were being made. Finn just noted the dark brown hair and the two-day-old stubble and never gave him much thought after that. Eli certainly wasn't present when Drew took Finn down in the gym.

Finn rounded the corner of the stairs and stopped in shock. Talon sat on the floor, his back propped up against Finn's apartment door, with Finn's bag from the plane resting beside him. Talon's head was lowered, and he hadn't looked up when Finn turned down the corridor, but somehow Finn knew Talon was very well aware he was there. So why wouldn't he acknowledge him?

"Oh cool, thanks." He took a step closer and fished for his key.

Talon opened his eyes and looked straight at Finn, and Finn came to a sudden halt. Desperation. Sadness. Futility. All those and more in the blue eyes that stared nearly unseeing into Finn's. Something had happened.

Finn swallowed and took another step. "Want a coffee?" he asked casually, and Talon heaved himself upright. He didn't reply, but he followed Finn inside. Finn walked straight into the kitchen and waved at the stool. "Take a seat."

He opened two of the wrong cupboards before he found the coffee. Talon still hadn't said a word, but Finn was never one to talk when he was nervous. Talon sat and didn't seem like he was in a hurry to leave. Finn could wait. He got two mugs and the cream and sugar out, and then stood awkwardly silent while it brewed. Finn turned to confirm Talon wanted it black as he had in the diner, but the words died in his throat. Talon had silently slid off the stool and stood so close, Finn took a step back when he turned around.

"What happened?" he asked, his fingers itching to touch Talon's bent head.

Talon sighed and took the coffee from the counter. "We were too late."

Finn sipped his own, but when there didn't seem to be any more info coming, he said, "Drew said it was at a school."

"I've never known a kid not to wake up with it, *ever*. It always happens overnight. But this one, he was playing ball and got into it with some other kid because he cheated. There was a fight, and he pushed him."

"Who? The enhanced did?" Finn asked.

Talon rubbed a hand over his eyes. "Yeah. Except the kid he pushed flew back straight into a brick wall and demolished it. He's currently in Tampa General with severe head injuries. They're not sure he's gonna make it."

"What happened to the other kid?"

"The cops arrived at the same time as the kid's parents. Apparently they live close, and the dad works nights, so he was home. By this time the kid was nearly hysterical. The teacher was trying to calm him down, and she told us the mark just grew before her eyes as the kid was crying. He wouldn't let anyone near him, just kept screaming for his mom." Talon looked up again, and Finn's heart seemed to tighten at the hollowness in Talon's eyes.

"And his mom and dad came?"

Talon nodded. "The kid was distraught. He was crying and shaking, and the mom and dad arrived. His mom called his name and started to go near, and then he looked up when he heard her. She just screamed, and the kid cried and ran toward her. The dad...." Talon stopped, his throat working. "He pushed him away," he whispered. "Told him not to come anywhere near his wife. Said he had to stay back. We arrived at the same time as the cops, and they took him out without giving us a chance to talk to him."

"Took.... You mean they sedated him, don't you?" Fuck, it sounded like they shot the kid.

Talon nodded. "But he wasn't completely out straight away. Crying desperately for his mom, and his dad just turned to the cops and told them to take him away. That he was no son of theirs. That they had to take him because he was never coming in their house ever again.

"There was nothing I could do," Talon said. "I thought Gael was gonna kill the dad. I had to get the team back."

"What will happen?" Finn asked in horror.

"State takes them. The ones no one wants. The ones who are thrown away."

Finn felt his own eyes burning, and he blinked.

Talon shook his head as if in complete disbelief. "That's why this unit has to work. We have to show we're not monsters. We have to show we don't need locking up. We could start all sorts of outreach programs—go to schools, even."

Finn closed the gap between them. He had no thought except comfort, except showing this man who hurt so badly that not everyone condemned them. He put his hand out to touch Talon's shoulder without thinking, and Talon raised his face. Finn stopped. Something changed. He couldn't swallow in his closed throat. The blue in Talon's eyes deepened and seemed to draw him in. His warm breath ghosted over Finn's lips, and Finn's heart seemed to slow.

Talon moved. Not so much moved as launched himself at Finn. It was only Talon planting his arms around Finn's back that kept Finn upright against the onslaught as Talon's mouth savaged his.

Finn was stunned, reeling. He froze for a second, and then, as he felt Talon react to his immobility, just as Talon stiffened and Finn knew he was about to step away, Finn's lips seemed to remember what to do, how to respond. He couldn't help the grunt as he latched on to Talon and feverishly hung on in case Talon thought he wasn't interested.

Talon responded just as desperately, and Finn felt his feet almost clear the floor as Talon dragged Finn's body against his. Finn arched as Talon threaded his fingers through Finn's hair and bent his head. Kissing didn't come close to the way Talon possessed Finn's mouth. He bit and pulled at Finn's lower lip with his teeth, and the groan that reverberated in Talon's throat traveled to Finn's cock.

Finn held on and tugged at Talon's hair, desperate for him not to move. Desperate for more. Never in his wildest fantasies had anything like this happened.

Then Talon moved his hand to the front of Finn's jeans, and Finn whined an urgent warning. His cock throbbed and pulsed, and he was desperate to feel Talon's fingers. Finn arched against Talon, blood pounding in his ears, blood pounding in his groin. He just needed…. Talon slid his hand down the front of Finn's jeans and cupped his cock through his boxers. Finn tried to pull away, tried to break the kiss, or he would come in his jeans. Talon just growled, and the sound went straight to Finn's balls.

"No." Talon nearly shouted the word and pushed Finn away.

Finn's knees gave out, and he staggered before collapsing on the floor. He blinked, completely dazed.

"I can't. I'm sorry." Talon dragged a hand through his hair, gave Finn one desperate look, and strode to the door. He banged it shut behind him.

Finn raised a shaky hand to his swollen lips. *What the fuck?*

He got to his feet and winced. He needed a shower. He didn't even know where to begin sorting all that out in his head, but in his limited experience with hand jobs, he'd just had the best sex of his life, and he never even removed his clothes.

What the hell did that mean for work tomorrow?

Chapter Eight

FINN DROVE his car up to yet another barrier the next morning. This was "the Farm"—the outside training area and shooting range. Apparently it was secure because the guy currently inspecting his security pass was in combat fatigues, but he knew it couldn't be the regular military because they weren't allowed to be armed on US soil. It was probably private contractors, maybe the National Guard.

The soldier directed him to where he should park and waved him through. Finn didn't know whether to feel excited or just plain sick. He was looking forward to showing some sort of knowledge, at least with a handgun and at least in theory, but he had no idea how to react to Talon this morning.

He recognized Talon's truck as he pulled inside three other cars. Finn turned the engine off and sat a few seconds, contemplating the large building in front of him. It looked like some sort of warehouse, with no names or any sort of designation on the small door set casually to one side. Finn had gulped two cups of coffee this morning, but his stomach was too tied in knots to be able to force any food down his throat. Maybe he'd feel better if he didn't make a fool of himself with a gun.

Not for one second did he expect to last even four weeks here, but maybe if he didn't make a complete idiot of himself, he might get a shot at Quantico. Or was he fooling himself? He knew he was here because he'd never had a chance at Quantico, not really.

Finn got out of the car and walked to the door. He smiled as he pushed open the door and was met by Gael.

"Hey, kid," Gael greeted him.

He grinned and unobtrusively scanned the room. The team was there sitting around a large table, drinking coffee, with the exception of one obvious person: Talon. *He's here, though.* Finn had seen the truck, so that meant Talon was avoiding him.

Finn accepted a coffee from Gael and looked quietly at the other agents. He was too nervous to really notice them yesterday. Gael and Vance were the biggest of the guys. Gael was roughly the same build as Talon, but Vance was… *huge.* He remembered what Drew told him last night, that strength was Vance's ability, and he wasn't surprised. He looked like he bench-pressed trucks, and that was without any enhancement. Eli and Sawyer were the smallest of the group. Sawyer was slim, with big shoulders, though, that tapered to a narrow waist. More of a swimmer's body than a wrestler. Finn remembered that Sawyer could deconstruct metal in seconds.

He glanced at Eli as Gael and Vance were chatting about some game. Eli never seemed to speak. He also never seemed to actually look at Finn, and he suddenly wondered if there was a reason why Eli didn't want him there apart from the whole "humans not working with enhanced" thing. Drew had told him about the agent with the burns.

At just that second, Eli lifted his head and stared right at Finn. His eyes were challenging, almost mocking, and Finn had an awful feeling the guy knew what he was thinking.

"So I'm assuming you wouldn't have gotten to the ripe old age of twenty-four and a fed wannabe without knowing something about guns, then?" Gael asked but didn't stop for a reply. He carried a plastic basket with four different guns and three boxes of ammo.

Finn blinked. What should he say? He did know about guns, in theory. He could rattle off the latest decision for the FBI deciding to change their handguns of choice to the Glock 19 because of the recoil. He could quote the statistics that proved most gunfights happened within three seconds and three feet of an opponent. He could also tell anyone who was interested that the national accuracy of police officers hitting their targets was only 15 percent.

He just hadn't actually ever held a gun, let alone fired it. *Shit.*

Gael held headphones and goggles out to him. "No one goes through that door without eyes and ears on."

He followed Gael's nod to the door behind him. The top half was glass, but Finn couldn't see anything behind it except for a wall. He took the headphones and goggles from Gael and followed him, conscious of three other people all getting to their feet and following them.

Where the hell was Talon?

TALON WAS a coward, he acknowledged in disgust. He'd watched Finn, and he admired his guts. It must have taken some to appear in front of the team like that, knowing Talon was here somewhere. He stood on the observation deck that ran alongside the range. There was a one-way glass so an instructor could watch a trainee in any of the lanes. There was also a microphone, so Talon heard everything Finn said—or rather, what he didn't.

He knew the purpose of this morning was to add another failure to Finn's tally. He agreed originally along with the team that, if by some miracle the kid made it to his second day, they would make sure he didn't get any further. The added bonus was Drew wasn't here to document anything. Talon had been convinced for months that an all-enhanced team was the right way to go.

There was no way anyone could know about Sawyer or Gael's extra abilities. They also weren't ready to tell an unsuspecting human population their abilities were evolving. The enhanced had always developed their powers instantly at the same time as the mark, even if some of the kids didn't know what they were. It wasn't something that ever grew or changed, and that was why the humans saw them as less of a threat. Gael certainly would never again see the outside of a laboratory if they knew what he could do. And Sawyer? It didn't bear thinking about.

The whole purpose of the unit was to turn the monsters into heroes.

Talon sighed. He was the furthest thing from a hero, but if he was going to do one thing, it was to make sure no more enhanced children were ever rejected by their parents. He already tried to visit the kid from yesterday and was barred. The hospital had cited that he wasn't family, but Talon knew that was complete bullshit. His *family* didn't want anything to do with him. The kid would be terrified. Gregory had agreed to make some phone calls to help him out.

Talon narrowed his eyes as he heard Gael offering Finn a choice of gun. Gael was subtly intimating he should go with the Sig Sauer P229, knowing full well Finn had slim hands and would be better with the H & K. He was deliberately setting him up to fail, and Talon wasn't sure how much longer he could watch. Gael never attempted to correct Finn's shaky stance. Never corrected his grip or his bent elbows. Never warned him the first shot would have the most recoil.

Like last night, how Finn had sought to offer comfort, and how Talon was the one responsible for taking it too far.

Fuck, he couldn't watch this anymore… not without doing something about it. Talon whirled around and raced out of the door. He clattered down the steps, grabbed a pair of goggles and headphones, and entered the range. The door slammed open just as Finn took his first shot and completely missed.

Gael smirked, especially when Finn nearly dropped the gun because of the pain Talon knew he would have felt in his wrist.

"You lot go get your practice in. I'll take over." Talon nearly growled the order.

Gael's eyebrows shot upward, but he gave a goofy grin. "About time," he said pointedly, and he turned and left with Sawyer, Vance, and Eli to go to the other end of the range.

Talon ignored the guns and looked at Finn. "Come on." He exited the range, and Finn shuffled after him to the large table. Talon took off his goggles and head-phones, and Finn copied him. "Sit," he ordered. Shit, Finn wasn't even looking at him. "How many times have you actually fired a gun?" Talon asked bluntly.

Finn looked up with resignation written all over his face. Talon suddenly wanted to see a different look. "Once," Finn admitted.

Talon opened his mouth to ask where but paused. "Just now?" he said incredulously.

Finn nodded again miserably.

"But how?" Talon asked. "It's not like it's diffi-cult to go to a local firing range. You told me you've wanted to be a fed for ten years. I can't believe you've never fired a gun before."

Finn's throat worked, but then he sagged a little in defeat. "My brother Deke's best buddy owned the range in town. There was no way I could get lessons there."

Talon sat down. He didn't know where to start. Normally it wouldn't matter at all, but condensing eight hundred hours of training into four weeks made it impossible. One of the requirements was that the trainee knew the basics, even if Talon personally pre-ferred someone exactly like Finn. No previous experi-ence meant no bad habits to break.

Allowing Finn a week that hopefully meant he might have a shot at getting into Quantico meant Talon was going to have to give him some lessons.

Talon stood and pointed to the light switch on the wall. "Make a triangle with your fingers until you're framing it completely in your line of sight."

Finn looked confused but did exactly what Talon said.

"Now close your right eye."

Finn did.

"Can you still see it?" Talon asked, and Finn nodded. "Good, now close your left eye." Talon nearly smiled at the look of surprise on Finn's face when he knew the switch had vanished. "That means your left eye is dominant, but you're right-handed. We need to know that to help with your stance. Now," said Talon. "The most important thing to remember is to always treat a gun like it's loaded."

WHEN TALON had answered every single one of Finn's million questions, he picked up the goggles and ear covers again. He'd covered everything from correct stance to sizing the weapon to fit Finn's hand. He wanted him to try the .40 and the 9mm so he could judge the recoil for himself. In a perfect world, there was a lot Finn could get to fit his hand better, but he would have to manage with standard department-issue weapons for now.

Finn brightened up considerably when he realized Talon wasn't about to humiliate him again, and Finn was a veritable treasure trove of information. He knew everything from the fact that there were over a million concealed-carry permits issued in the state of Florida to the current stats arguing feds shouldn't be armed anymore. They were never the first responders in any situation, and there was currently a lot of government noise suggesting special armed units similar to SWAT teams.

Whatever Finn was, he wasn't dumb, and Talon was beginning to understand what Gregory saw in him.

Talon directed Finn to the nearest lane, well out of the way of the others. He let him try the VP first, as it would have the least recoil and he wanted Finn to get comfortable. He corrected Finn's loose grip and bent elbows and tried very hard to ignore his seeming apparent need to touch Finn to correct his arms, his fingers... even which foot he threw out behind him.

"One of the reasons you shot low last time was adrenaline. Squeeze the trigger slowly. The recoil on the first shot is the worst. Aim for the chest."

Finn lowered his chin like he'd been shown and pulled the trigger. The hole was bang smack in the target's center area. Talon chuckled, and he saw Finn visibly relax. They spent another thirty minutes with two different guns, simulating firing from a holster and at different distances. Finn was actually pretty good. He was especially accurate with the head shots, which were the hardest.

"Always go for the spine area in defensive shooting," Talon encouraged. "Even if you hit an assailant's heart or jugular, it takes minutes to bleed out, in which time he could have shot a lot more people, including you. Anywhere in the spine area or the hip is going to stop him."

Finn emptied the last round and placed his gun down exactly as Talon said. He turned triumphantly, and Talon heard clapping behind him.

Gael and Vance stood grinning widely. "You did good, kid," Gael called out, and Finn blushed.

Talon wanted to groan. Why the fuck did he get so turned on because the guy blushed like a teenage girl?

Because you want to put that look on his face....

"I sent Eli and Sawyer for supplies," Vance added.

Good, thought Talon. He was actually starving. They all walked back into the main area, and Vance gathered up all the training guns and ammo to lock them away in the cupboards. "Every day you can at 7:00 a.m., come down for practice with one of us," Talon decreed, and Finn nodded eagerly. "Vance is gonna show you how to take care of your weapon while we wait for lunch." Talon watched as Finn followed Vance.

"You changed your mind yet?" Gael said.

Talon chewed the inside of his cheek while he thought about brushing off Gael's question. "About?"

"Wonderboy over there," Gael said, and Talon could hear the laughter in Gael's voice.

"You know we can't." Talon turned to Gael. "You of all people know we can't."

Gael shrugged. "Just so you know, I like the kid. If we had to have someone, I don't think he'd be a bad fit."

Talon didn't reply. It was impossible. He had to protect the others. Finn seemed nice, but if Gregory or any of his superiors asked him a direct question, Finn wouldn't be able to lie, and Talon wouldn't risk his friends' lives with that chance.

Chapter Nine

FOUR DAYS later no one was more surprised than Finn that he was still there. His shooting was improving to the point where he could now draw from a holster. He still hadn't attempted any moving targets, though, and Finn knew assailants didn't just stand still and threaten. They were usually moving very fast.

His hand-to-hand was improving, even if his bruises had bruises. He'd still only fought Drew, but Vance, surprisingly, had started giving him little pointers. Things like controlling balance and tricks to distract Drew into expecting one thing while Finn did another. He wasn't sure Drew could still easily take him out, but Drew didn't let his guard down around Finn at all after Finn took him down the first day. Finn comforted himself with the fact that Drew had been an agent for two years to his whole four days.

He now knew the proper way to arrest a suspect, and Gregory even coached him himself in giving evidence at trials. Gregory also opened up a little about the team. Apparently he knew Talon's family, and Talon secretly underwent months of training last year, along with Vance. The rest of the enhanced were brought in slowly by Talon. Gregory had a small team of instructors who gave their time quietly to keep this under the radar. Everyone at the field office knew because the enhanced weren't exactly easy to hide, but they all thought they were being brought in for consultation only, not to be made agents. That made Finn uncomfortable. Hannah Bishop, Drew's friend, certainly knew, and he wasn't completely sure Drew hadn't told the agents the night they were at the bar. He wasn't about to rat him out, though. Drew was helping him out in the hand-to-hand, and besides which, it would be good to have some friends here.

Finn was also getting on better with the team. Gael and Vance were quite relaxed around him, and they seemed to be his biggest supporters. Sawyer was unbending a little. Eli, however, still ignored Finn completely, but Talon was still the biggest enigma. He was courteous but distant. Finn no longer thought he was setting him up to fail, but he never came within three feet of him unless he was demonstrating hand-to-hand or correcting his shooting stance, and he didn't seem to do that anymore.

Talon never mentioned the night he turned up at Finn's, and Finn definitely wasn't going to. Talon obviously wanted to forget it. Finn had tried to bury the memory anyway. Being in the gym with a hard-on wasn't conducive either to his training or his self-respect. Every second of every day, he was more determined to make the team a success, and if that meant keeping it zipped in his pants for the foreseeable future, well, it wasn't something Finn wasn't used to.

Even Agent Gregory had started looking jovial.

"We want to make you all aware of a new domestic threat that seems to have emerged," Gregory said. He stood at the front of the "classroom," as the team jokingly called it, where Finn had taken the first written test in the day he started. Gregory clicked on the monitor and moved to the side. There was a picture of a middle-aged guy standing at a podium. He seemed professional, wearing a suit, but the photo showed the guy's mouth turned up in a sneer.

"This is Judge Benedict Cryer. He retired last year and has taken up local politics. It's widely accepted that he'll get elected to represent district four. When he was serving, he was notorious for his hard-line stance on anything juvenile-related. He has repeatedly been quoted insisting that society, in general, is too soft on kids, so any coming through his court weren't given any favors." Gregory clicked on the next screen, showing Cryer speaking to a large group of people. "He's narrowed his opinions on juvenile crime recently, specifically targeting one group of people."

"Enhanced," Eli said flatly, and Finn jumped, not used to him saying anything. Eli continued. "Same age, same circumstance, same misdemeanor, but if you were enhanced, you would get locked up. I came into contact with the judge a few years ago."

Finn swung his head around back to Gregory, feeling uncomfortable. He might try to get his boss on his own if he could. Surely it was only fair to know a little of his team's personal history? He knew damn well they all knew his.

"What's he up to now?" Vance asked.

"He's making noises about registering enhanced," Talon replied and shrugged. "Not that he hasn't done that before, but he's also saying it's in the child's best interests for them not to live at home even if the parents want them to."

Finn gaped. There had been noises about registering enhanced over the years, but the mark made it obvious who they were, so it died down. *But the kids?* "How could they do that, though?" Finn asked. "It's gotta break so many laws. It's impossible."

"Remember Oliver Martinez from the school a few days ago? The boy he threw against the wall died last night. He never recovered from his head injuries," Gregory said solemnly.

The room was silent.

Gregory blew out a breath. "There's a demonstration and a rally outside city hall being hurriedly set up for this afternoon. It's widely reported, and it's likely Isaac Dakota will be there."

Finn looked up from where he had been staring at the floor. He'd seen that guy on the TV a lot of times. Isaac Dakota was an enhanced. He came from a huge political family, and as Judge Cryer fought against the civil liberties of the enhanced, Dakota fought just as hard the other way. Isaac was likely to cause trouble.

"There's a possibility that he may bring some friends. Other enhanced." Gregory looked at them all. "The powers that be have decided they are going to stage a press conference at city hall. The

formation of the human and enhanced unit is going to
be announced."

Everyone was silent. Finn glanced at their
shocked expressions and tried to judge their reactions.
They'd mostly been cool to him the last few days, but
he still didn't think they wanted the unit to include
regular humans.

Sawyer threw his pen down. "So you're saying
the kid stays?"

Gregory looked embarrassed, and Finn wanted to
crawl under the table. "I'm saying the unit goes ahead
with both regular and enhanced. Each of you will get
partners, but steadily, over time. It isn't something anyone wants to rush, and we are still reviewing whether or
not we should be using trained agents or not." He glared
at Talon. "What works for one of you might not work
for everyone. They have organized the press conference
to take place ahead of the rally, and they want you all
there to keep the peace without the EnU."

Finn knew the EnU, or Enhanced Unit, stood for
the cops' special unit that carried the tranqs in case an
enhanced needed sedating quickly. No one said anything. Finn risked a look at Talon, but his face was a
hard mask.

"One last thing," Gregory added. "They want
Finn front and center."

"No way!" Talon lurched to his feet. "Absolutely
no way. He's been here five days."

Gregory put his hands out in supplication. "I
know it's not a perfect scenario. But they want Finn
obvious to give the public confidence in the unit."

Finn's heart was pumping so hard, it was a wonder no one else heard it.

"And they want you in uniform." Deathly silence met Gregory's last statement.

"We don't have a uniform," Gael said slowly, as if expecting to be challenged.

"Yeah, you do now. You'll find them all hung in the locker room."

Vance and Gael stared at each other in astonishment. "This I gotta see." Vance lurched to his feet.

Finn glanced at Talon, equally torn whether to follow them out or to wait and see what being front and center actually involved. He took one look at Talon's grim face as he headed for Gregory and decided to go see his new uniform.

"Well, shit," Gael drawled, holding up the black shirt. "This is so not my color."

Vance chuckled, but he'd already stripped down and was pulling a shirt the size of a tent over his massive shoulders.

Finn gazed at them with his mouth wide open. They were all acting like a bunch of kids playing dress up. *Even Eli.* Finn watched as he yanked his pants up.

"Here."

Finn turned just in time to catch the armful of clothes Sawyer threw at him.

"Oh my God, it fucking fits." Vance stood in front of the mirror in the corner, turning to his left and tightening the belt, and Finn suddenly laughed. Vance could demolish a house, and he was excited because he'd gotten a pair of pants that fit him.

Gael grinned. "Hey, Finn. Let's see you in yours."

Just at that moment, Talon stormed into the locker room and stopped in astonishment.

"Look, boss," Vance said eagerly.

Talon shook his head in disbelief and caught Finn's gaze. "Sit down, everyone," he barked. Everyone sat, Finn still clutching his uniform. Talon paced. "Right. We need to introduce ourselves."

Finn glanced in astonishment at Talon. He caught the grin Vance and Gael sent each other.

Talon stared at Finn. "This was never supposed to happen five days into your training." He looked around at the other guys. "On the off chance that we get into a situation out there, Finn needs to know who has his back and how to use it to his advantage. The press will have a field day. Apparently they're flying in Deputy Director Cohen to make the announcement."

Sawyer stood. "But I thought this was just an experiment?"

Finn swung back to be pierced by Talon's cold blue eyes as he spoke. "I've just been told either the joint enhanced unit goes ahead or they are disbanding the unit entirely."

Eli stood next to Sawyer. "You're shitting me. There's no way." He looked scathingly at Finn. "We're gonna be nothing but guard dogs for the show pony we're gonna trot out for the press."

"Hey," Finn protested. "I—"

"Be quiet, all of you," Talon snapped.

Finn seethed. He was sick of being belittled. He'd worked his ass off for the last few days, and he had every intention of being an active member of this unit.

"We have no choice," Talon grated out.

Wonderful, thought Finn. That was really going to endear him to his teammates.

Sawyer scoffed. "So we're either stuck with him or the unit doesn't happen?"

Finn bristled again, but Talon sent him a warning glance.

"I want you to go around and name your official enhancement," Talon said carefully, and Finn whipped his head back around to him. *Official enhancement?* That implied there were unofficial ones. Ones that maybe even Gregory didn't know about.

Finn leaned back against the locker. That was it. He would bet his last dime that was it. The reason they didn't want a human in their unit was secrecy. Shit. His day had gotten even more fucked up. What was he doing, really? Did he really want to work with people who clearly hated his guts? Was being in the FBI that important to him?

For the first time in ten years, he suddenly wasn't so sure.

"Well," said Vance, seeming loud in the quiet of the room. "What you see, Finn, is what you get with me." He shrugged.

Finn smiled cautiously. Vance and Gael had been nothing but helpful this week. He put his head to one side. "Do you actually know how strong you are?" he said, suddenly curious.

Vance shrugged. "The Guinness World Records puts the heaviest lift at over sixty-two hundred pounds, but I've beaten that." He glanced at Talon. "How much does your truck weigh in at?"

"You've lifted his truck?" Finn said in astonishment. He gazed at Talon. "It's gotta be at least eight thousand pounds."

Talon nodded slowly.

"You're also good at hearing accents," Finn added, and Vance smiled in acknowledgment.

"Although to be honest, that's not necessarily an ability. Some humans are good at that," Vance said.

"Voice recognition," Gael added. Finn raised his eyebrows, and Gael glanced at him. "He's like a computer. He only has to hear someone talk once and he can pick them out in a crowd."

"I don't actually think many computers can do that," Finn said faintly. "Speech recognition was aimed at recognizing a preprogrammed voice." He brightened. "Although the UK's Air Force is doing experiments with speech recognition in cockpits."

"Where do you know all that stuff from?" Gael interrupted.

"Enough," Talon said, exasperation coloring his voice, and Finn shut up.

"I can deconstruct metal," Sawyer said—grudgingly, it seemed to Finn.

He frowned. "Meaning?" He suddenly fell with a whoosh as his chair gave way.

Sawyer grinned and stood, holding his hand out to pull Finn back up.

Finn turned, amazed to see the plastic seat flat on the floor surrounded by what looked like a bunch of metal filings. "That is so cool!" Finn exclaimed and sat gingerly on the next available seat Sawyer pulled out for him.

Sawyer grinned. "It only works at around six feet so far, though."

"I demonstrated my ability when you came for your interview," Talon said.

"I remember not being able to move." It was the closest he had ever been to a full-blown panic attack.

"I'm able to slow everything down in your body—your blood flow, your breathing. It brings on a state of near paralysis, but we think that's the body's defense, not something I actually induce."

Finn waited to see if he offered anything else, but he didn't, unsurprisingly, so Finn looked at Gael.

"I can translate anything without ever being taught a foreign language," Gael said. "Unless you count the Spanish I was taught in middle school."

Finn shared his grin. "Just hearing or written?"

"Both," Gael replied. "Wewe kuuliza maswali ya haki."

Finn blinked. "What does that mean?"

"It means 'you ask the right questions,'" Gael said. "In Swahili."

"Wow," said Finn. "I'm surprised they didn't want you for the foreign office or something."

Gael shrugged. "They're too ashamed of us. Did you know none of us can get a passport?"

"Why?" Finn asked in astonishment. He hadn't known that.

"Because they're too frightened we might accidentally blow up the plane or something," Talon said.

"Because no other country wants us either." There was a short silence when no one said a word, and everyone looked at Eli. After a few seconds, he shrugged. "I'm a pyromaniac," he drawled. "That means—"

"I know what it means." Just because he couldn't set things on fire didn't mean he was dumb.

"So that's our little group," Gael said, grabbed his uniform jacket, stood, and put it on. "Is Gregory waiting for us to go back in?"

Talon shook his head. "No. We leave in an hour. Get something to eat, and then he wants us in full uniform. He's arranged for a press conference inside the city hall before the demo starts. He's hoping it will take the attention away from them." Finn could hear the disbelief in Talon's words.

"Fuck me."

Everyone turned at Sawyer's outburst and followed his gaze. Gael had turned to the door, but he twisted around at Sawyer's exclamation.

Vance barked out a laugh and grabbed his own jacket. "Did you know about this, boss?"

Finn stared at the lettering on the back of the jacket, and his face broke into a grin. "They've given us a cool name."

Talon looked heavenward in exasperation. "Gregory mentioned it, but I thought he was yanking my chain."

"H.E.R.O." Finn spelled it out slowly. "What does it stand for?" he asked Talon in awe.

"Human Enhanced Rescue Organization." Talon winced as he said it.

"That's completely awesome," breathed Vance.

Gael took off his jacket and stared at the letters. He glanced at Talon. "You have to admit, boss. It's kind of cool."

Talon looked around at all their faces and shook his head. "This could still go very wrong." He looked at Finn and nodded to the jacket Finn was gripping. "You need to get that uniform on."

Finn stood nervously. "I think I'll eat first."

Vance was just leaving the room, but he turned at Finn's words. "Shit, that's actually a good idea." He slowly unbuttoned his shirt and glanced at Finn. "My whole family's either cops or in law enforcement of some type. Dad and four brothers. I've wanted to put this uniform on since I was a kid, and I don't dare risk mayo all down the front of it." He laughed.

Talon made an exasperated sound. "I'll see you in the cafeteria." And he walked out.

Finn stared after Talon.

"Don't mind him. His family is all in law enforcement too. They live in DC."

Finn nodded. "Yeah, I know. Drew told me."

"I bet you think we're all complete dumbasses." Vance sighed heavily.

Finn paused before he let out the immediate easy denial that had sprung to his lips. He sat on the bench opposite Vance and leaned back on his locker door. "You are stronger and faster than me. You outran me on the track yesterday, even though technically I should be able to sprint faster because of your bulk. You had much better endurance." Vance looked up hesitantly. "Most people use the phrase 'can kill with their bare hands.' Vance, you could take me out with one tied behind your back." Finn's grin widened as Vance started to look uncomfortable at the praise. Seemed he was shy.

"All my life I wanted this," Vance said slowly, as if he were picking through his own memories. "It was a given. I'm the youngest of five. Cops came around to our house all the time. My dad is a lieutenant, and all my brothers wanted to be just like him when we grew up." He smiled. "Drove my mom nuts."

Finn kept quiet. There was more. He knew there was more.

"It was my birthday. I was thirteen and felt on top of the world. A few of us had been laid up with a mild flu the week before, so when I woke up not feeling too great, I shook it off. We had a huge barbecue planned for the afternoon, and the house would be full. Full of cops and their families. Dad had promised to take me to the shooting range for my birthday. He made us all wait until we were official teenagers. He used to joke it was a good age. How old you were when you had to start becoming a man. I never even stopped to brush my teeth, or I'd have seen it in the mirror." Vance touched his mark self-consciously. "We always had breakfast together. Whoever was in the house. Breakfast was our thing. I knew the presents would be laid on the table next to my plate, and I couldn't wait." Vance leaned his head back against the lockers and swallowed. "I ran into the kitchen. Mom was just frying the eggs, and she turned around with this huge smile on her face."

Finn watched Vance struggle with the memories. The everyday noises from outside faded into the distance. Someone closed a door. Someone else was talking.

"I'll never forget how she screamed. She dropped the pan, and my dad and eldest brother came running into the kitchen. They all looked at me like I had two heads. Then my dad kissed my mom's head and opened his arms. To me. I nearly ran to my dad. I didn't know what the matter was. Mom was scaring the crap out of me.

"Mom calmed down in seconds, and two of my other brothers had turned up by then. I knew something was wrong with how tight Dad was clutching me, like he was real scared."

Vance sighed and opened his eyes. "They showed me in the mirror. Mom had a small one in her purse because Dad wouldn't let go of me to even go to the bathroom." Vance shrugged. "And just like that, my life was over."

"Your dad sounds wonderful, though," Finn said cautiously.

Vance grinned. "Yeah, he was. They all were. I stayed on and finished every bit of school. There was no way anyone would dare go against a Connelly. My brothers were all fiercely protective of me, and I was incredibly lucky. I even did college and got a job for a security company. That's how I met Talon. Private security companies loved us because perps just took one look and ran, but it was the only way I ever thought I was gonna get the chance to put on a uniform."

Vance smoothed out his jacket. "Talon had a similar background to mine, and we decided to train ourselves. We both wanted to be ready if this chance ever came up. To prove we can be more than the monsters the public seems to think we are. This is our chance, Finn, and I know you understand that."

"You've seen my file." Finn smiled.

Vance nodded. "Different set of circumstances, but I can respect that you want this as much as any of us." Vance stood and pulled on his T-shirt. "Lunch?" He'd obviously finished sharing, and Finn took his cue from him.

Finn grimaced. "I don't know how hungry I'm going to be."

Vance grinned. "I'm always hungry." He stuck his hand out. "Welcome to the team, partner."

Chapter Ten

FINN HAD stared at himself in the mirror in the bathroom as long as he dared. The black pants and shirt were made of some stretchy material he couldn't put a name to but definitely wasn't just cotton. It seemed a mixture of an official dress uniform and combat clothes, and he loved the badass boots he now wore as well.

He didn't blame Vance and the others one bit for their excitement, but the thought of him doing something to mess things up for the team made him feel sick. He barely ate a sandwich at lunch, and Talon had dismissed them for five minutes to get their shit together.

The team had ribbed one another over lunch. They all made a huge joke out of the name, but it was obvious they were each affected in their own way. Vance and Gael were the loudest, as usual. Sawyer had relaxed and was teasing them both. Eli was silent, but Finn caught a smile once before Eli realized Finn was looking at him, and it turned into a scowl pretty quickly.

He hadn't known what to make of Talon. Talon stayed quiet but glanced at Vance indulgently a couple of times when Vance asked Gael to take a photo of him in the uniform so he could send it to his mom and dad. Talon told them everything Gregory knew about the demo, citing a couple of the judge's sentences in regard to the enhanced to demonstrate his bias. Then they piled into Talon's truck, although it was a bit of a tight squeeze even when they put Vance in the front.

"I think you ought to requisition a vehicle, boss. We need something we can all fit in, for starters," Gael grumbled.

"We need a 6.7L BearCat," Finn said eagerly. "Lenco does a V10 Triton gas as well, but I'd go with the diesel." He looked around the car at the five astonished faces in the sudden silence.

"Yeah." Gael grinned and put his hand up for a high five.

Finn didn't leave him hanging.

"So give me a good reason to ask for one?" Talon turned around. "And I'm not just saying they would match the uniforms," he drawled.

Finn started counting off the reasons on his fingers. "The diesel engine's gonna last you, but it's a lot more costly upfront. It can seat up to ten people comfortably, plus their gear. There are many documented incidents relating to the armor shielding. In Texas in 2010, a BearCat withstood thirty-five rounds from an AK-47. It—"

Talon laughed and held his hand up. "Okay, okay. I'm convinced."

Gael bumped shoulders with Finn.

"Actually, boss, Finn's right," Sawyer said. "Tampa's already buying an extra armored vehicle for this year's round of political conventions. Nearly every SWAT unit in the entire country has them. If the team gets the go-ahead, I don't think getting the funding would be difficult," Sawyer said to the shocked faces in the car.

Finn was dumbfounded. *Sawyer* was agreeing with him. Before he knew it, Eli would be acknowledging his existence. He glanced at the stony-faced guy staring at the roof. Mmm, okay, maybe not.

"So," said Gael, looking at Finn. "You've just got to convince them."

Finn swallowed. How had it suddenly become his responsibility?

Vance glanced back. "We're on Kennedy. Five minutes." He turned back around, then quietly breathed, "Shit."

Talon's knuckles whitened on the steering wheel. "Get Gregory on the phone. I don't think they were expecting this."

Finn leaned forward and felt his heart thud angrily in his chest. The cops were rushing to cordon off the hastily erected podium right outside of the old city hall. Even with the noise of the truck, the shouts of the crowd were easily heard.

"I'm going to pull the truck right up to the barrier and block the rest of Kennedy," Talon said. He fixed a hard look on Finn. "Put your jacket on."

Finn nodded. It was well over seventy degrees, but Finn knew exactly why Talon gave the order. If this was going to work, it was down to him.

THIS IS why the whole thing is such a complete fuckup, thought Talon. Finn had been here five fucking days. He could shoot a gun, barely, so long as the perp stood still and waited for him to fire, he couldn't take Drew down now that he was ready for him, and he was still missing 750 fucking hours of training. Talon scrubbed a frustrated hand over his face. He should have gone with his first instinct and had Finn fail the written test on the first day. Then his own heart wouldn't feel like it was going to stop on him.

You shouldn't care. He shouldn't, but all of a sudden, his team's future rested on the shoulders of some scrawny kid who couldn't read properly.

Talon bit his lip. He knew better than that. Of all people, he knew better than to judge at face value. He might struggle sometimes, but Finn was quick and clever. He rattled off random bits of information all the time, and Talon smiled at how he'd known the engine sizes on the BearCat. His own feelings aside, Finn wasn't a bad fit for the team. Gael and Vance certainly liked him, and he was pretty much sure whoever they sent wouldn't be liked by either Sawyer or Eli. It just wasn't fair.

He looked over at Finn's pale but determined face as he leaned forward and gazed at the crowd as Talon pulled the truck to a stop. It wasn't fair to the team, but most of all, if he were honest, it wasn't fair to Finn. He needed to sit them all down without Finn and talk.

They couldn't risk anyone knowing about Gael or Sawyer.

Talon turned around and looked at five serious faces. "Remember, every TV network will show this around the world. They all want us to fail. Don't give them any excuse." He looked at Finn. "You ready, *Agent Mayer*?"

Finn looked startled at Talon's words, but Talon had used them deliberately. He needed Finn to have a little confidence. At the very least, he should know they all had his back.

Finn took a breath and nodded.

Eli opened the back of the truck, and one by one, they all jumped out. Talon immediately saw a sergeant jogging toward him and wondered what reception he was going to get. The cop looked relieved, though.

"Agent? I understand your team will be handling this. I've asked for additional backup, but to be honest, the size of the crowd has taken everyone by surprise, and the Yankees are playing the Orioles this afternoon. Being spring break, we're already spread thin."

Talon nodded, relieved the sergeant clearly had no problem taking direction from an enhanced. The cop barely glanced at his scar.

He gazed over the crowd as murmurs arose. People started pointing at his team as they exited the van, and one or two defiantly raised placards. Talon sighed silently. The word "mutants" was scrawled over two in dripping red paint. Done, he assumed, to look like blood. He felt Vance stiffen as a shout came from the crowd, and Talon glanced to where Vance was looking.

A woman raised a placard and screamed as she saw them. "Monsters!"

Another guy joined in. "Filthy perverts!"

Gael glanced at Talon. "That's original," he said sarcastically, but Talon knew it hurt.

"Just ignore them, and let's get in there," Talon said gruffly, and they walked to where another crowd stood huddled around the entrance to the old city hall. Talon counted at least fifteen press vans as they walked past, and he was thankful when a truck pulled up and more cops piled out.

They hurried toward the building, Talon leading. Vance and Gael were firmly on either side of Finn and Eli, and Sawyer brought up the rear. They flashed IDs as they walked past human agents and through the doors, all of them looking astonished at enhanced turning up in uniform. Talon led his team toward where he could see the press conference being set up. He stood respectfully as Deputy Cohen raised his head from the sheaf of papers he was reading.

"Mr. Valdez," he said, and Talon's resentment never registered on his face. He knew the director had deliberately not given him agent designation to get under his skin. He knew the deputy director wasn't in favor of his unit, but he also knew he would have his team face on in public.

"Deputy Director," Talon acknowledged respectfully.

Cohen glanced behind him, and his disapproving gaze fell on Finn. "Mr. Mayer. I'll make no secret of the fact that I think this is an incredibly bad idea. However, you have thirty minutes to convince the world otherwise." He waved to the desk with a row of chairs beside it. "Mr. Mayer and Mr. Valdez, I would like you to sit beside me."

Talon paused as Finn went to sit, and Cohen looked up when he didn't immediately move. "I assume, sir, you wish to present a united front for the press?" Talon said.

Cohen frowned but nodded stiffly.

"Then may I suggest you call me Agent Valdez?" Talon said quietly.

Cohen stared assessingly at Talon, finally giving him a sardonic smile. "You've got balls, anyway, Valdez. I can understand what Gregory sees in you."

Talon didn't reply, just waited until Cohen nodded to the desks.

"Agent Valdez, perhaps you would join your trainee?"

Talon walked slowly over to where Finn was watching him anxiously, and cursed. Now wasn't the time to be grandstanding. Cohen was right in one thing. For better or worse, Finn was his trainee, and Talon should be sitting next to him. He nodded to the rest of the team to take their positions in the corner just as the press started filing into the room and TV cameras started rolling.

Agent Cohen cleared his throat and stood. "I will be taking questions in a few minutes, but I have a statement that will explain the intentions behind this incredibly important initiative.

"As the world knows, our naturally evolving human population has had some remarkable individuals born in the last thirty-plus years. Enhanced individuals, all with unique abilities that can be utilized in a way to strengthen and reinforce America as one of the leading countries in the world. You all know that the mission of the FBI is to protect and defend the

United States against terrorist threats, and to uphold and enforce criminal law. In all our history, America has welcomed diversity, and it is our responsibility to defend and protect the rights of all law-abiding citizens." Cohen paused. "Including all the ones you see before you in this room.

"Ladies and gentlemen, the FBI has always prided itself on leading the world in innovation and security, and with that in mind, I would like to introduce Agent Talon Valdez, the team leader for the new Human Enhanced Rescue Organization, and trainee Finlay Mayer, his regular human partner."

Nearly every hand in the audience rose, and Cohen pointed to the first guy with a microphone.

"Agent Valdez. How are you going to ensure that your team doesn't use excessive force?"

Talon barely blinked as he answered each question evenly and succinctly. Every so often when a reporter pressed for further details, Cohen would intervene and say, "Asked and answered," and point at another reporter to answer a different question. They covered everything from training techniques to abilities of the team, which Talon flatly refused to answer, citing measures of national security.

"But what happens if you have to kill an enhanced?" a woman reporter shouted from the back.

Talon put his head to one side. "Are you asking me if I, as an FBI agent, would kill someone if they posed a threat to other human life as I am trained to do, or are you asking if"—he looked around and spotted one of Cohen's agents standing behind him—"that female agent there couldn't kill a female terrorist simply because she is a woman?"

Talon relaxed a little as the reporters chuckled at his response.

Finn seemed to be coping as well. He fielded a few questions, but apart from saying what an honor it was to be chosen to be on the team, the reporters were more interested in Talon than in him. Talon didn't care. He'd been used to difficult questions since he woke up with the mark.

"Last question, please," Cohen stated, pointing to a guy off to the side who hadn't spoken so far. The reporter stood eagerly and looked at Director Cohen. "Deputy Director, can you explain how you would re-assure the public that the enhanced working on your new team are fully in control of their abilities and present no danger to the public they are supposed to be protecting?"

Talon stiffened imperceptibly. He'd been expecting this.

Cohen answered immediately. "I have every confidence and faith in our new team. With the exception of our new trainee, they have all undergone the same rigorous training as every single other agent."

The reporter nodded and glanced at Talon. His heart beat once, hard.

"Then perhaps you could explain why your team leader is the same enhanced who lost control of his abilities to the extent that he was responsible for the death of his own father?"

For another heartbeat the room sat in stunned silence, and then every reporter erupted with their own questions. It was pandemonium. Talon suddenly got about ten microphones shoved in his face. How was he going to be able to control himself? Wasn't he a

bullet was talking at all. Gael raised a hand and stood slowly as Finn got to him. He shook his shoulders and winced.

"Gael, be careful. Sit," Finn said desperately, searching for blood, but despite the hole in the jacket, he couldn't see any.

Gael ignored him and turned to Cryer. "Sorry I knocked you down, sir. Are you hurt?"

Cryer mutely shook his head, looking at Gael as if he were some sort of alien. Then all of a sudden, the paramedics were there, and a lot of people were talking.

"Gael." Finn closed his fingers around his arm.

Gael turned to him and grinned. "I'm fine, honest." He looked at the remnants of the crowd and saw Talon and Eli jogging back to them. The cops had also rounded up the reporters who hadn't scattered in the panic.

Talon nodded to them. "They're hoping the cameras might have got some footage to identify the shooter. Anything is going to be sent directly to Gregory."

"Where's Sawyer?" Vance asked.

"He thinks he saw the shooter, but the guy seems to have vanished. He's directing the cops, but I think it will be a waste of time." Talon looked at Gael. "You okay?"

Finn had had enough. "Okay?" he shouted incredulously. "He got shot!" He turned to Gael. "You need the paramedics. You should be in the hospital."

Gael stepped closer to Finn. "Shh, kid. I'll explain in the truck, but the bullet didn't penetrate my skin. I'm fine. Just a little bruised."

Finn swallowed. He didn't know what to say.

More cops had arrived, and Talon was talking to them. One of them shook his hand, and Talon turned. "Gregory wants us back at the office."

Finn looked as the paramedics finished with Cryer. He wasn't looking at Gael. He wasn't looking at the man who just saved his life, and as Finn glanced at Gael, he realized Gael wasn't expecting any acknowledgment either. This was their life. He knew cops, military, and thousands of others put themselves in the line of fire every day without getting thanks, but Cryer was deliberately keeping his gaze lowered.

Cryer wasn't going to publicly acknowledge an enhanced had just saved his life, and that sucked big-time.

Chapter Eleven

"I WANT to know what just happened," Finn demanded as they shut the truck doors.

"You okay?" Vance asked Gael, as Gael winced a little and took his shirt off. Vance brushed a hand over Gael's back. No bullet hole, no blood.

Finn looked at the material on the shirt suspiciously, then picked it up. He carefully poked his finger through the hole in the back where the bullet had gone through, and with a sinking feeling, raised his eyes to where Vance was watching him steadily.

He thought a second before he ran his mouth off. Then he turned to Talon, who was sitting quietly in the front seat, watching him. "So next time someone's waving a gun around, can I stand next to Gael, boss?" Finn asked innocently.

Gael guffawed and slapped Finn on the back. Finn tried not to wince.

"I take it this is your other ability? What is it, rapid healing?" Finn frowned. That still didn't explain the lack of blood, though.

"Not exactly," Gael answered.

"Gael," Sawyer said warningly.

Gael looked at the guys sitting around the truck. "We've got a decision to make. We can't work as a team without trust." He looked at Finn. "To be honest the TV cameras saw me take the bullet, saw me move fast. There's going to be questions anyway."

Finn took a breath. "I know you don't trust me."

Talon interjected. "It's not as easy as that. Even Gregory doesn't know all our abilities, and we can't expect you to lie if you're asked a direct question."

"I can change the…. I dunno." Gael shrugged. "Last year I got skin cancer."

Finn gaped.

"Cutaneous melanoma, to give it its full title." Gael's scars twisted when he tried to smile. "It was shit, really. It's the most aggressive form of cancer, and you're pretty much out of luck if it's spread." Gael gazed at Finn. "Mine had. Anyway, Talon and Gregory gave me a chance. We can't get health insurance, and because the team wasn't official, the bureau wasn't gonna pay for anything…. So you met the doc?"

Finn nodded.

"Well, turns out her daddy is one of the most renowned dermatologists there are, and he was fascinated with me. I had a shit-ton of tests, and I was waiting for the results when we were asked to help with a special op last year. Drug running, but they thought an enhanced was behind it, so they asked for our help… unofficially."

Finn returned Gael's smile automatically, even though his heart was doing its best to escape his chest.

"Things went wrong, and Talon got knocked out so he couldn't help. They had Vance pinned down and were just going to shoot him. I thought, what the hell. It was likely I was going to die anyway, so—"

"What he means is, he threw himself at the dickhead with the Tec-9 that was just about to blow my brains out," Vance interrupted.

Gael chuckled. "The thing happened with my skin like you saw today. None of the bullets touched me. I went for a load of tests, and they found out there's something called a KLF4 gene in everyone that is responsible for making human skin a barrier. Anyway, I won't bore you with science, but basically the levels of it in me are off the charts. This gene doesn't just protect the skin, though—it can have something to do with melanoma and other cancers. The doc called it 'a double-edged sword.'"

Finn swallowed. "It's an activator and a repressor. That means it helps as well as harms."

"How the hell do you know all this shit?" Sawyer burst out.

Finn shrugged. "It took me so long to learn to read, once I had, there was no stopping me."

"Anyway, my skin changing didn't just save Vance. When I got back and went to Doc's, all traces of my cancer were gone, and Gregory doesn't know because Doc's father doesn't work for the FBI. Doctor-patient privilege."

"We keep it secret because we don't want to end up as lab rats," Talon said quietly, his blue gaze resting on Finn's.

Finn frowned. "Secrecy won't necessarily help that, though. The public knows you saved Cryer's life—they're gonna be more on your side."

"Agreed with provisos," Talon said. "I don't want a perp suddenly deciding to see if Gael can withstand armor-piercing rounds."

They all winced.

Talon started the truck and looked around at everyone. "We agreed on secrecy a long time ago. I get where Finn is coming from, but I'm not gonna insist on it. You all will have to come to your own decision." Without waiting for a reply, Talon added, "Gregory wants us back at the office."

Finn stared at Talon's back. He hadn't forgotten what that reporter said, and despite his nice little speech there, he hadn't done any sharing. Finn now knew more about Gael than Talon. What he knew about Talon, Vance had told him, and Talon was supposed to be his partner, not just a member of the team. It all came down to trust. Talon gave him no direction out there. He didn't even tell Finn to stay with him. That showed a glaring lack of trust as far as he was concerned.

He gazed out of the window. He was squashed up against the door, as Gael's bulk sat next to him. He thought about what that reporter said about Talon. Had Talon really lost control and killed his father? Finn remembered the tightness in his chest when Talon demonstrated his ability on him, how he couldn't breathe, how he couldn't move.

Maybe Finn should be the one not trusting the team, not the other way around.

"Hey, kid," Gael said.

Finn sighed. It looked like they were all gonna call him that.

"There's a bar near my place. How about we all meet up later?"

Vance protested, "That bar's got the most expensive beer in town. Why do you always want to go there?"

Gael shrugged. "It's quiet."

Sawyer piped up. "That's because it's only tourists who can afford to drink there."

"What do you think, kid?" Gael asked. "It's about four miles away from your place."

Finn looked up eagerly, then remembered he barely had any money left, and he still was a good eight days from getting any wages. There was no way he could go to a pricey bar. *Shit.* "I-I can't," he stammered. "Maybe next week?"

Gael shrugged. "Sure, kid." He turned to talk to Talon.

Finn cringed. He could have screamed in frustration. Just as they were giving him the opportunity to get to know them better, they thought he wasn't interested.

They pulled up at the office a little subdued. Well, Vance was silent, anyway, and he usually carried the conversation for the rest of them, so maybe that was why they seemed a little quiet. They trooped into the classroom, and Agent Gregory appeared a few minutes later.

He beamed. "Congratulations. All the networks are covering how you saved Judge Cryer's life. We haven't been able to secure the shooter, unfortunately, but that's someone else's problem and not this team's."

"I'm surprised the papers aren't blaming it on an enhanced, though. He was quite vocally against us," Gael said.

"He has put a lot of criminals away in the last thirty years," Gregory replied. "Most notably the leader of the Al Cairo drug cartel the year before he retired. We had already warned him that a new territorial leader had been appointed, and Cryer's execution would make a good first week. He chose to ignore the warning, and a few of the papers have run with that story." Gregory pinned a stare at Gael. "You look remarkably well for someone who just took a round in the back," he said dryly. "But we'll discuss that later." He sat at the table, passed out a bunch of brown folders, and leaned back as everyone opened one.

Finn stared at a photograph of a young boy with light brown hair, freckles, and brown eyes. He looked about seven or eight. He quickly turned the pages and saw three more photos of kids, all boys. The oldest was probably about sixteen.

"Those of you who were present at the school on Tuesday will remember the child, Oliver Martinez. He was the enhanced who transformed and, after rejection from his parents, was taken into state custody."

"Who are the others?" Talon asked. "There is only one with the mark."

Finn looked back at the photos. He was right. The older child only, and he was staring quite defiantly at the camera.

"They are all enhanced children who have transformed in the last year, year and a half. The ones without marks are merely because we were provided with no recent photographs."

Vance grunted in disgust, and Finn understood why. The implication was that no one wanted photos of their kids once they became freaks, as Talon had told him.

"They are also all the children we know of who have disappeared in the last six months—most notably, Oliver Martinez."

"He's disappeared?" Talon looked up quickly from the folder.

Gregory ignored the question and continued. "Apparently his mom had a change of heart she didn't tell her husband about and turned up requesting a visit. When she was escorted to his room, Oliver had vanished sometime in the night, and no one knew how or why. The group home in DC and the one here are monitored. Cameras have been interfered with and put on a repeating loop. We have no way of knowing if Oliver ran away or was taken, and no way of knowing what time. We know he was still there at midnight when the last rounds were done."

Finn listened in horror. Kids? Kids were going missing, and he didn't even know there was a unit in Tampa. "Why is this only being flagged now?"

Agent Gregory looked uncomfortable. "There is a thorough investigation starting. Apparently the unit in Tampa wasn't as strictly controlled as the one in DC. They're saying it's not uncommon for kids not to return after school or trips out. They're reported, but in a state that ranks third in cases of missing persons, often children, those numbers are not uncommon."

"Not uncommon? Not return?" Talon repeated incredulously.

"What he means is that no one looked. That's right, isn't it?" Sawyer asked bitterly. "None of these kids have families who care where they are. These kids are just swept under the carpet and forgotten about. They're probably happy to have one less to worry about when someone doesn't get off the school bus."

Finn stared at the photos of the kids. One photo of a little boy with blond hair had obviously been cut out of a family group. His head was bent, but as Finn looked, bruises were visible on the bottom of his cheek.

"This is our case now," Talon said defiantly, as if he were daring Gregory to disagree.

"Start reviewing the files," Gregory said. "Oliver was not only the youngest to disappear, but he was the only one who had any family to kick up a fuss. Deputy Director Cohen wants daily updates, but how you handle everything is up to you."

Gregory got up and walked to the door, then glanced at Gael. "I want the doctor to look at you before you go anywhere. There will also be vests issued for everyone included in your lockers." Not waiting for a reply, he left the room.

THEY SPENT the next few hours going over the files. There was barely any investigation after each disappearance. The first and oldest boy was Luis Rodriguez—fifteen when he went missing. He spent the day at school but never got on the school bus to return home. He would have been sixteen two months ago. The cops interviewed his teachers, the staff at the unit, and his friends, but no one reported seeing him after school. The cops noted no one seemed surprised, as he was such a loner.

"He'd been in trouble a few times with the cops for stealing cars before he disappeared," Gael read aloud. "No one could ever work out how he did it, as there was never any sign of the cars being broken into, even the ones that had immobilizers and electrical kill switches, so the cops had tentatively noted that he may have some sort of ability."

"What about the other two?" Vance asked. He had the photographs laid out on the table in front of him.

"Mark Brady," Gael continued. "Twelve when he transformed two years ago. Says his ability is incredible speed, but it's never been measured. And Lee Miller, nine when he transformed three years ago. He seems to be able to stop any sort of electrical power. Can just turn things off. It's noted that all the power was cut to the entire street where the unit is the night he disappeared."

"So the youngest by quite a margin is Oliver," Finn stated. "How many other kids are in the unit now?"

"Three. One who seems to have some sort of telekinetic powers." Talon whistled. "There's a couple of reports of chairs flying at school when he lost his temper. He's not allowed back at school and has tutors instead. The other two are of a similar age to Oliver and have transformed in the last few weeks. Neither of them have demonstrated any ability."

"Even defensive." Finn felt nauseous. Apparently another child who never went into the foster home, Dale Smith, was being attacked and beaten by his stepfather when the cops were called. His mom was a crack addict, and the so-called stepfather her pimp. She was glad to see the back of him when the cops said he could go into the unit. Something happened to the car and it crashed. Both cops were knocked unconscious, and when the EMTs arrived, Dale had vanished.

Talon looked at his watch. "It's late. First thing tomorrow, Sawyer and Vance go interview Oliver's mom. Gael, you and Eli go see what cops you can get any more information out of. In fact…." Talon paused. "Scratch that. Vance, you do the cops. Throw your name around a little."

Vance chuckled.

Talon looked at Finn. "I want to visit the unit. When a new child, an enhanced, gets admitted, they aren't permitted to go to school until assessments are done and the ability is deemed non-life-threatening. If they are safe, they can attend school with provisos. If they are designated as dangerous, they get transferred to the nearest locked facility."

"Kiddy prison," Vance said in disgust. "Which is why we need to stop this shit from happening."

FINN SHUT the washer door with a snap and rubbed the crick in his neck. None of the team mentioned anything else about their abilities after what Talon said in the truck, so Finn quietly got his gear from his locker and went home when they finished going through the files. He pulled his towel around him a little more securely after stripping off his swimming shorts to add to the pile in the wash.

The pool was just as good as he had been expecting, if a little crowded because of spring break. He'd hoped by nine o'clock at night it would be fairly empty, but no such luck. He tried a couple of lengths, but then he joined in with some kids playing water volleyball, or trying to. Finn chuckled. The oldest had to be about thirteen. He had fun, though. He was on the same team as a kid who could barely swim, and he quickly worked out that he could swim up behind him and lift the kid up so he could catch the ball. The mom came to thank him afterward, and he got an invite to a barbeque next week. Lifting the kid was a better work-out than any gym, and he made friends, even if they were children.

Finn was stepping into the bathroom to take a shower when someone rang his doorbell. He gathered his towel tighter and looked through the peephole on the door. Surprised, he immediately opened the door to Drew.

Drew looked sheepish, holding a six-pack of Buds. He grinned and waved at them. "Thought you might have some questions from today? I saw the news and heard you got a case."

Finn hesitated, but Drew had already taken a step inside, so if Finn hadn't stepped back, he would have blocked him. *Awkward.* He had a ton of questions, but he didn't think he should be asking Drew any of them.

"Just let me grab some clothes," Finn said, walking toward the bedroom and glancing back when he didn't get a reply.

Drew slowly slid his eyes up to his face, and Finn's body heated a little. He didn't pause to meet Drew's eyes, just dove into his bedroom and raced to grab a pair of shorts and a T-shirt. He would swear the guy was checking him out, but Drew had never given off any gay vibes to him, ever. But then, Finn didn't give off any gay vibes either. He'd never dared.

Liar. Talon's face swam in front of him, and he thought about something gross to stop his dick from deciding to get *any* sort of vibe. Like his mom getting a boyfriend—or even worse, Deke getting a girlfriend.

Finn pulled on some old shorts. He really was gonna have to go to the store, and soon. No, he was really gonna have to wait until he got paid. It was a good thing the office was so casual and they were given uniforms. He'd rushed out of his house and didn't even think to grab his laundry pile. He had more books in his bag than clothes.

He took a deep breath and walked out. Drew sat on his balcony, already on his second beer. Finn sat and pulled the top off a bottle.

"So I bet you've got a ton of questions, huh?" Drew asked, almost eagerly.

Shit. Finn covered his indecision up by taking a long pull from the bottle, wondering what he could ask without feeling like he was going behind the team's back. He put the bottle down. "Do you know what made Gregory want to set up the unit in the first place?"

Drew looked surprised at the question, but he tilted his head to one side and put his empty bottle down. "I'm not totally sure, but I did hear that he has a kid that's an enhanced." Drew squinted. "Or maybe a younger brother."

"What's the oldest age of any enhanced?" Finn asked.

"Recorded thirty-nine, but it's entirely possible we've still got quite a few under the radar." He paused. "Gregory's fifty-seven. There was talk he was putting in for retirement before this came up, or maybe he's here because he's putting in for retirement." Drew smirked.

Finn frowned. "What do you mean?"

"It's quite common for agents to request the last transfer to wherever they want to retire." He grinned. "You'll have to ask him."

Drew took a small silver flask out of his pocket, and Finn watched him in surprise as he took a drink and offered it to Finn. Finn shook his head and gazed at him assessingly. Drew had knocked a few back the other night as well, even though he'd been driving.

"I thought you might want to ask about what that reporter said about your partner," Drew said.

Here we go, thought Finn.

"Just in case you were worried," Drew continued without pausing.

Finn shrugged and tried to laugh it off. "To be honest the whole thing is kind of freaking me out. The press conference made no difference."

Drew nodded and grinned, stretching his legs out. "I tell you, it's like being on vacation every day, living here. All I've been doing today is monitoring wiretaps."

Finn took a cautious sip and tried to think of another easy question. "How long have you worked in Tampa?"

"Three years straight out of the academy. There's not much action, though. I was thinking of trying to specialize. Get some extra training. Everyone says field agents are the way to go to get a solid career, so I'm just keeping my nose clean and an ear to the ground." He gestured at the scene below. "Although I can't complain about waking up to this every day."

Finn smiled and watched carefully as Drew popped his third bottle. "Is your family from around here?" That was a safe subject, surely.

"We used to live here around ten years ago—that's how I know Hannah—then Dad got a transfer to upstate New York. He retires in two years, so I think they'll come back. He's a bank manager," Drew said. "You?"

"One brother, an insurance salesman from Cookeville, Iowa. Mom's alive. Dad died three years ago."

Drew picked up his silver flask, and it slipped through his fingers before he could take a swig. "Oops," he snickered.

Finn grinned; he'd definitely been at this awhile. "So no girlfriends, significant others in your life?" Finn teased, stretching his legs out.

Drew looked at him steadily. "Nah, wouldn't want a girlfriend."

Finn blinked. Drew was gay? He hadn't imagined being checked out? Was that what he was trying to tell him?

"What about you?"

Finn just shook his head mutely. He had no intention of telling Drew anything.

Drew grinned and got up, swaying slightly. "Just gotta go take a piss."

Finn waved him to the bathroom and stood when he heard the washing machine finish. He needed to throw his stuff in the dryer if he wanted some clean clothes for tomorrow. He heard the toilet flush and the bathroom door open as he was bending down to the washer. He straightened up and turned to find Drew suddenly right in front of him. Finn swallowed. He couldn't back away because of the washer.

Drew stepped up next to him. "Hey, I'm not wrong, am I? I'm getting the right signals from you?"

Finn opened his mouth like a fish. *Signals?* No. No way. No signals. Even if Drew weren't an agent. Drew lunged for him, and Drew's lips met his in an uncoordinated rush of tongue and teeth. Finn froze for a millisecond, then pushed away. Drew brought his arms around him and pressed in. Finn put all his weight behind the next push.

Drew stumbled back, windmilling his arms. "Aarghh!" Drew yelled as his arm struck the side of the counter, taking two plates, a coffee cup, a glass, and a box of cereal with him. Everything hit the floor and shattered in a huge crash.

There was complete silence for a beat as the noise echoed around the room.

"*Finn!*"

Finn turned to the door as it banged open, and Talon burst into the room. He gaped at Talon, then stared at Drew, who was rolling on his side, laughing hysterically.

"Fuck me! You playing hard to get?"

Finn closed his eyes in horror and exasperation as Talon stiffened at Drew's words. He glanced at Talon. "He's been drinking," Finn said, pleading for understanding as Drew rolled around laughing.

Talon just stared at Drew, then bent down and hoisted him to his feet. "Which apartment," he growled, but Drew seemed to sober up and realize Talon was there.

"I can manage," he said, pulling his arm away from Talon. He gave them both a murderous glare and stumbled out the broken door, which was hanging from only one hinge with a busted lock.

Talon huffed and stalked after Drew.

Finn was astonished. Talon broke his fucking door, and he was just gonna leave? And what the hell was he doing here anyway? Wasn't he going drinking with the rest of the team? Finn heaved an angry breath and bent to pick up the broken pieces that littered the floor. Glass was everywhere, and he didn't so much as have a vacuum cleaner to get it up with.

He sighed and dug out the dustpan and brush. He started sweeping the glass shards and emptying them into the trash. He heard another sound at the door as he reached for a piece, taking his eye off it for a second. He parted his lips in astonishment.

Talon was back, carrying a toolbox.

"Ahh, shit!" Finn yelped and brought his hand up quickly. *Fuck me.* He went and sliced it on the glass, not looking what the hell he was doing.

"Let me." Talon was suddenly in front of him, pulling his hand down. Finn forgot about the cut, forgot blood was dripping down his finger, forgot the pain. With his large hand wrapped around Finn's, Talon gently directed him under the faucet and turned it on with his free hand, and Finn didn't seem to be able to get his brain to work to say a word about it.

He stared at Talon, who was looking questioningly at him, as if he wanted an answer. Had he asked him something? Finn tried to clear his throat. "W-What?"

Talon's lips tilted in a wry smile, and Finn suddenly couldn't drag his gaze away from Talon's mouth. He stared at Talon's tongue as Talon slowly licked his plump pink lips. "I said, Vance's mom would have said you need a keeper. You got any Band-Aids?"

Finn blinked, completely dazed, small shocks racing up his arm from where large fingers were clasping it. "I—"

Talon frowned a little. "You okay?" He glanced at the beer bottles sticking out of the trash.

Finn shook his head a little to clear it. "Yeah, I haven't even had a whole one. I think Drew had something before he got here. He'd only been here fifteen minutes," he added hurriedly. Finn snatched his hand back in embarrassment, and Talon shrugged.

"None of my business, but you need to be careful around the office."

"We weren't." Finn started again. "I wasn't...."

Talon turned his back and walked the three feet to the door. "You go see to your hand, and I'll mend the door."

Finn's heart sank. Why did he insist on making a complete fool of himself every time he was around Talon?

He thought there were some Band-Aids under the sink. The apartment was stocked with the basics when he arrived. He'd clean the rest of the glass up after he'd taken care of his finger. He turned and stepped into the bathroom, crunching glass under his flip-flops as he went. At least he had them on.

When Finn had gotten his hand sorted, splashed water on his face, and given himself a stern lecture to calm the fuck down, he opened the bathroom door and spied Talon screwing the hinge back on the door. He looked down. All the glass had been swept up. "You didn't have to do that."

Talon opened and closed the door, ignoring the comment. "Call maintenance in the morning before you leave and report it. It's okay because the block is fairly secure, but it's just temporary. It won't stop anyone serious about getting in."

Finn huffed and leaned on the counter. "Ya think?"

Talon glanced back and had the grace to look a little uncomfortable. "I heard the shout. I didn't realize you had company," he said steadily.

And just like that, Finn was fiery red again. Although it should have been Talon who was embarrassed for the BS line he'd just given him. *Heard the shout, my ass.* He glanced at the floor, desperately trying not to groan.

Talon's shoes appeared, and he felt a finger raise his chin. "You must have got the shit kicked out of you at school for that."

Finn swallowed but didn't answer. He was too busy gazing at pink lips again. He closed his eyes on barely a whimper as Talon brushed a thumb up his jawline.

"You turned Drew down," he said flatly. "Was it because you're not gay?"

Finn shook his head, just a little.

"Was it because of work?"

Finn barely shook his head again.

Talon slid his thumb to Finn's neck. "I can feel your heart pounding. Do I scare you?"

Finn's eyes shot open to deny any such thing, but the words stuck in his throat. Talon was so close. So fucking close, he could almost taste him. Finn inhaled slowly, filling his lungs with whatever fresh scent Talon was wearing. Like leather—a deep, almost buttery smell. Fuck, he didn't know what it was, but it was so Talon. Finn could feel his dick grow heavy in his shorts.

"Not scared?" Talon mused to himself as he repeated the question.

"No," Finn whispered.

Talon took another half step closer until they were touching. "You ought to be."

Finn closed his eyes as soon as Talon crossed an invisible line and made the decision to kiss him. He almost braced himself for the onslaught like before, but the soft, ghostlike brush of Talon's lips went straight to Finn's knees, more shocking because of its gentleness than if he'd been wrestled to the ground.

Finn heard a sound, a groan, but couldn't have said whether he or Talon made it. He raised his leaden arms around Talon's neck, silently begging to be closer. Talon slid his arms around Finn's waist, and he deepened the kiss a little but still kept it light. He drew back, and Finn's heart jumped, hard. Would Talon leave him again?

"I can't have this affect work." Talon gazed down at him. "If we're going to do this, it has to stay separate."

Finn nodded eagerly, desperate to feel those lips once more.

Talon pulled back again. "I mean it. This can't affect work ever."

Finn sighed. "I understand," he said solemnly. He nearly crossed his heart.

"Shall we go in there?" Talon held his hand and glanced toward the bedroom.

Finn's heart was beating so fast, he was worried it was gonna stop. Would Talon want everything? What if he wanted to top? Should he ask? Shit, what did he say?

Talon looked back at Finn when he didn't get an answer and narrowed his eyes a little. "Am I reading this wrong?"

He paused, but Finn walked past him purposefully. "No, no, absolutely not." Shit, now he was talking too much. He was such a dork. What on earth was Talon doing here? Why would he want to be here with him?

Finn walked into the bedroom and stopped. Now what? Did he get undressed? Did Talon undress him? Crap. Sweat broke out along his top lip, and he yanked at his T-shirt.

"Hey." Finn paused as Talon closed a hand over his own. Talon was looking at him, mildly puzzled. He gave out a short sigh. "I think we're maybe getting ahead of ourselves. I don't want you thinking…." Talon pulled Finn close to him sharply. "Finn, please, God, don't tell me you think refusing this will ruin your chances on the team." Talon dropped Finn's hand as if it had burned him. "Fuck," he spat. "I knew this was a bad idea."

"No!" Finn exclaimed.

Talon backed away. "I am so sorry. This has no bearing on the team."

"Will you listen?" Finn said in exasperation. "I…." He felt his face flame again. "I've never done this before." That was it. At that moment in time, Finn would have been quite happy to die. Maybe have a heart attack. His face was so hot, he felt like he was going to spontaneously combust anyway.

Talon just looked at him blankly. "You mean with a guy? You're bi?"

Finn dropped to the bed and buried his face in his hands. Maybe terrorists would level the building. Of course, they'd have to get everyone out first, but still, where was a gas explosion when you needed one?

He felt a hand on his, and Talon hunkered down in front of him, pulling his hands away. "Look at me," Talon asked quietly. "Finn?"

Finn allowed Talon to pry his hands from his hot face, and he looked into Talon's gorgeous eyes. Funny, they didn't seem as cold as they usually were.

"You mean you haven't done this with anyone, period. Don't you?"

Finn closed his eyes. He couldn't bear to see the derision he knew would be there.

Lips barely grazed his own, and his eyes shot open. Talon's eyes weren't cold. They were warm. A lazy crinkle flashed at the side of each one as his lips pulled up into a soft smile.

"We don't have to do anything you don't want to," Talon murmured, rubbing his jaw along Finn's cheek.

Finn shook. His cock was suddenly hard and pulsing. He moved his face a little to be closer to those lips, and Talon obliged. Finn felt the kiss down to his toes, and it certainly didn't skip over more desperate, needy places. He pushed forward, heat thrumming through his veins, hyperaware of every sound, every brief touch.

"Let's get you undressed." Talon gazed at Finn steadily, and Finn scrabbled eagerly at his shorts. Talon chuckled and swatted his hands away, then nodded to the bed. "Move up, but I'm gonna undress you."

Finn shuffled up the bed so quickly, it was likely he set a new land speed record. He was past anything other than a desperate need to feel Talon's hands on his body. He couldn't be cool or casual if his life depended on it.

Talon stood, and in one move, lifted his shirt over his head. Finn's mouth went completely dry. The muscles in his neck wanted to swallow, but he seemed to have lost the ability to do so. He stared in awe. Talon was gorgeous. Huge shoulders and powerful arms tapering to a flat, hard abdomen. Talon looked up and caught him staring, but Finn couldn't look away. Talon smiled that slow, lazy smile again for him, and Finn clenched his ass as need swirled in his gut.

Talon dropped his pants, and Finn might have actually whimpered. Talon had nothing on under them. Finn blinked, mildly alarmed at the size of him. His long, thick cock rose from a messy bunch of blond curls and slapped his belly as he stepped out of his pants.

"Like what you see?"

Finn's lips curled upward. He might have lost all higher brain function, but his body seemed to know what to do.

"LIFT." TALON pulled a wrapper out of his pocket and tossed it on the bed. He knelt on the bed and grabbed Finn's T-shirt. Finn obeyed the order instantly, and Talon felt the response as his cock thickened even more. In another ten seconds, he had Finn's shorts off. He was wearing plain blue briefs, and Talon's mouth watered at them barely holding in Finn's lengthened cock.

"What happened to Superman?" Talon teased, and Finn groaned and brought his hands to his face again. Talon chuckled as he pulled the briefs down, then Finn's hands. "I'm sorry. I shouldn't tease."

He stroked the side of Finn's jaw with his finger and dipped it down his throat, heading for a nipple. As soon as his nail scraped it, Finn shuddered and his eyes widened. Talon smiled to himself. Finn was sensitive there; good. He could play. Talon continued his downward trail until he brushed the dark hair around Finn's balls. Finn gasped. His cock was jutting out proudly, beads of precum on the tip. Talon bent down, swallowing Finn's whole length in one go. Finn yelled and stiffened, and Talon sucked purposely.

"Talon!" Finn cried in desperation, but Talon didn't even stop to smile at the sound of Finn falling apart.

Talon scraped with his teeth and hollowed his cheeks as he sucked. It only took Talon a few minutes to get him off, and he swallowed in satisfaction.

Finn's harsh panting surrounded the room. "Oh God," Finn groaned. "I can't believe…."

Talon lifted his head and let Finn's cock slide gently from his lips. He didn't know how sensitive he was afterward. "We have plenty of time."

Finn groaned again and raised half-lidded eyes to Talon. "I. I can—"

"Lie there and relax." Talon finished the sentence for him and eased himself alongside. He grazed a finger over Finn's other nipple, and Finn shivered. Talon smiled in satisfaction. He wanted Finn relaxed before he did anything else. "Have you got any lube?"

"Uh-huh." Finn pointed to the drawer.

Talon was quite pleased that Finn didn't seem to have regained the full power of speech.

He nearly hadn't come to Finn's. He'd had one beer with the guys and then pleaded paperwork, which everyone knew was a lie. He was on his way over before he'd even realized it. Then he'd stood in the hallway and willed his feet to take him back to his truck, but the second he'd heard the crash, his heart had slammed so hard against his ribs, he thought they would break.

Talon glanced up and looked at Finn. Really looked at him. Soft brown hair that was just long enough to run his fingers through. Green eyes, currently closed, but he'd seen them. Ridiculously long fair lashes. A smattering of freckles across his nose he would swear had multiplied since yesterday. His chest was rising sharply with each breath, nipples still erect and begging to be touched.

Finn opened his eyes slowly and caught Talon staring. His eyes were unfocused, pupils wide.

Talon grinned. He looked well-fucked now, and Talon hadn't even gotten started. He was going to blow his mind.

He reached over and got a tube of lube from the bedside drawer. He caught the flush on Finn's face and then realized it had never been opened. He wanted to laugh, but he didn't. It had probably taken all Finn's courage to actually go and buy it. He clicked the top and wondered what Finn planned on thinking about as he jerked off. Talon's cock pulsed. The thought of Finn jerking off to thoughts of Talon really did it for him.

"It will probably be easier if you get on your knees the first time, but there's no rush, so I'm just gonna play. Bend your knees and relax."

Finn cautiously bent his legs but held them closed.

Talon smiled a little and reached underneath. "You ever played a little down there?" he asked softly as he lubed a finger and traced it under Finn's balls.

Finn swallowed. "Yeah." He laughed. "Since I was about thirteen."

Talon's smile widened. He hadn't meant just jacking off. He slid his finger down Finn's taint. "What about there?" he whispered. Finn moaned a little, and Talon eased his knees apart. He reached up and grabbed a pillow and put it under Finn's ass, lifting him up a bit. Finn let Talon move him wherever he wanted.

Talon had never been into inexperienced guys. He didn't like someone cutting their teeth on him. He liked a guy who wanted a hard, fast fuck. No questions. No awkward promises.

But teasing Finn? This was probably the most erotic thing he had ever done.

Talon settled back down, stifling a groan as his own dick scraped the sheet. Fuck, he was so hard, it was damn painful, and no one had touched him yet.

"Talon?"

"Mmm?" He raised his gaze from where he had just been sliding his finger under Finn's balls.

"Do… do you like kissing?" Finn's words rushed out. "Because I—"

Talon sealed Finn's lips with his own.

"Mmff," Finn moaned as Talon thrust his tongue inside, and Talon felt the action harden his belly. Whatever Finn lacked in experience, he made up for in enthusiasm, and Finn returned the kiss eagerly.

Talon moved his fingers back down to Finn's cock and gave it a hard tug.

Finn whined in protest, and Talon did it again. There was no sound except a groan from the back of Finn's throat, but he pressed further into Talon and deepened the kiss. Talon ignored the small insistent voice inside him wanting to analyze Finn's reactions. Finn was getting off. Talon wasn't a selfish lover, but this was purely a mutual fuck, and Talon didn't need to start giving it any deeper meanings. He could feel Finn's cock start to stiffen in response and gave it one or two more tugs before he went back to playing underneath. Talon gentled the kiss, cautious, and skimmed his finger over Finn's hole.

Finn shuddered.

Beautiful. He did it again and broke the kiss. "You ever played there?"

Finn's whole body shook again, his head diving into Talon's neck. Imagining the pink flush on Finn's skin, Talon slowly inserted a finger up to the first knuckle. He heard the small gasp and desperately tried to ignore his growing satisfaction at Finn's responses. Somehow he went from consideration that this was Finn's first time to an almost possessive need to make every second blow his mind.

"How's that, beautiful? That good?" he murmured, bringing his finger out to get some more slick. Finn moaned a little as he did so. "Want more?" he whispered. Talon was mesmerized. What was Finn doing that Talon seemed to need validation from him? He never questioned. He never spoke during sex. Words were too powerful, too intimate.

Finn had brought his head out of Talon's neck and arched his neck on the bed as Talon inserted his finger again, playing around the rim of his hole. Finn gasped, and Talon inserted it past the second knuckle and curled his finger upward, searching for the small gland.

"Oh my God," Finn gasped and nearly jumped off the bed, and Talon grinned. Finn's cock jerked and a little precum oozed around the slit. Talon's mouth watered. He loved giving head, really loved it, but his macho image always seemed to make guys assume he always had to be on the receiving end.

He wouldn't go down on Finn again; he had other plans. Talon brushed Finn's lips again, and Finn opened them eagerly. He shyly crept his smooth arms up Talon's back as Talon leaned in, pressing his dick into Finn's thigh and groaning in need.

Finn's kisses were getting sloppier and more uncoordinated as Talon added a second finger. He broke off. "Please," he begged. "Please fuck me."

Talon groaned again. He would have to go slow, use every bit of his iron control. He withdrew both fingers slowly. "Turn over," he said, pulling out the pillow and placing it so Finn could burrow his head in it. Finn eagerly rolled over.

"Up," he ordered and raised Finn to his knees, head down. Perfect. Finn's ass was gorgeous. Talon wanted to take a bite out of it. *Maybe next time.* He also kneeled up behind Finn, quickly donned the condom, and slicked himself up real good. "It'll hurt a little. I'll try to go slow."

Finn moaned. "Just do it." He even wiggled his ass a little, and Talon slapped it affectionately.

"Who's in charge here?" Talon chuckled, and then all humor fled his brain as he lined his cock up and brushed Finn's hole with it. *Fuck.* He held Finn's hips firm and pushed. "Push out a little."

Finn froze as if panicked, and Talon bit down on his lip and held himself completely still. He stroked a hand up and down Finn's spine while he felt him relax slightly. He pushed a little until he felt the first ring of muscles give, and Finn groaned. Talon nearly swallowed his tongue trying to keep still when every muscle in him screamed at him to push deeper.

"Are you okay, baby?" Talon asked before he could think. Before he could stop the endearment that spilled from his lips. Before he could remember that asking gave people the impression that he cared about the answer.

"Mmm." Finn's reply was smothered in the pillow.

Talon reached under Finn and fondled his balls gently, feeling them pucker and draw up into his hand. He pushed again and then he was in.

Finn shuddered. "Oh fuck."

Talon smiled. It wasn't a bad "oh fuck"—more an incredible acknowledgment. He stilled for a beat, then pulled back out gently, and Finn groaned. Talon let go and grasped his hips properly. "Jack yourself."

Finn didn't need to be told twice. If Talon hadn't been holding him up, he would have face-planted. His movements were jerky, but from the sounds coming from his throat, he was clearly getting the job done.

Talon closed his eyes in utter bliss. Finn was completely perfect. A glorious wet heat surrounded his dick and gripped him tight. He was helpless to stop himself thrusting and could feel the pressure building in his spine and circling to his balls. "How close are you?" Talon ground the words out.

"I'm—Ohhh…." Finn arched and shuddered.

Thank fuck. Talon gasped and shot into the condom. He thrust once, twice. The rush started in his balls but nearly took the top of his head off.

Talon just managed to hold Finn up while he withdrew, but then Finn collapsed on the bed as Talon let go to deal with the condom. He staggered to the bathroom to wash his sticky hands and to get rid of it. He walked back to the bed with a damp cloth and heard a soft groan from Finn. He sat down cautiously. "You okay?"

Finn turned his head to face Talon. Sweat slicked his hair back. A pink sheen dusted his shoulders and neck. His pupils were dazed and his smile was lopsided. He was possibly the best thing Talon had ever fucking seen.

Talon lay down on the bed, telling himself they would just take a minute to recover, and then they had to have another awkward talk about it not affecting work.

Finn lay in his cum, and he'd need the cloth. Talon wouldn't do it, though. Too personal. *I need to go.* Put a little distance between them. All the words, all the phrases he had used jumbled and echoed in his head. He took a breath as his heart sped up. Finn sighed and grabbed Talon's wrist, heaving his arm up at the same time as he shuffled into Talon's side.

Talon reached for the cloth and wiped Finn without thinking. It was as if he could see himself doing shit even though he knew it was a bad idea. He needed to go, and he wasn't going to analyze the fuck out of why he suddenly didn't want to. Talon's breath caught at the sound of Finn's satisfied sigh, and he froze. Finn rubbed his head on Talon's shoulder and promptly closed his eyes. Talon blinked in confusion as the lithe warm body *snuggled* into his side like it was meant to be there… which was *dangerous*, fucked-up in all sorts of ways Talon could list. Finn was a threat to the team. They had all sorts of secrets that couldn't be trusted with a regular. He had to protect the team, and he couldn't let his dick get in the way of that.

He threw the cloth haphazardly toward the bathroom door, and it landed somewhere in that general direction. Finn settled in a little more, and Talon gazed down at him in astonishment that he could seem so at ease when Talon was so conflicted.

Talon blew out a slow breath and tightened his arm around Finn. He was right. Finn was dangerous. He was very dangerous, but Talon wasn't entirely convinced he should worry for the team.

It was Talon's peace of mind that was the most at risk.

Chapter Twelve

FINN WOKE to a sound in the bathroom, and he remembered everything instantly. He looked over and put a hand out. The Talon-sized dent in the mattress was still warm. He picked up his cell phone: 5:00 a.m. He sat up as he heard the toilet flush, then lay back down quickly. Would it be awkward? Should he pretend to be still asleep? He needed a piss and, ugh, he needed a shower. He vaguely remembered Talon wiping him with a cloth, but the sheet he had lain on most of the night was stiff. Maybe they could get breakfast before they went to the enhanced kids' unit. Go to Betty's diner? Then he remembered his lack of cash. He looked up eagerly as the bathroom door opened.

Maybe not. Talon was dressed. He was clearly leaving.

Talon blinked, seeing Finn awake, almost as if he weren't expecting it.

"Hey," Finn said. Okay, as a conversational opener, it wasn't original, but this was awkward, and he didn't want it to be.

"I was just leaving," Talon replied, stating the obvious.

Finn's heart sank. It *was* going to be awkward. He sighed and sat up. "Do you want a coffee? I need a shower." He wanted to scream. What he really wanted was for Talon to join him in the shower.

Talon shook his head and picked up his keys from the side of the bed.

Oh shit, thought Finn. *Here goes nothing.* "Wanna join me? You said last night we were going to interview the manager of the unit." And then he fucked Finn into the mattress.

Talon shook his head again, then sighed and fixed his cool blue stare on Finn. "I'm sorry. Last night was a mistake. I shouldn't have let things go that far between us. I'm sorry. This is all on me."

Finn's jaw fell.

"I—" Talon took another breath.

"Bullshit," snapped Finn. "I can't believe you're going with the whole 'It's not you, it's me' speech. You had just as much of a good time as I did. We agreed it wouldn't interfere with work."

Talon looked exasperated. "I can't. I'm sorry." He swallowed, whirled around, and strode to the door. "Don't forget to get your door fixed."

Finn nearly threw something at him. The apartment door closed carefully. All the more deafening because it was quiet. Finn sighed and picked a thread from his sheet. He wanted to pout, to throw a fit. But he wouldn't. Being a grown-up sucked sometimes.

Humiliation turned to anger. Disappointment turned to hurt. Finn had spent his life not measuring up to other people. He shouldn't be surprised, and he should really, really know better by now. He rubbed at the hurt in his chest and tried hard not to wish this time had worked out a little differently.

On the plus side, he wasn't some loser virgin anymore. One never knew what would be around the corner, what was waiting just outside that door, and he threw his legs over the edge of the bed and winced. Okay, maybe he wouldn't be rushing to the door quite yet. Maybe he would have a bath and check if he could walk first.

By the time he had a leisurely soak and stripped and shoved his sheets in the washer, he felt a ton better. In fact, he would be hard-pressed to keep the smile off his face all day. He'd just had the most awesome sex of his life—the *only* sex of his life—and nothing was gonna spoil his mood. He'd loved every second and wanted more of it, and if Talon was just gonna act like a dick instead of doing something useful with his dick, well, then, he'd look elsewhere.

Finn sighed and thought of the sight of Talon naked last night. He felt his cock stir at the memory. Look elsewhere? *Yeah, you keep telling yourself that.*

Finn pocketed his phone and his wallet and picked up his car keys. The bath had sorted him out. He wasn't even wincing. He glanced at himself in the mirror and smiled. He had one of his oldest T-shirts on and jeans. Talon had said they could dress casually as they would either be working out, training, or in uniform from now on. The T-shirt was unavoidable due to his serious lack of clothes. The fact that it showed a picture of Superman on it wasn't.

He flung open the door just as Drew was lifting his hand to ring the doorbell. Finn paused, embarrassment rushing through him—although to be fair, Drew looked worse.

Drew put his hands up. "I am so sorry. I made a complete ass of myself last night." He sighed. "I don't—"

Finn grinned. Nothing was gonna spoil his mood. "It's fine."

Drew looked relieved. "Have you eaten?"

Finn shook his head.

"I know this awesome diner. Totally my treat."

"Betty's?" Finn asked hopefully. He really shouldn't, but he couldn't afford to go and pay for himself. He would return the favor when he'd gotten paid.

"Of course." Drew grinned, and Finn followed him out.

DREW GROANED and put his fork down. "Have you tried their breakfast platter?"

Finn smiled, stirred his coffee, and took a sip.

Drew looked awkward. "Do you know what's on the agenda for today? Are you starting work on your new case?"

Finn hesitated. He really needed to know what he was supposed to say to Drew and what he wasn't. He knew Drew was an agent, but….

"What about you?" he countered. "Are you with us today?"

Drew shrugged. "I'm assuming so. Gregory told me to be early." He leaned forward. "I hope I didn't make it awkward for you last night... you know, with Talon."

"Nah," said Finn. It was Talon who made it awkward with Talon.

"Look, I want to say something, and it's got nothing whatsoever to do with you shooting me down last night. I was drunk, and I never get involved with anyone at work. You were right to turn me down. *Way* too awkward," Drew said.

Finn stiffened slightly. What was he trying to say?

Drew sighed and stared at his cup. "My bedroom window looks out the back where the cars are. When I woke up feeling like death this morning, I saw Talon's truck still parked outside."

Finn's heart sank, and he took another sip to cover the fact that he had no clue what to say.

"I'm the last person to get all sanctimonious with you. And this has nothing to do with last night. It's just—you have to be real careful."

"We're not allowed relationships on the team," Finn said flatly. He knew that. It was standard.

Drew looked really uncomfortable. "No, we're not, but that wasn't what I meant." He dumped some sugar into his own coffee and stirred it thoughtfully, so Finn took another nervous sip. Drew lowered his voice. "That reporter wasn't joking when he said Talon had killed his dad."

Finn's eyes shot up. With everything that happened last night, he'd forgotten that. "What do you mean?" he asked cautiously. They wouldn't let someone on the team who had killed someone unless it was in self-defense. Maybe that's what Drew meant.

"It was when he was a kid."

Finn parted his lips in astonishment, and he felt uncomfortable. This was his team leader. This was his partner. He felt disloyal for listening.

"It was when Talon first got his abilities. He can... slow the body."

Finn knew that. He remembered that day in Gregory's office, that feeling of suffocation.

"I was told that Talon was hysterical, and his dad tried to calm him down, even restrain him. Talon did his thing. To be honest, he may not have realized it, but... his father had a massive heart attack. There was only Talon and his dad in the house. A neighbor heard Talon shouting, called 911. The paramedics couldn't revive him, and he was pronounced dead at the scene."

Finn didn't know what to say, and even if he did, he shouldn't be talking about it with Drew.

"So that's why I'm telling you to be careful." Drew leaned forward. "They're all fucking dangerous. I'm not even sure if they all know exactly what they can do. Michaelson only just got discharged from the burns unit."

Finn barely heard Drew. He was too busy questioning his sanity. Not because his first thought was to get out of there like any normal person's would be, but because it wasn't. He wanted to believe that trying to protect his team was one of the reasons Talon seemed so closed off. Not because it was something Finn had done or something he hadn't done. Was that why he suddenly did the about-face on his emotions? Did he dare hope there was another reason that sent

Talon running, and not because he wasn't as affected as Finn? He had so many questions, but he still felt uncomfortable asking anyone except the team.

Drew pressed on. "They lose control. Eli lost it when he was sparring with Michaelson."

"I thought you weren't there?"

"I wasn't, but Dennis was working at the time."

"And he saw it?"

Drew sighed and put down his empty cup. "Look, I'm just giving you a heads-up. Gregory is so desperate for this to work, he's letting dangerous precedents slide."

Finn paused as a young girl he hadn't seen the other day put the check down.

"I got this," Drew said.

"No," Finn said firmly. "We split it." He barely had any cash left, but he suddenly didn't like Drew paying. He felt awkward about the whole conversation.

"Okay." Drew stood. "Please don't say anything about what I've told you. I still have to work in this office."

Finn nodded.

"I'm just trying to help," Drew added. He'd obviously taken Finn's silence as censure.

Finn smiled. "I know. I'll see you at work." He paid his half of the check and left a tip. He didn't see Betty before he walked out.

He got into his car, started the engine, and blasted the air conditioner. It had to be eighty degrees already. He was wearing his second pair of jeans, and they were really too hot.

His thoughts drifted back to what Drew said last night.... Not that they were ever far away. He remembered what Vance told him about how hard it was even with the support of a big family. What would it be like to go through something like that without support? He remembered Oliver from the school, and his childhood best friend, Adam. As soon as he got some money together, he would see if he could get a cheap flight to New York. In fact, if Gregory was as sympathetic as he seemed, maybe he could find some information out on Adam.

Which brought him back around to his partner. Talon. Did Finn think Talon deliberately killed his dad? It was an accident. For all Finn knew, Talon's dad might have had a weak heart and Talon was a scared kid. If something like that had happened to him, he would have freaked out too.

Did he trust Talon? Or was he being naïve? With everything he had learned in the last few days, he should be running for the door. He wasn't. Was that because he was *too* trusting?

Or if he were honest, really honest, was it because every second he spent with Talon made it more impossible to walk away?

Chapter Thirteen

FINN DROVE around to the underground garage behind the field office. Like most Florida buildings, it wasn't exactly underground because of the high water table. It was more like the garage was the ground floor, and the offices were above. He turned the engine off and looked around. He was early, but Talon's truck was already there, thank God. He half wondered if Talon would go visit the kids without him. He noted some of the other cars and wondered if they belonged to the rest of the team, and where they lived. Vance was the only one who had shared any personal information, really. In fact, Finn learned more about his partner from other people than the man himself. He still thought there was an ability Talon was hiding from him, and he had no clue about the others.

Finn got out and walked to the elevator, making a decision. He was going to see if he could get Agent

Gregory on his own today. He wanted to ask about the team, but he wanted to see if Gregory would help him find some information on Adam. He'd also stopped at an ATM and realized he had less than thirty dollars he could withdraw. Mr. Jacobson deposited his latest check early, but it hadn't cleared. He could have kissed the man, especially as he kind of ran out on him, just leaving a voicemail.

He was going to have to talk to Gregory before he did anything else.

Finn reached the top of the stairs, electing to miss the elevator, pleased he wasn't too out of breath, and decided whatever else he was doing exercise-wise that day, he was going for a run when he got home.

He walked into the small reception area and stopped in surprise when he saw Sawyer doing some paperwork.

Sawyer looked up as he came in. He didn't smile, but he didn't frown either. "They're all in the gym. Gregory wants a final word before we all leave."

"I was hoping to see Agent Gregory first," Finn answered. He looked to the closed office door. "Is he in?"

Sawyer nodded disinterestedly, so Finn knocked on the door and waited for the "Come in" before he opened the door. He went to close it, but Gregory waved his hand to leave the door open.

Shit. He didn't want to talk about money with Sawyer sitting there.

"Unless it's private?" Agent Gregory asked, to which, of course, Finn said no because that would look worse. Sawyer didn't trust him already.

"I actually wanted to ask about my wages, sir," Finn started nervously, and Gregory looked away from the computer screen he had been frowning at. "The plane ticket kinda wiped me out."

Before Gregory could answer, the phone on his desk started ringing, and Gregory snatched it up. "Shit," he said and stood. "I'll be right down. Find Talon." He looked at Finn, who stood the second Gregory sounded agitated. "The press are camped out at the front of the building. Apparently someone has told them where the HEROs are." Gregory smirked a little as he said it. He pulled his jacket off the back of his chair and turned. Finn noticed the shoulder holster he hadn't seen before, along with the gun neatly tucked in there, and followed Gregory out.

Sawyer was standing respectfully, holding the door open. Finn wanted to cringe again, knowing he would have heard him trying to explain he was broke.

Gregory marched to the elevator, and they all climbed in. He didn't say a word until they exited on level two. Finn got a quick glance at a large open office and around twenty different people all staring at Gregory when Talon came through a door at the other side. Gael was with him. They were both in shorts, looking like they were just working out. Finn's mouth went completely dry, but beyond a bare glance, Talon took no notice of him.

Gael spoke first and handed Gregory a piece of paper. "It's on every network."

Gregory scanned whatever was written, sighed, and turned to Finn. "I'm sorry. I'm afraid your family has been contacted by the press. The networks are alternating coverage of them with the press conference and Gael taking the bullet for Judge Cryer. They want a statement."

Finn cringed. Deke was on TV? His mom?

"They're saying you disappeared in the middle of the night. Thought you'd been kidnapped," Gael said a little stonily. "You never told them where you were going?" he said in disbelief. "This doesn't help, you know. It makes the unit look bad."

"I was told to keep it quiet—"

"Not from your family," Talon interrupted in exasperation.

"It wasn't that simple," he snapped. "I left them a note, and I certainly wasn't going to get grilled about something I didn't know enough about." He fumed. "He wouldn't have bothered reporting me missing. In fact, until someone tracked him down, I'd bet they hadn't noticed," he added bitterly.

Finn swallowed at the silence. It was one of those sentences he really wished he could take back. He'd sounded like a spoiled child.

"Go get in uniform." Gregory sighed.

Finn turned and followed the others, ignoring the curious faces of everyone else in the room. In a week he'd never been in the main office, and apart from the bar, he hadn't met anyone else from the field office. Talon and Gael didn't look at him as he walked with them back to the locker room. Great. Now Gael was pissed at him as well.

Eli opened the locker room door just as they reached it, a tablet in his hands. "You might want to see this, guys," he said quietly.

Finn came to a horrified standstill when he heard the high-pitched quivering voice of his mom—the voice she used every time she wanted his dad to agree to something. Finn stared at the screen in mortification.

His mom sat in Deke's lounge, talking to reporters. He parted his lips in astonishment at the photograph of his dad on the wall behind her. It was the one of him over forty years ago, standing quietly in uniform beside the helicopter, handing out candy to the local village kids outside of Saigon. His dad didn't even know that photo was being taken until the news team sent him a copy when he was sent home. It was one Finn rescued before his mom threw them all away after his dad died. There were no pictures at all after he lost his legs. It was also never on display, and Finn knew it had been put there for the cameras.

He blinked a couple of times and swallowed around the tightness in his throat.

"It's a disgrace," his mom cried. "Disappearing in the middle of the night like that. If they're so proud of this new thing, why does it have to be so secretive?" She put a handkerchief up to her eyes and dabbed.

Finn turned. He couldn't look at it anymore. He felt like he was going to be sick. He stormed into the locker room and heard the door open and close behind him. He smelled Talon's scent before he turned around.

"They're just worried. Everything will calm down."

Finn whirled around, not even noticing the rest of the team had trooped in. "Worried," he spat. "She's only *worried* about herself. That photo of my dad? It's been buried in a box in the shed for ten years. It was the only one I could save from the trash. That's what she thought of him, and her opinion of me hasn't ever been any better."

Fuck, he had to get out of here. Finn ignored everyone and pushed past Gael. He'd had enough. First Talon and now his mom. He was going to get his thirty dollars and get drunk. Maybe if he turned up at the bank, he would be able to get some cash. Fuck the job. He was going to lose it anyway.

TALON HELD his hand up as Vance took a step after Finn. "Let him go. We can catch up to him later."

Gregory appeared at the door and instantly tossed the vests he was holding to Gael and Vance. "They will fit," he said sternly and looked around. "Where's Finn?"

"Running home to Mommy, I expect," Eli drawled.

Talon opened his mouth to tell Eli to shut the fuck up when Gregory frowned, turned, and shut the door behind him.

"Sit down," he barked. "I want to tell you a little about Finlay Mayer." Everyone looked at Gregory in surprise, but they all sat on the benches in front of the lockers. "His father and my elder brother served together in 'Nam. Around three years ago, my brother got a letter from Finn's dad. Said he was going to try out for the FBI, but that his older brother would deliberately try to mess it up for him on the interviews because he was a dick and wouldn't want Finn bettering himself. He never asked for any favors from either of us other than to ignore the reference. He hadn't realized that my brother no longer worked at Quantico." Gregory sat and loosened his tie. "Finn's dyslexic. He's never been formally diagnosed, but his file also contains a letter from his college English teacher urging us to look past his grades. Apparently she'd done an IQ test on him without Finn knowing what it was. He scored 133."

Gael whistled. "That's impressive."

Talon almost smiled, but then remembered he wasn't supposed to care one way or the other.

"I had a ton of applications I could have chosen from." Gregory paused. "I'll admit the letter made me curious enough to look, and, well, why not? There are too many applicants at Quantico for them to take an outside chance. Finn knows this."

"You mean he's least likely to make waves because he knows this is his only chance," Talon said flatly.

"Not just that. He's a poster boy for small-town America. Unthreatening. Polite. Eager. The public would lap him up."

"Think Captain America before he went badass." Vance grinned.

"So you just want him for the press?" Sawyer asked.

"No. Absolutely not. I still firmly believe the partnership is the only way to go." Gregory looked carefully at everyone. "At some point the world is going to find out your abilities are evolving."

Talon looked up sharply, and Gregory smiled.

"You thought I didn't know? You thought I just wouldn't question the bullet not even causing a bruise on Gael? I know you have things you only share with each other, and I kind of understand that. But you have to believe me when I say this is the only way to go. Get the public on your side, and they won't be able to lock any of you away in a lab." Gregory grinned. "Hell, they'll be wanting autographs."

He paused and stood. "I'll handle the press today. I think you need to go find Finn and go do those interviews Talon briefed me on this morning. The regular cops haven't uncovered anything else about Oliver's disappearance. He seems to have just vanished. Oh, and unofficially I hear the Vice President is making noises about wanting to meet you."

Talon blinked in astonishment as the locker door swung shut behind Gregory.

"Shit," Gael said. "I feel lousy now."

"It's not just on you, Gael," Eli said. "He turned down going for a drink the other night. He can't be that keen on being part of the team."

Talon firmed his lips. Yeah, and then he happily drank beer with Drew.

"Actually," Sawyer said slowly, "much as I hate to give the guy any credit, I think it's simpler than that. I don't think he's got any money."

Talon looked up, but Vance beat him to it. "What do you mean, he's got no money?"

"I was upstairs filling in some requisition forms, and Finn started to ask Gregory about his pay. He said the flights getting here wiped him out."

"But he would have got that back in expenses, surely." Gael looked at Talon, and Talon squirmed. Gael sighed. "Let me guess. You've never told him about claiming expenses."

"I'm not some fucking secretary," Talon snapped. "Edwards in payroll would have seen to that."

"When?" Gael exclaimed. "I'm willing to bet today was the first time he's even seen the main office. How the fuck was he supposed to know?"

Talon stood and paced. "Why the fuck is it my responsibility to tell him?"

"Oh, I don't know," Gael thundered. "How about because you're the team leader? How about because you're supposed to be his fucking partner?"

Talon whirled around, the words dying on his lips. He brought his fist hard into one of the locker doors, and it immediately crumpled. Shit. Gael was right. He remembered the bag Finn had brought and the old suit he was wearing. Every time he saw him, he seemed to be doing laundry. He never thought it was because he didn't have any clothes. He blinked. What the hell was he doing for food? Guilt slammed into him. He'd been fighting that feeling since he left him that morning, and that had nothing whatsoever to do with food. It had everything to do with what else they shared.

He looked at Vance. "Vance, try to get him on the phone. Find out where he is. We're all gonna take him out for food and then split up. We'll meet back here later." He looked at Gael. "You're right."

Gael grinned. "Of course I am."

FINN GLANCED down at the gas gauge on his car. Shit, it was nearly empty as well. This was all kinds of messed up, and he'd noticed the gas prices in Tampa weren't as cheap as back home.

Home. If seeing that video of his mom told him anything, it was that he was never going back there, ever. Maybe if he went in the bank with his ID, they'd give him an advance on his check without waiting for it to clear. He needed to find a job, and he needed to find somewhere cheap to live. He'd noticed a local branch of his bank when they drove down Kennedy yesterday, so at least he knew where it was. He found parking down the street from First National. It was an hour maximum stay, but he doubted he'd be anything like that long. He wasn't going to discuss his finances today. He knew he'd need to do all that, but he just wanted to get some cash. His stomach growled, and he thought longingly of Betty's breakfast platter. Maybe he could get a job there waiting tables. They could always pay him in food.

And it was raining. Wonderful. Finn sighed. Why was his life always so full of crap?

The question echoed around his head for a few seconds until he sighed again. It was ridiculous. He was fit, healthy, reasonably intelligent, and more than capable of holding down a decent job. There were a ton of others far worse off than him, and he needed to grow the fuck up and stop feeling sorry for himself. Something would turn up.

Finn blinked as an idea came to him. He had no intention of going back anywhere near his brother, and he was really liking the whole Florida vibe. Just because he wasn't going to be an agent didn't mean he couldn't look at the local sheriff's department. Agent Gregory had been cool with him. He bet if he asked, Gregory would give him a recommendation, and there was the sergeant from yesterday.

Finn smiled a little as he pushed open the doors to the bank and joined the line. There was a mom pushing a crying baby in a stroller in front of him. She was clutching the arm of an older child who looked about eight or nine. He had a baseball cap tugged down his face.

A security guard stepped forward and pointed to a sign. "I'm sorry, ma'am, but the boy will have to remove his cap."

Finn looked at the wall and noticed the sign. It used to request that any motorcycle helmets were re-moved, but now it seemed they included any sort of headgear that could hide people's faces. Finn sighed. He knew what that was for: enhanced.

The kid ducked his head farther down into his neck, and his mom pulled him closer, almost defensively.

Every hair on Finn's neck stood. He took a step forward, and immediately the security guard noticed and unholstered his weapon.

What the fuck? Finn froze. How was he any threat? "Whoa there." Finn immediately put his hands up.

The guard swiped a hand across his forehead and pointed to the kid. "Cap off now."

The mom drew the child closer. "I'm sorry, sir. He's shy. We'll leave." And she tried to turn around the stroller with the crying baby.

"No." The guard grabbed the kid's arm and swiped the cap off.

The few people who were in the bank stopped to watch in fascination. The guard looked horrified, as if his worst fear had come to fruition. Finn glanced at the boy's face, knowing exactly what he was going to see. Dark brown spiky hair and brown eyes brim-ming with tears, and a red mark under the left one. The mom tried to get the stroller past the guard, but he was blocking it.

"Sir," Finn said again with some mad idea about showing his ID to get the guy to calm down. The guard was sweating profusely, which was ridiculous because the air was on full.

Finn realized what an insane thought that was when, twenty seconds later, he was facedown on the floor with a shotgun pressed into his cheek, listening to the screams around him and the gunfire that preceded it.

He also had the insane thought that they were pretty dumb bank robbers, because the guard had fired at the ceiling as soon as three other guys walked in instead of quietly locking the doors. The guard was obviously in on it and panicked. Finn wanted to shake his head at their stupidity. Waving the guns around would have gotten them as much cooperation, but a lot less police attention. He knew someone would have heard the gunshots and called 911.

Finn breathed through his nose, trying to keep calm while the bank staff were dragged out with the customers. The boy was crying along with the baby, and Finn wanted to get closer to him to help.

A lanky guy wearing a ski mask dragged Finn to his feet, immediately patted him down, and took out his wallet.

Finn suddenly realized it was going to get a whole lot worse.

The guy opened his wallet. "Who the fuck are you?" he screamed at Finn. He looked at his friends. "He's a cop. He's got ID."

A bigger guy marched over and snatched Finn's wallet out of the first guy's hand. "Fuck, he's not a cop. He's a fed." He threw Finn's wallet across the floor in disgust, turned around, and pushed the guard into Finn.

Finn tried to stay on his feet. "I—" Pain exploded in his jaw and his legs buckled. Fuck, the guy had hit him.

"I ask the fucking questions!" the bigger guy screamed, and Finn saw the first one wince at the second one's shouting. Through his pain haze, he registered guy number two was definitely in charge.

"Then we need to get out of here," the first guy shouted, panicked. "They'll have heard the gunfire."

"Are you kidding me? After all it's taken to get our man down here?"

Finn dropped in a heap.

"Dave, the cops will be here soon," the first guy whined, and the second one marched over.

"No fucking names," he growled, turning his own gun on the cowering customers.

Finn wanted to help, but it was all he could do to stay conscious.

The one called Dave motioned with his gun. "Everyone get on the floor, hands behind your heads." Finn started to comply but was hoisted up again. "Not you. You come with me." He nodded to the other gunman to follow, the one Finn noted was just standing silently. He carried a gun but wasn't waving it around like the other two.

"You two watch them," Dave said, and the security guard and the first guy held guns over the customers and staff.

Finn stumbled but kept his head down while he was pushed toward where he assumed the safe was. The guy gripping his arm nodded to the smaller one. Finn gazed at the third guy in the mask. He was quiet, and he seemed to be staring at Finn.

"Go do your shit," Dave shouted. "You know what will happen if you don't."

That caught Finn's attention. The quieter guy was being forced?

He walked up to the safe and shakily put out a hand. Finn couldn't believe what he was seeing. The bank was open, so that meant the huge safe door was unlocked and open wide. There was an internally locked gate with black metal railings. The gate groaned as if it were under some unseen pressure, and with a loud click, the gate swung inward. Finn stared in shock at the guy. He was enhanced. He must be. He was willing to bet the mask wasn't just hiding his identity—it was also hiding a mark.

"Dave, Dave!" The other guy rushed into the room, but Finn didn't have to be told what was wrong. They could all hear the sirens.

Crap. Now what was going to happen?

Chapter Fourteen

"JUST GOES to voicemail," Vance said in frustration. "Maybe he's turned it off?"

"He knows better than that," Talon countered.

"I don't know, boss," Sawyer said. "He was pretty pissed when he left."

Talon pulled down his T-shirt. "Let's head over to his place. It's likely he's just gone straight there anyway." Talon was running out of ideas as to what to do with Finn. He was an absolute joy last night. He mulled the word over in his mind. Joy? He didn't think he'd ever used that word in his life, and he had no idea where he had come up with it to use for Finn. He paused as he fastened his pants. Yeah, he did. It was that jubilant, bubbly feeling he'd gotten last night. Unwrapping Finn was like unwrapping a birthday present as a kid.

Except better—way better. Talon grabbed his keys and wallet and took a step just as the locker door opened.

It was Drew. "Gregory needs you in the command center ASAP."

They all glanced at each other, but it was the urgency in Drew's voice that kept them silent. Talon jogged out of the room, sickness swirling in his gut. He had no idea why, but he knew something was very wrong.

Talon and the others ignored the stares for the second time that day as they rushed through the main offices. The front office had about ten telephone and computer terminals—everything to run any joint operation from. He looked at the large TV feed as they walked in. There was a police lieutenant on a video feed talking to Gregory. Gregory paused the monitor as they all trooped in.

"We've got a hostage situation at the downtown First National Bank. We have no reason to think there are any enhanced down there, but I've been asked for your input." Gregory nearly rubbed his hands in glee. "This is outstanding. What happened yesterday has caused the lieutenant to reach out. I can get regular SWAT, but they've asked for you." Gregory paused, realizing what he had said. He had the grace to look embarrassed.

Talon paused and glanced at Vance. "We'll go get into uniform."

"What about Finn?" Gael asked.

"Vance, keep trying to get him on the phone. If he hears about this, he may come back anyway."

They rushed back through the office, heading for the locker room once more.

"What do you think they'll need us to do, boss?" Eli asked.

"I'm not sure," Talon admitted, and then he paused when they got into the locker room. "But this is our chance, guys. We've trained for this. Let's go see what the lieutenant has to say first."

TALON PARKED his truck in the same place as yesterday with an ominous feeling of déjà vu. He blocked off the street, but was pleased to see around four times as many cops as there were the day before.

He got out and saw two cops walking toward him. He stood respectfully, recognizing the lieutenant as he neared him. The guy put his hand out. "Agent Valdez? My sergeant had good things to say about you yesterday, and I saw the video myself. Name's Dobbs."

Talon shook hands. "Do we have any indication that there are enhanced involved?"

"No." Dobbs paused. "But we have reason to believe this is the same gang that struck in Miami and in Atlanta last month. I wasn't told you were exclusive to enhanced activities only."

Talon shook his head. "No, that's right. Our A-SAC was especially keen to help."

The lieutenant nodded, visibly relieved. "Our negotiator is on his way, although as yet, there has been no communication."

Talon nodded. "Cameras?"

"Disabled nearly immediately. It shows them entering and a security guard firing at the ceiling, people panicking. There seemed to be a little altercation between the bank's security guard and a child, and we're a little worried about one of the hostages. He got involved in whatever was going on with the kid and the security guard just before three men in masks ran in. They examined wallets and took cell phones straight away, but they didn't like what was in the guy's who was talking to the guard. They brought the guy to the floor and shoved a shotgun in his face."

Talon's ears pricked up. "Was he in uniform?"

The lieutenant shook his head. "To be honest he looked like a college kid. He was wearing a Superman T-shirt."

Talon heard the gasp from his team as he froze. No, surely not. Talon's heart sped up.

"What is it?" the lieutenant asked.

"One of my team fits that description," Talon said carefully, refusing to respond to the fear churning his gut.

"Come with me to see the feed," the lieutenant said immediately.

"Boss," Sawyer whispered.

Talon shook his head. He knew what Sawyer was offering, but he had no intention of letting Sawyer go in there unarmed, and any metal Sawyer was carrying would be destroyed immediately with his body's change. He'd never simultaneously gone through a wall and gotten rid of more than one gun in practice. Sawyer would need a few seconds to recover before he could attempt to take out all the weapons the gunmen had. Talon wanted to see the vid first.

They stepped up to an iPad some tech guy was holding. Talon gazed in horror as he recognized Finn lying on the floor. He took a slow breath. "Play from the beginning, please."

The tech restarted the feed, and it showed various customers standing in line, Finn among them. They saw a security guard step up to a child wearing a baseball hat, and there was some sort of altercation. Finn took a step closer, and the guard reached for his gun. Finn stopped and seemed to be trying to talk to the guy. The mom and child were getting upset. Then all hell broke loose. Three guys in ski masks ran in at the same time as the guard panicked and shot his weapon at the ceiling. Within seconds Finn was laid flat on the floor with a boot on his face and a gun pointed at him.

Talon breathed through his nose and tried to calm down. Finn had his head turned away from the camera, but Talon didn't need a reminder of those luminous green eyes and what they had looked like the night before. The bastards were going to regret ever laying a finger on him.

He stepped away, and his team surrounded him.

"I still think I should go in there first," Sawyer insisted.

The lieutenant called over to them. "The negotiator has arrived." Talon looked over his shoulder. A balding, middle-aged guy was getting a hurried briefing from the cops. Good, they were distracted for a minute.

"Gael, take Sawyer around the back. See if there's anywhere he could enter that he wouldn't be seen by the cops." Gael nodded, and Talon clasped Sawyer's arm. "I want an assessment first before I give permission for anything." They ran off.

Talon interrupted Dobbs. "How thick are the walls? It looks an old building."

The lieutenant frowned. "No different than normal. The security is within the vault itself, but the bank is open. The outer door would be unlocked, and the inner cage just usually requires two keys."

Talon breathed out again and tried to unclench his fingers. They'd been like that since he saw the gun in Finn's face. "So they're not relying on finesse here, just speed?"

"That's exactly what's happened in the other two robberies, but there's been no delay like this up to now, and never any weapons fired. Straight in, straight out," the lieutenant confirmed. "We think the guard wasn't supposed to lose control like that, and I have no idea what was up with the kid."

Gael stepped forward and pointed to the screen. "He entered wearing a baseball cap." He moved the video until it stopped, showing the guard reaching for his weapon after he yanked the cap off the boy and the look of fear on his face.

"I would bet he has a mark on his face in the same place as I do," Talon said in resignation.

The lieutenant peered at the screen in surprise. "That had never occurred to me," he admitted. The more the lieutenant spoke, the more Talon liked him.

"It would also explain why our teammate tried to de-escalate the situation," Vance said.

The lieutenant looked up. "Of course. This is your partner. I saw him on the video yesterday." He shook his head. "I would never have recognized him."

"Yeah, he looks about fifteen," Vance added dryly.

"That explains the reaction to seeing his ID," the lieutenant said. "I'll go update our negotiator." The lieutenant stepped away.

"What we going to do, boss?" Eli asked.

Talon tapped his earpiece. "Anything?" he asked quietly.

Gael answered straight away. "Yeah, there's a parking lot behind. Quite a few cops, but there's some dumpsters Sawyer could maybe get past without them seeing him if we can arrange a diversion."

Talon watched as the negotiator picked up the telephone to try to see if someone would answer inside the bank. He knew what would be asked. Was everyone unharmed? What did they want? Yadda yadda.

He was torn. He wanted to send Sawyer in. Fuck, he wanted to take a battering ram to the bank doors, but he had to think about his team as a whole, not just the one inside. Sawyer had never changed himself, walked through a wall, and deconstructed metal simultaneously. He was always exhausted after changing his body composition, and that's why they never asked it lightly. Talon didn't want a second member of the team in danger, as desperately as he wanted Finn out.

Sawyer had to be unarmed as well. He was never able to take any metal objects with him, and he always wore plastic buttons or simple ties to his clothes. They had a few laughs in the last few months when Sawyer reappeared without the zipper in his pants. He couldn't take a gun in without the metal part deconstructing, rendering it useless.

"How long is Sawyer up to for maintaining it now?" Talon knew he'd been practicing, but the longest he could stay hidden seemed to be a maximum of forty minutes. Talon heard the negotiator ask for some of the hostages to be released. "Wait one second," he instructed Gael quietly and moved back to the lieutenant. "Have we established how many hostages we have?"

The lieutenant took a step away from the negotiator. "At least six bank staff. We saw four customers, plus the child and the baby, plus your guy."

The negotiator winced a little and put the phone down. "He wants a fully fueled armored car, and I asked for a hostage release as a sign of faith."

Everyone looked at the bank as the door opened. They heard a baby crying straight away, and the sobbing mom pushed the stroller out and ran with it straight at the armed police. Talon stepped up to her as soon as she was brought behind the barricades and had a blanket wrapped around her. She quickly bent to unfasten the crying baby and pick it up.

"Bobby. They still have my Bobby," the mom cried.

Vance leaned in to Talon. "That's odd. You would think the perps would want the kid out of the building in case his abilities are a threat. It makes no sense to keep him there."

Talon stepped closer to the mom and hunkered down in front of her. He smiled reassuringly. She seemed to start in surprise when she saw his scar. It stopped her crying, anyway. "Are we right in thinking your boy is enhanced?" he asked gently.

She hesitated, then sagged and started crying again. "S-Six months ago. The day after his eighth birthday." She looked completely bewildered. "He just woke up with it."

Vance sat and covered her hand reassuringly, and she gave a watery smile. "Is there someone we can call? What about Bobby's dad?"

She looked up at the baby, who had stopped crying and was currently playing with Vance's handcuffs. Sadly, she turned to Vance. "He left. He wanted us to take Bobby to state, to give him up," she said in bewilderment. "We had a huge fight, and I asked what would he do if Jack suddenly woke up one morning with a scar? Would he stop loving him too?" She choked the last words out, and Vance wrapped an arm around her. "What's going to happen? Why wouldn't they let him come out with me?"

Talon almost shook his head. A lack of confidence on his part wasn't what she needed right now. He stuck his hand out. "My name's Talon. That's Eli and Vance." He gestured to the other two.

She gave a wobbly smile. "I'm Jenny Anderson."

"I need to know, ma'am—"

"—Jenny."

"Jenny." Talon smiled. "What's Bobby's ability?"

She looked at him in confusion. "He doesn't have any yet. He's only eight."

Talon looked sharply at the others. Sometimes the most dangerous abilities only came out later. "Ma'am, all enhanced have their abilities as soon as they transform. Get the mark," Talon added hurriedly and touched his scar.

Jenny shrugged. "Well, whatever it is, neither of us know. He's just a normal little boy, as far as I'm concerned."

Talon subsided. He wished there were more moms like Jenny, but he knew a lot of enhanced weren't so lucky.

"Have you ever known an enhanced to transform as young as eight?" Eli asked.

Vance shook his head. "The child from the school was only around that age, and that was unusual. And it's perfectly possible that the ability is rare enough that it's not something that would occur to an eight-year-old to do."

They all looked up as the telephone rang, and the negotiator answered it. They heard him speaking re-assuringly on the telephone and asking for more time for whatever it was. "They've given us an hour," the negotiator said as he replaced the handset.

"Or what?" Jenny asked, her voice cracking again.

Talon stood and tried to sound reassuring. "We're just working that out. We have a few tricks up our sleeve."

"What can you tell us about the other hostages, ma'am?" Vance asked, getting a notebook out.

"There are at least five people who work there, maybe six. To be honest I wasn't totally sure if one lady was a customer or an employee."

Talon nodded. They knew this.

Jenny screwed her eyes up in concentration. "There was a really nice boy."

Vance looked up. "Another child, ma'am?" he said, concerned.

"No, sorry. I shouldn't call him a boy. More a teenager, I suppose. Probably around seventeen, eighteen, maybe."

Talon smiled to himself and shared it with Vance. Only Finn fit that description from who they'd seen on the vid.

"Nice?" prompted Eli. Talon looked at him in shock. Eli asking about Finn?

"Yes," Jenny said. "He tried to keep the guard from reacting so badly to Bobby, and even when they hit the young man with the gun, he stayed close to Bobby."

Talon's heart thudded in his chest. "They hit him with the gun?" he repeated.

Jenny wiped her eyes. "Yes. One of the guards who was the loudest. He hit him when he tried to stop them from threatening Bobby. He seemed to be in charge. In fact—" Her eyes widened. "Oh. I just realized what they said. They looked at all our wallets for ID, and they said the young man was a fed."

Talon couldn't get words past his throat.

"He's actually part of our team, Jenny," Vance said carefully.

She smiled. "That's wonderful. I-I mean...." Jenny reddened as she realized what she'd said.

"Yes," said Vance firmly. "He's going to help us coordinate our efforts to get everyone out safely."

Talon barely heard the rest of Jenny's words as she tried to remember who else was being held. His brain was stuck on the thought of Finn getting hit with the gun. Apparently one of the older ladies had a scarf she gave him to try to stop the bleeding, and the loudest gunman hit him another time when he put himself in front of Bobby to stop him from crying. Jenny thought he might have gotten knocked out for a few seconds, but she couldn't be sure.

What have I done? Why was I such an asshole this morning?

He distantly heard Vance finish questioning Jenny.

"Boss?"

Talon blinked, bringing Eli into focus.

"Gael's waiting to hear what you want them to do."

Talon took a deep breath. What he wanted to do and what was a good idea might not be the same thing. "Let's walk." He turned. Vance quickly joined them, as Jenny's mom had arrived. Out of the corner of his eye, he saw Gael and Sawyer running over.

"What are our options?"

"They have eleven hostages," Vance replied. "Six bank staff. An elderly couple and a middle-aged man we haven't been able to identify yet."

"Finn and Bobby," Talon finished.

Vance quickly filled in Gael and Sawyer on the details of the child and what they found out about the robbers.

"There's three robbers plus the security guard," Eli confirmed. "I don't get the guard, though. He was completely freaked out about the whole thing, but Jenny says he definitely sided with the robbers and has a weapon, which no one has tried to take off him. There wasn't enough said for her to tell whether they knew each other or not, but apparently the guy who seems to be the leader was pissed at the guard for firing his gun."

"It ruined the whole surprise thing for them," Gael agreed. "They seem to be very smash-and-grab type. In and out as fast as they can."

"Jenny said one of the robbers didn't look like he was participating much," Vance said. "He just stood there until the one in charge ordered him into the back. They made Finn go in with them. Apparently the guy in charge completely freaked when they found out Finn's a fed."

"How trigger-happy do we think these guys are?" Gael asked.

Talon tried to bank down the sick feeling in his stomach. "If they're the same group that did the banks in Miami and Atlanta, there were no shootings at all."

"Then much as I would love to see what Sawyer can do, maybe we ought to see what the negotiator can do first," Gael said slowly.

The lieutenant walked over to them. "All the blinds have just been closed. I have cops with telephoto lenses, and they can't see a thing."

Talon took a breath. "Sir, we have no reason to think that the gunmen won't give up peacefully. Both their previous raids were carried out without one single shot fired."

"What do we know about this guard?" Gael asked.

"This is his first day," the lieutenant answered. "Divorced dad. No red flags except a hefty judgment for child support. Apparently the agency he works through recently received instructions for his wages to be garnished."

"Money might be a problem, then?" Sawyer said what they were all thinking.

"So we're agreed we let the negotiator take point?" the lieutenant clarified. "We have absolutely no eyes and ears in the place, and no easy way of getting any. The building is stand-alone. We have a hostage crisis team, but they are an hour away."

Talon agreed. "Unless we are faced with the possibility of injury to any of the hostages, an incursion is the absolute last resort."

The lieutenant walked back to his negotiator.

"There are many possible complications, boss," Gael started. "My biggest worry is the enhanced child. I know his mom said he hadn't demonstrated any abilities, but we don't know what he will do if he's scared or threatened."

Talon sighed. He hoped to God Finn managed to keep him calm. They all knew it could go badly wrong very quickly.

Chapter Fifteen

FINN LOWERED the cotton scarf. His head wasn't bleeding anymore, just felt like it was threatening to explode, and his vision kept blurring, which he didn't think was a good sign. He sat with his back to the counter and the kid close by. For some reason they were keeping the two of them separate from the rest of the hostages—the bank staff, a guy in his fifties, maybe, and an elderly couple. The older guy looked pale and shaky. His wife seemed in better condition. Finn tried to give them a reassuring smile a couple of times if his guard, or "Slim," as he had nicknamed him, wasn't looking. Bobby, as he heard his mom call him, surreptitiously shuffled closer to Finn, and Finn tried to give him an encouraging look, even if he couldn't speak without the threat of a gun in his face.

The idiot guard was in the far corner, watching the bank staff. If he had to guess, the guard was in on it, but he'd definitely never done this before. He didn't have the swagger of the guy who was in charge. Finn glanced at the clock on the wall. Three hours since he'd stormed out of the field office.

"There's no fucking food in here," Slim grumbled.

Finn risked speaking. "Get on the phone and ask for some." He gestured to the phone.

Dave opened his mouth, but at that second, the phone rang. Everyone jumped a little, and Dave snatched it up. "You got my car yet?" he said gruffly. He glanced at the clock on the wall. "Yeah," he said, looking at Finn. "We're hungry. Yeah. Wait," he demanded and slammed the phone down. "They'll bring food and water, whatever we want, if we let a hostage go." He pointed to Bobby. "They want him."

Bobby ducked his head and pressed into Finn's side.

"That makes sense," Finn agreed. "You want hostages who will be cooperative and sensible. Adults, not children. The more you give them, the more likely it is we will resolve this soon."

He realized his mistake as soon as the big guy turned.

"More likely?" Dave said incredulously. "Maybe we should give them a hostage in a body bag and then they'll cooperate."

One of the bank tellers burst into tears, and Dave rounded on her.

"Shut the fuck up, you bitch."

One of the other women put her arm around her and tried to calm her down.

Dave leaned over and snatched the phone up. "I want food and water brought to the door and left.

And everything in packets so I know it hasn't been drugged." He lifted his chin toward the old man. "Stand up, Grandpa."

The old man shook his head. "No, please. Take my wife."

His wife shushed him. "The boy," she said pleadingly. "Please let the child go."

Dave grinned and looked at the old man. "Uh-uh. See the scar on his face? That means he can do cool shit. He's going nowhere."

Finn was surprised. He hadn't met any humans who seemed to be in awe of enhanced before, and he noticed Dave kept glancing toward the quieter one standing in the corner. After Finn saw him open the safe, he didn't get involved in anything, just kept out of the way. He seemed to glance at Finn one or two times, though, and Finn had no idea why.

Finn looked up sharply, wishing he could see behind the mask. What if Dave was an enhanced? Was that why he wasn't scared? *No*, thought Finn. That made even less sense. If he were an enhanced, he wouldn't need the child. In fact, he would understand how unpredictable any ability was in so young a child. Finn would have thought he was more likely to want to get rid of him.

Slim peered out of the blind. "There's a guy putting an open box down with stuff in."

The phone rang again. Dave snatched it up and said, "Yeah, hang on." He put it down and walked to the old man. He grabbed his arm and tried to pull him upright. "Come on, Grandpa," he said derisively.

The old man struggled and wheezed. "I'm not going. I insist you take my wife."

Dave got impatient. "Do as you're fucking told."

Finn wasn't sure what happened next. Whether it was an accident or whether it was deliberate, as the old man went to grab at Dave for balance, he caught his ski mask and pulled it off. Dave went nuts. He put his hands to his face, then brought a hand around and cracked the old guy on the side of his head with the gun. Blood burst from the side of his head, and his wife screamed as he went down. Cries went up from everyone. In a second all the guns were raised.

Dave was furious. "You fucking idiot," he spat.

The old man's wife sobbed and pulled her husband's head onto her lap. He seemed unconscious. Finn opened his mouth and was suddenly looking at a gun again.

"Don't even think about it," threatened Slim.

Dave pointed the gun at the security guard and hoisted one of the bank tellers to her feet. "Send her out and get the food."

"Me?" the guard asked hesitantly.

"Yes, you," Dave ordered, bringing his gun up to the guard.

Finn put his arm around Bobby, who was shaking in fear and trying to get as close to Finn as possible. This was escalating, and he was worried. Finn nearly laughed. Worried? He was scared to death and completely out of his depth. An hour's lecture on hostage negotiation in no way prepared him for any of this shit. An image of a blond-haired, blue-eyed giant came to mind. What he wouldn't give….

The guard grabbed the woman Dave had pulled upright and nodded.

"Get the food in first," Dave instructed, keeping his gun trained on the guard.

The guard clasped the woman in front of him and cautiously opened the big door. He looked outside and pushed at the woman to move her.

Dave stood behind him, out of sight of the cops.

"We're coming out," the guard shouted, then pushed the woman as he took a step outside. The security guard cried out, "I surrender, I surrender," and Finn saw the woman go sprawling onto the sidewalk.

Dave cursed and, as if in slow motion, sighted his gun. The shot took them all by surprise, and Dave stepped back and slammed the door as answering bullets hit it.

One of the tellers started crying quietly. The old woman was still sobbing over the unconscious body of her husband, and Finn's heart plummeted. Dave had shot someone. Finn was completely convinced he shot the guard because the guy tried to escape. Whatever happened, Dave was now a murderer in a state that still had the death penalty and had little to lose.

Everything had just become a hundred times worse.

THE COPS got off a few rounds before Talon yelled at them. They'd nearly shot the hostage. He put his hands straight up and calmly walked toward where the woman was crying hysterically. He glanced at the security guard who had been shot in the back of the head and was obviously dead. He nearly had to carry the woman back with him, as she couldn't stand on her feet, and immediately passed her to the paramedics. He heard a noise behind him, and for the first time, noticed what a large crowd had gathered behind the barriers the cops had quickly erected. He could count at least five news vans. *Wonderful.*

He glanced at his team, and without being asked, they all stepped to one side.

"The stakes just changed," Talon said. "Sawyer, go see what you can find out, but for fuck's sake, be careful."

Sawyer gave a lopsided grin in acknowledgment. "Gael, Vance? You might have to distract the cops while I get behind the dumpsters."

Talon stared at his team as they all moved to do his bidding. He saw Sawyer surreptitiously hand his gun, keys, and phone to Vance. This was the bit Talon hated. He knew part of being the leader was some-times sending people in who had a better skill set than he did. Talon remembered the day when Gregory named him their team leader. He'd thought it might be Vance, with his connections, or Gael, maybe, with his levelheadedness, but it was given to him, and he'd made a crap job of it so far. He wasn't even a good partner, as Gael so ably pointed out.

Talon glanced back at the building and wished for just five minutes to tell Finn that he, Talon, was an ass. That he hadn't meant a word. That… he *liked* him.

He grunted. He was fooling himself. *Like* didn't begin to describe how he felt about Finn. He wasn't sure exactly how he did feel, but he suddenly desper-ately wanted to get the chance to find out.

Talon raised his eyes at a movement from Gael. Gael nodded at Talon, and Talon watched them walk away.

"NOW WHAT do we do?" Slim asked nervously as Dave pulled the box into the middle of the room.

Finn kept quiet. He wasn't sure bringing attention to himself or Bobby at that moment was such a good idea.

Dave looked up and glanced over at the quiet guy. "You keep an eye on them two," he ordered to him and then looked at Slim. "Get over here."

Slim went eagerly to the box, pulled out a bottle of water, and unscrewed the cap. Dave did the same, except he pulled out a sandwich also. They both dragged the box over to the corner and sat where they could see all the people huddled together.

Bobby shivered slightly and then turned his face up to Finn. "I need to pee," he whispered. Finn wrenched his gaze away from the old man and looked up at the quiet guy, convinced he had heard Bobby speak.

"Dave," the quiet guy shouted over. "The kid needs a piss. I'm going to take them both in there so I can keep an eye on the fed." He looked over his shoulder to where the restrooms were.

Dave looked up from ramming a sandwich down his throat. He got up, marched to the restrooms, and peered in. "You've got five minutes. Go in with him to make sure the kid isn't up to anything."

Finn stood shakily, his head swimming a little, the pain making him nauseous, and felt a small hand slide into his bigger one. The quiet guy gestured with his gun for Finn to walk in front of him.

Finn stumbled a little, and the guy grabbed his arm to steady him. Finn stared in shock, wishing the guy would take the mask off. They walked into the restroom, and he let go of Bobby so he could use the toilet. Finn walked up to the mirror above the sink and winced at his white face and the blood that had run down into his collar.

The quiet guy came up behind him and seemed to stare at Finn through the mirror. Finn stared back. There was something about him. He had a gun, but he hadn't been a dick with it at all. Finn decided to take a chance.

"You know things will go better for you if we get the old man and the kid out of here. You didn't shoot the guard, and something tells me you don't want to be here."

The man shrugged. "Be here? In a bank with SWAT outside waiting to put a bullet in my brain? Whatever gave you that idea?" he asked mildly.

Finn registered the faint sarcasm. "This isn't gonna to go well for anyone. I can help you before this gets any worse and before more lives are lost."

The guy stared at Finn quietly. "You can't help me. I lost my life a long time ago."

Finn's lips parted at the bitterness in the whispered words. "We need to get the old guy out of here. You know where I work," he added desperately, trying another argument. "My partner is enhanced."

The guy reared back a little in surprise.

Slim opened the door. "Out. Whatch'ya doing in there? Feeling each other's dicks?" He sneered and waved his gun threateningly.

Finn didn't dare say anything more and quietly walked back with Bobby, concentrating on putting one foot in front of the other and trying to ignore the dizziness and the pounding in his head.

Dave was throwing a few bottles of water to the rest of the hostages. The old man's wife never glanced at anyone except her unconscious husband. The middle-aged guy stared at Finn pointedly as he came out. A few of the bank staff also looked at him. Finn felt expectation settle on his shoulders. What would they all say if they knew he'd been a trainee for a week?

Finn, Bobby, and the quiet guy all walked back into the room. Finn hesitated. "Can I look at the old guy? See how he is?"

Dave glanced at the old man, who was still unconscious, and nodded briefly. "Knock yourself out." He smirked at his choice of words.

Finn knelt next to the man's wife, who looked up at him, tears rolling silently down her cheeks. Finn had done plenty of basic first aid. He'd taken classes at school, and he'd even managed to get a few free courses while he was at college. The man wasn't having any breathing difficulties. Finn raised his eyelids, and the man turned away from the light slightly and tried to shut his eyes against it. His wife gasped a little, and Finn covered her hand with his. He turned to Dave. "He needs a doctor. They are more likely to negotiate if they think you will cooperate."

Dave sneered. "You mean come in with guns blazing?"

Slim glanced at Dave with a frightened look on his face. "Dave?"

"No, they won't," Finn urged. "Not if they think they're getting somewhere. They'll only risk coming in if you start shooting people."

Dave glanced at Slim as if he were suddenly unsure. The telephone abruptly started ringing again. Dave swiped it up. "Yeah." His face changed. "I want the fucking car," he shouted. Finn pointed to the old guy, and Dave seemed to think about it. Then Dave laughed at something the negotiator said. "Are you fucking kidding me?" he shouted again and slammed the phone down. He shook his head in disbelief. "Dicking us around with the car, and then they said they'd send in a doctor to check everyone out."

"A doctor?" Finn repeated, puzzled. They wouldn't send a civilian into a hostage situation.

"Yeah, some guy called Sawyer. As if I care what his fucking name is," Dave spat and got up. "I'm going for a piss," he said to Slim. "Watch them."

Sawyer? Finn sat back with Bobby. He was sure that was a message for him, but he didn't know what it meant unless they hoped to get Sawyer in here so he could do his thing with the guns. That must be it. He glanced back at the quiet guy, who had tucked his gun in his waistband and was making no attempt to aim it at anyone.

Slim went to the front of the room and started counting stacks of bills even as he had his gun trained on the rest of them.

The middle-aged guy looked over as Dave came out of the restroom. "I think I might be able to help you get what you want," he said cautiously.

Dave ignored him.

"I have plenty of money, and I'm a personal friend of Governor Jackson. Alan Swann. I'm CEO of Swann Industries."

Finn wanted to tell the guy to shut up. He was painting a target on his back.

"It's interesting you show no fear that the child may use his abilities against you," Alan continued.

Finn was trying to get his sluggish brain to think. He'd heard of Swann industries.

"Is it perhaps that you have some protection in place that makes you unafraid?" Alan mused, glancing at the quiet gunman.

Dave shot Swann an irritated look, and Finn stiffened in alarm. Did Swann suspect the third gunman was enhanced? No one had seen what he did in the vault except Finn. Dave lifted his gun, and Swann shut up immediately. Finn was relieved. He thought he might have guessed correctly.

Bobby moaned a little and slumped against his side; unbelievably, he was dozing. Not an unsurprising reaction to shock. Finn put his arm cautiously around him. The bank had been on lockdown for over two hours now, and they weren't getting anywhere. He stared aimlessly at the pile of wallets and cell phones on the counter to his side. None of them were any good to him, though.

He spied his own cell phone on the pile and narrowed his gaze slightly as it vibrated while he was watching it, and Finn glanced around to make sure no one else noticed. It was the phone Agent Gregory had given him, and no one else had the number. That was ridiculous. He couldn't exactly answer it. Surely they would know that.

Finn surreptitiously glanced back and saw it vibrate, and then, unbelievably, it just disintegrated. He blinked at the small pile of metal shavings and the empty plastic case sitting on top of them.

Sawyer. It had to be. The name of the doctor, but.... Finn looked to his side carefully as Dave paced restlessly. He didn't know Sawyer could do that sort of thing remotely.... Sawyer's words from the intros came back to him: *It only works at around six feet*

so far. It couldn't possibly be Sawyer. There was nowhere he could hide by the counter, and he wouldn't
be able to get behind it without being seen. Finn was
behind it when they went to the safe. He knew there
was no one there.

Every hair suddenly stood up on Finn's neck as,
behind the counter, a framed aerial photograph of
the building's grand opening suddenly titled an inch.
What? No. That was ridiculous. There was no way
Sawyer…. Finn stared at the ground carefully, his
mind working furiously.

Was it really beyond the realm of possibility that
he could make himself invisible?

It sounded like something out of a movie, but
then, so was Vance's strength, Gael's language skills,
and Talon's freaky thing he did with Finn's body. And
he hadn't even started with what exactly Eli could do.
Finn glanced at the phones again, but saw the quiet
guy move a little and follow Finn's stare, so he quickly looked away.

Two of the women had asked to use the restroom,
so Slim was standing guard outside. Dave was getting more and more agitated. Finn watched him for a
second, then threw a worried glance at the quiet guy.
He seemed to sigh, then walked over to where the old
guy was still on the floor, even though he was blinking
every now and then.

"Dave, I think we should let the old man go," the
quiet guy said. "He's not doing us any favors staying
here, and I think Finn's right. We'll have more chance
of getting what we want if—"

Finn managed to control the gasp, but the guy
stopped abruptly as soon as he realized what he'd said.

Dave paused in his pacing and looked incredulously at the guy.

Finn. He'd called him Finn. It said Finlay on his ID, and as far as he knew, no one had said his name, and the guy never looked at the wallets. He knew him. He had to know him.

Dave marched up to the guy in fury, grabbed the ski mask that covered his face, and yanked it off even as the guy tried to duck and stop him. "There, ya little fucker, seein' as how you two know each other." He spun the guy around so Finn could see his face, and Finn stared in complete shock.

Adam.

Dave yanked the gun out of Adam's waistband and pulled him back against his body with one arm while he pointed the gun at his temple with the other. "You're an undercover cop," he screamed.

Finn looked at Dave quickly, realizing things were getting even worse. "We were at school together. He was a neighbor." He tried not to sound as panicky as he felt.

Adam looked completely defeated. "We haven't seen each other since we were eleven."

"I don't give a fuck," Dave shouted, and Finn stopped breathing as Dave's finger moved to the trigger. "What the fuck?" Dave yelped as the gun dropped to the floor in pieces at the same time as the door burst open.

Slim raised his weapon at Finn, and Adam leaped to shield him, except the cops bursting into the room didn't know that. To Finn's team it looked like Adam was attacking Finn, and the bullets hit Adam before he knew what had happened.

"No!" Finn screamed, lunging as he caught Adam's body. He looked at Talon, who was lowering the gun he had just fired.

People screamed, and suddenly the room was very full. Paramedics swarmed all over Adam and the rest of the hostages. Swann lurched to his feet clumsily and stumbled against Finn in the panic. He tried to steady himself, knocking Finn out of the way, and the jolt to Finn's head was one more than his body seemed to be able to cope with.

"Finn." Talon choked out his name and held out his hand, but Finn wasn't listening.

Adam. Talon shot Adam, thinking he was going to shoot Finn. Adam was dead, and it was all Finn's fault.

Everything blurred. Finn put up a hand to his pounding head and struggled to stand.

"Finn," someone shouted again, but it seemed like Finn was falling down a tunnel. People were shouting, and he couldn't hear them. He wavered, and the last things he remembered were the strong arms that caught him and the smell that he knew.

FINN BLINKED, trying unsuccessfully to open his eyes, but the ten-inch spikes currently hammering at his skull made him wish he hadn't bothered. He whimpered slightly and felt a strong hand cover his own. He swallowed to stave off the nausea and work out where he was before he had another go.

"Hey," the quiet voice he recognized said. "Just lie still. Are you in pain? I'll get a nurse."

"No." Finn's voice cracked, and he winced. "What happened?"

"All the hostages are okay. The gunman I took out is in ICU. Stable. They operated." Talon paused as Finn valiantly tried to open his eyes without wanting to vomit.

"Sure?" he managed to croak.

"Of course," Talon replied. "The other two went for their guns and were killed by the cops."

Finn gave up attempting to move, the relief overwhelming. He heard the door open and either a nurse or doctor talking cheerfully. He was okay until someone tried to force his eyelids open and shine a light in them. He jackknifed up in bed and promptly vomited everywhere.

He must have passed out again, because the next time he woke, he was convinced he was having a nightmare. He could hear his mother's strident voice telling someone to get the hell out of her baby's room.

Finn opened his eyes again groggily, and his mom was all over him. He could have quite cheerfully vomited once more. Talon was nowhere to be seen. He breathed slowly through his nose for a few seconds while he worked out that the top of his head wasn't going to explode. It still felt like evil elves were in there with ice picks, but it was better than before.

He opened his eyes properly as a man in a white coat walked in, followed by another guy in blue scrubs. He guessed at least one of them was a doctor.

"Doctor," his mom exclaimed. Finn absently noted the stupid cow had managed to make sure she was wearing lipstick. "How's my son?"

The guy in the white coat came close to the bed. "I don't know. Mr. Mayer, perhaps you can tell us how you are feeling?"

Finn took a deep breath and pulled his hand out
of his mother's vicelike grip. "Get her out of here."
He ignored his mom's horrified gasp. "I want her out
of here now."

"He's hysterical, the poor boy," his mom said.
"He has a head injury, doesn't know what he's saying."

"I am perfectly lucid," Finn ground out.

The guy in the scrubs grinned at him and turned
to his mom. "Either you leave, ma'am, or I will have
to call security."

"You ungrateful child," his mom fumed. "After
all I've done for you."

Finn shut his suddenly stinging eyes and waited
while his mom's footsteps and loud protests could no
longer be heard in the corridor. He opened his eyes again.
The doctor was quietly writing notes on the chart.

"Doctor? A patient…. Adam Mackenzie?"

The doctor put down the chart and smiled. "We're
keeping him sedated to give his body a chance to heal.
He will make a full recovery." He came and stood by
the bed. "And before you ask, you were brought in
yesterday. Severe concussion, but your scan was clear.
You can be discharged if your boyfriend will be staying at home to look after you. There's no way you can
be on your own."

"My b-boyfriend?" Finn stammered in shock, and
the doctor looked up quickly.

"I'm sorry. Did I make assumptions?"

Finn looked around the room as if he were waiting for his imaginary boyfriend to appear.

The doctor sighed. "Your partner, then? Agent
Valdez? He was here all night with you until your
mom arrived and had him banned from your room."

"She did what?" Finn said incredulously.

"I'm afraid until you were awake to make your own wishes known, she is your next of kin, and the hospital had no choice but to abide by her wishes."

Finn rubbed his eyes. His head still hurt like shit. Talon stayed with him all night? A warm feeling settled somewhere in his chest. "What? I mean, where?" Finn tried to get his sluggish brain to sort the words he needed.

"They're in the other waiting room," the doctor said, correctly guessing at Finn's question as he hung up the charts. "You have quite a crowd waiting for you. I had a feeling you might feel differently when you woke up, so I just put them somewhere out of your mom's way."

Finn smiled. "Thank you so much."

The doctor grinned. "You're welcome. My husband's always telling me I'll get into trouble with the hospital one of these days." Finn's smile widened, and the doctor left.

He laid his aching head back down and wondered if he could get some painkillers. He heard the door open again after a few seconds and opened his eyes. He stared as it seemed like everyone trooped in. He looked in shock as Talon, Vance, Gael, Sawyer, and finally Eli came in.

"Hey, kid," Gael said. "Nice to see you're finally awake."

"Yeah," chuckled Vance. "These probies are always lazy. Lying in bed while we've sat in waiting room chairs all night." Vance flushed slightly as he realized what he said.

Finn swallowed. They'd been in the waiting room all night? He looked at Talon, but Talon was looking at the floor. "How is everyone, the hostages?" Finn asked.

"They're all fine. Even the old man," Gael said. "Bobby wants to know if he can visit you as soon as you feel up to it. He's got a serious case of H-E-R-O worship." Gael spelled the name and chuckled.

"They said I can go home," Finn started.

Talon looked up and spoke immediately, his blue eyes clashing with Finn's own. "Not on your own, though."

"What about your mom?" Sawyer asked cautiously.

"I said she was to leave. I hope the security guard's thrown her out."

Gael and Vance laughed.

Finn remembered something and glanced at the closed door and then looked at Sawyer. "That was you, wasn't it?"

Sawyer smiled sheepishly. "Yeah."

"Does Gregory know?" Finn asked.

"Not officially," answered Talon, "but he suspects our abilities are evolving."

"That is so awesome," breathed Finn and did a double take at Eli. "I swear," he said, putting a hand to his head. "Hallucinations are caused by a head injury, aren't they?"

Talon took a hurried step forward. "Why? What is it?"

Finn closed his eyes and leaned back. "Eli just smiled."

Chapter Sixteen

FINN OPENED his eyes and looked around in shock as Talon turned off the truck's engine. "Where are we?" He seemed to be in a garage, and for one moment, Finn thought they were back at the field office.

"My place," Talon answered.

"Your place?" Finn parroted.

Talon smiled. "I have a dog, and you weren't allowed to be discharged if you were going to be on your own. So we're here."

Finn looked around in surprise as Talon got out of the truck and started walking around to Finn's side. He scrambled for the door handle, and in his haste to not have Talon waiting on him, he jumped down.

Really fucking stupid thing to do, Finn.

Talon lunged for him just as his legs refused to hold him up, and he nearly face-planted.

"What the hell, Finn. You trying for another concussion?" Talon said in exasperation.

Finn's head swam sickeningly, and he leaned into Talon, his legs refusing to cooperate. Talon grunted, and the world swayed as Finn was swung up into Talon's arms. Finn hovered between shock, embarrassment, and trying not to lose the small breakfast he'd had to keep down in order to be discharged. To be honest he felt too bad to give a fuck, and he relaxed as Talon tilted him safely against his chest in his strong arms.

Leather. Finn breathed it in and closed his eyes. He didn't bother opening them even as Talon jostled him a little, and from the movement, they were clearly in an elevator. *Talon must have an apartment* was Finn's thought, but to be honest, he was past caring. He figured if Talon needed to put him down, he would. Talon moved him again as the elevator doors opened, and Finn heard a key in a lock, then claws scratching on tiles and a whine.

"Hey, Charlie. There's a good girl. Let's get him settled, and you can say hello."

Finn giggled helplessly at the inane thought that Charlie was a girl. More words drifted over Finn, but his eyes were so heavy, he couldn't summon the strength to look at the dog.

He felt Talon lay him down gently on a bed, heard him say something about having to wake him up a little later, but that he was okay to sleep for a little while. Finn was happy to agree.

TALON STRAIGHTENED from laying Finn on his bed. Finn hadn't questioned his insistence about looking after him. They were partners, and Finn's mom was an absolute joke. He also hadn't questioned Talon's decision to bring him back to his place because, as he said, he had a dog to look after.

But as he stared at Finn's white face against the chocolate-brown sheet, Talon had to admit he had no justification for walking straight into his own bedroom and laying Finn down on his bed. He had a perfectly good spare bed. One or more of the team had crashed there on a few occasions. It seemed automatic, bringing Finn in here. Talon stared at him and absently petted Charlie's cold nose as she shoved her head under his hand. She whined and sniffed at Finn.

Talon hesitated. He'd thought he might have to help Finn undress to get into bed, but he didn't expect Finn to go out like a light as soon as he got him laid down.

The doc was clear. Mild painkillers. Plenty of rest and water. Check for alertness every few hours for the first twenty-four, but the CT scan was okay, so they weren't expecting further problems, just being cautious. He could expect Finn to be dizzy and confused for a while. Maybe have some short-term memory loss. Apparently concussions were never the same for any two people. Some only took a few days to recover; some could take weeks. He had a list of indications to watch out for that meant Finn had to be brought back to the ER immediately. He spoke to Agent Gregory briefly at the hospital and told him he was taking Finn home. Gregory said to keep him posted, and Talon could worry about work later.

Vance and Gael both said they would handle the debrief, as the team had been camped in the waiting room for twenty-four hours. All Talon had to worry about was Finn.

If only it were that simple.

Talon leaned over and flicked the top button on Finn's jeans. He couldn't decide if he was hoping for the Superman shorts or the delicious blue briefs that hugged his package so firmly. Talon frowned and lectured his dick about not lusting after unconscious young men. His dick wasn't getting it, though, especially when he spied a red pair of briefs exactly the same as the blue.

Finn turned his face and moaned slightly in apparent pain, and Talon held his breath and glanced at Finn's face. Talon felt his own dick wither almost at the livid swelling and purple bruising down the left side of his face. Talon left Finn in the plain white T-shirt he had dressed in at the hospital. Something told him it was Sawyer's, since after sending Sawyer and Eli back to Finn's apartment to get some things, they said the only clean clothes were wet in the washing machine. They brought his shaving things and a toothbrush, though. Whatever else he needed, Talon would send the team out for it.

Talon covered Finn up but made sure the air was at a comfortable temperature. He got out the pills they were sent home with and a glass of water. Then he quickly took Charlie out to the dog park opposite his apartment block. She wouldn't need much. Talon paid his neighbor's kid to take her out twice a day, and the way she ignored her full food dish told him she'd been around at their house for lunch also. Charlie was getting on in years and a gentle soul. Mr. Takei's youngest had Down syndrome. Andrew and Charlie bonded nearly straight away, and he often lost Charlie next door even when Talon was at home.

He checked on Finn immediately when they came back in, and he was sleeping soundly. Talon resisted the urge to brush some hair that was lying across Finn's forehead. He inhaled sharply as he remembered the image of Finn's flushed face with his hair sticking to him as they both lay there panting.

Talon replaced his jeans with an old pair of shorts and stretched out in the armchair next to his bed, his long legs easily balancing on the end of the bed.

"UGH…."

Talon snapped his eyes open immediately at the soft sound. Finn was struggling to sit up. "Hey," he said softly and stood to put an arm around him to draw him easily and slowly upright. "What do you need?"

Finn blinked his dazed green eyes. "Where am I?"

Talon sat on the bed. "My place. I have a dog," he repeated in case Finn didn't remember him saying so before. Even as he said it, he was half expecting to get called out on it. He'd used Charlie as a justification for bringing Finn home when he knew full well all he had to do was call Mrs. Takei and Charlie would spend the night curled up on the bottom of Andy's bed.

Finn didn't reply, though, and Talon felt him sag a little against Talon's shoulder.

"Are you thirsty?"

Finn groaned as if remembering the reason he'd woken. "I need to piss."

"Okay," Talon said quietly and stood without rocking the bed much. He'd been warned Finn might be nauseous for a few days.

Finn slowly slid his legs to the edge of the bed, but even in the half light from Talon's drawn blinds, he saw the grimace on Finn's face brought on by the movement.

"Go slow," he cautioned, steadying Finn as he stood.

"Fuck," Finn groaned and swayed a little. "Hangover without tying one on the night before." His lips tilted wryly. "Not fair."

Talon chuckled in relief. Finn didn't protest the help, and he seemed to be aware of what was happening. He'd even tried a joke. The doctor had scared him shitless with all the things he had to look out for that could suddenly go wrong with a head injury.

He led Finn into the bathroom but didn't turn the main light on. Apparently bright lights weren't doing anything for Finn's headache, but he worked that one out himself when the hospital was less than sympathetic, as they needed the lights on full all the time. Talon noticed Finn shielding his eyes more than once. He eased Finn toward the toilet. "What do you need?"

Finn groaned in embarrassment. "I can manage."

Talon wanted to protest with the death grip Finn had on the sink, but he got him as close to the toilet as he could and then left to stand outside the door. He was back in the second he heard the toilet flush.

Finn wiped a bead of sweat off his forehead, then bent to pull up his briefs. His knees gave out, and Talon caught him before he hit the floor. "I bet you played ball when you were a kid." Finn gasped as he let Talon take his weight.

Talon ignored the briefs on the floor and the fact that Finn was now almost naked. "Huh?" he grunted, wrapping his arms firmly around Finn's waist.

"You keep catching me," murmured Finn.

Talon didn't have an answer, as the innocent statement seemed so loaded.

He deposited Finn on the bed and handed him the water as he took two pills out of the plastic bottle. He stood over Finn while he obediently swallowed them. "Are you hungry?"

Finn shook his head and winced.

"You're only allowed over-the-counter meds," Talon said in sympathy. "But the doc thinks you'll start to improve tomorrow after a decent night's sleep. It's hard to get any rest in the hospital." Talon pressed his lips together firmly to stop any more verbal diarrhea from spewing from his mouth.

Finn bent forward to put the glass down and yawned widely. "Sorry," he muttered and brought up his hand gingerly to his face.

Talon smiled. "Don't worry. You're still beautiful."

Finn looked at him, puzzled, as the words registered, and Talon now wanted to slit his own throat. He was bashed up, sick... and Talon was *flirting* with him?

"What time is it?" Finn asked.

"A little after eight." Talon looked at the closed blinds. The light around them was dimming. Finn sighed, his shoulders drooping, and Talon lifted the sheet. "How about you try to get some more sleep?" He managed to not offer the platitude of feeling better in the morning.

"Have you heard how... everyone is?"

Talon swallowed hard at the stilted question, but there was no censure in it. He was sure for a second Finn was going to ask something else, but he wasn't thinking clearly and his words were still a little slurred.

The gunman didn't get a weapon drawn, but Gregory was satisfied it was a valid shot. They hadn't found out much about the enhanced gunman. He had no ID on him at all, and the other two were dead. The cops were waiting to be given the all clear to question him, but that wouldn't be anytime soon. EnU were guarding his hospital bed, but the guy was still doped up from the surgery.

"The older couple have both been discharged into their daughter's care this afternoon. The gunman is out of danger." Was that what Finn meant?

"What will happen to him?" Finn asked quietly.

"You know he's enhanced?"

Finn nodded carefully, as if the movement hurt.

Talon shrugged. "There are two specially made prison units for enhanced, both in New York. But they're altering one at the moment here, seeing as how our unit is based here."

Finn's eyes widened. "Really?"

Talon stared at the huge green eyes in the pale face that was covered in bruises. He didn't understand why it was worrying Finn. Finn didn't shoot the guy. Talon had.

He checked Finn didn't want another drink, and the room grew quiet.

"Where are you sleeping?" Finn murmured suddenly, the catch in his voice betraying the reluctance to voice the question.

Talon considered his answer. It wasn't an invitation. Did he know he was at Talon's? Did Finn think he was somewhere else? Whatever it was, Talon recognized the need for reassurance when he heard it.

He stretched out. "Right here," he said firmly. "Go to sleep, kid."

He wasn't immediately sure what woke him the next time he opened his eyes. The room was black, but it didn't take him long to distinguish furniture. He got up quietly and switched on the low bedside lamp. It was about time he checked if Finn was okay. Talon took a step to the bed and caught Finn's arm suddenly as he thrashed it across his side. Talon searched Finn's face. His eyes were tightly closed. He shuddered, parting his lips as if he were going to say something, then moaned in distress. What the hell?

Talon sat on the chair and reached to take Finn's hand. Were you supposed to wake people from a nightmare? "Finn," he urged. "Finn, wake up." Talon smoothed the hair away from his eyes. "Come on, kid, wake up. Finn," he tried again a little louder.

Finn opened his eyes on a gasp. "Talon?" he said, and Talon's heart broke at the fear behind the question. Finn had been having a nightmare, and Talon was well used to those.

"You're safe, Finn. You're here to rest up, and the docs say you're gonna be fine." He tried to keep his voice soothing as Finn took a few hurried breaths and calmed down a little.

Finn took a steadying breath and gazed at Talon. "We're at your house," he said as if asking for confirmation.

"Uh-huh," Talon agreed, relieved that Finn knew where he was, and held Finn's head while he sat up enough to gulp some water.

Finn swallowed and looked at the chair Talon was in. "That's dumb," he said.

Talon looked over at the chair, suddenly non-plussed. "What is?"

Finn heaved another sigh. "You sleeping in the chair. The bed's huge." He lay back down and closed his eyes, a dimple flashing at the side of his mouth. "I promise not to jump you."

Talon couldn't have formed the words for a reply if his life depended on it. He was too busy wondering why he never noticed the dimple before. Even with the bruises, Finn was gorgeous. Talon shook his head and glanced over to the empty side of the bed. He had to admit the offer sounded tempting. Stretching his six-foot-five frame out in a chair was hell.

He glanced back at Finn, but he seemed to have gone back to sleep, so Talon stood and walked around to the other side of the bed. After a brief moment of indecision, he stripped off his T-shirt but kept his shorts on. He crawled in the bed, relieved to find his california king still left a good two feet of space between them. Talon sighed and closed his eyes.

FINN WAS toasty warm and having the best dream of his life. He was at that stage where he was just awake enough so he could appreciate his vivid dream in perfect detail. He could feel the hot puffs of breath on his neck, the heavy arm that was slung over him, trapping him down securely, and his dream boyfriend's delicious hard-on that was currently jabbed into the crease in his ass.

Finn sighed gustily and couldn't help the enthusiastic wiggle in his hips.

Dream boyfriend's breath caught, and as sudden awareness flooded him, Finn knew with perfect clarity where he was and who was in bed with him. He considered feigning sleep but knew that wouldn't work, as he had stopped breathing altogether.

He took a deep breath, gathering courage, shuffled around as the arm pinning him moved back, and winced as his bruised face scraped on the pillow. Talon's blue eyes were fixed on his. He didn't seem to be doing much in the way of breathing either.

"Good morning," he said, acknowledging that, as an opening comment, it wasn't very original.

Talon raised his eyebrows slightly, and Finn, emboldened, tried a shy smile. Talon blinked but didn't return it. Finn sighed again and regretted turning around. They were close but no longer touching. Finn took a mental tally of how he felt as he waited for Talon to decide if he was going to speak. His face was sore, but his headache had faded to a dull ache. He wasn't dizzy, but then, he hadn't tried anything that didn't involve him staying horizontal. His mind shied away from the questions he had over the events of the last few days, and he focused on how other parts of his body were recovering. In fact, if the ache in his balls was anything to go by, he was feeling much better.

He searched Talon's face for any hint of how he was feeling. Talon still hadn't said a word. He was just staring at Finn in rapt concentration.

"How are you feeling?" Talon seemed to bring himself out of his daze.

Finn considered the question carefully. He took a big chance. "Horny," he whispered beseechingly and wriggled his hips, even though Talon's big dick wasn't pressed into his butt anymore.

Talon's smile flashed across his face, and he chuckled. "You're injured."

Finn looked up. "So make me feel better?" He held his breath as Talon looked at him, astonished. To be honest Finn was shocking the hell out of himself as well. "I mean," Finn continued, deciding to go for broke, "you're my team leader. Don't you have to check all my injuries?"

"You hurt your dick?" Talon drawled.

Finn swallowed, drawn to Talon's full lips. "It's very painful. I think you ought to check it out."

Talon blinked, a half smile curving his lips. "Turn back around," he urged softly.

Finn's breath caught again at the way the blue in Talon's eyes deepened. Arousal. He cataloged the re-action for future. He liked having that effect on Talon. Lord knew his head injury wasn't the only thing that had him currently going weak at the knees.

Talon put an arm around Finn's side and slid him back so he was flush with his chest. "Tell me if any-thing hurts." He paused. "*Anything else*," he clarified.

Finn closed his eyes in complete rapture as Talon's dick scraped between his asscheeks. Even through the shorts, it was as hard as nails. He pushed back a little, silently asking for more.

Talon put a steadying hand on his shoulder. "No. I'm not going there. You had a head injury, for fuck's sake. Lie still and just enjoy it," he added, a little mel-lower, and Finn heaved a huge sigh and settled down to being teased a little.

Talon wrapped his huge hand over Finn's dick, and Finn let out a strangled squeak. Talon hesitated.

"Don't you dare stop," Finn ordered.

Talon chuckled. "Lie still. Knew you'd be a pushy bottom."

Finn thrust his hips a little again and got another chuckle, but Talon tightened his fingers when he brought his hand up Finn's length and twisted his wrist a little. Finn decided Talon definitely knew what he was doing and needed no further prompting from him.

Finn gasped as Talon pressed his dick into him harder. He desperately wanted to feel Talon inside him again, but he was thankful for anything he could get. Talon leaned over Finn and dropped kisses on his neck, avoiding anywhere that was bruised. Finn melted at the gentleness from Talon's lips, the complete opposite of his fingers. He had a moment to acknowledge that he never seemed to have any staying power where Talon was concerned as he felt the familiar heat pool in the base of his spine and spread to his groin. Talon stopped jacking him for a second and cupped his aching balls, scraping one fingernail down them as they tightened.

"Talon." Finn was prepared to beg.

Talon dropped another gentle kiss behind his ear and wrapped his fingers around the base of Finn's dick. Finn moaned long and low and felt Talon's puff of hot breath on his neck at the same time incredible pressure started in his balls and rushed the length of his dick.

"Fuck. Fuck. Fuck. Fuck," Finn chanted as Talon sped up. Finn cried as ecstasy exploded in his mind and white heat blurred his vision as he came. He hissed as Talon kept pressing, and Talon eased off immediately. Finn mourned the loss of Talon's fingers, even knowing how sensitive he was immediately after he came.

Finn was floating. He vaguely felt the bed dip and then Talon clean him with something. He heard the soft chuckle once more and briefly worried Talon might leave. He breathed out a huge contented sigh as Talon slipped back in bed behind him and pulled him close to his chest. He registered Talon's hard-on, and the vague thought that he ought to do something about it was the last one he had for a long time.

Chapter Seventeen

FINN WAS still asleep when Talon slipped out of bed in the morning to get in the shower. He woke up with a cock as hard as granite and knew he had to remove himself from temptation. He had a very satisfying, if quick, jacking-off session in the shower to the images of Finn's face each time an orgasm hit him. He already thought Finn was gorgeous, but at that second, with his head flung back in rapture and his lips parted, it was likely the best thing Talon had ever fucking seen.

Too soon the light of day poked into his postorgasmic bliss, though. The team was coming over, and knowing Gael and Vance, they would turn up at the ass crack of dawn just to see if they could catch him out. In fact, he briefly thought about messing the covers up in the spare room, but none of his team would believe Finn hadn't slept under Talon's very watchful eye all night, so it would be a complete waste of time.

Talon shrugged and turned the water off, stepped out of the shower, and briskly dried himself down. If he were honest, he had no idea what to say to Finn. Finn had to understand he couldn't be demonstrative with him... at all. But he didn't want it awkward either. Talon sighed. He had no clue what to make of his feelings this morning; he didn't tend to acknowledge having any, as a rule. Maybe it was a good thing the team was coming. Distract them both.

He pulled on some shorts and a T-shirt and stepped into the bedroom to see Finn sitting up and blinking sleepily. Talon swallowed and felt his dick lengthening slightly. It was no good. Any expression on Finn was gorgeous, not just the one he jacked off to.

He walked over to the bed and put a finger under Finn's chin to tilt his face slightly, and Finn acquiesced. "How sore are you?" Talon asked. "Headache?" Without waiting for a reply, he moved to get the pill bottle. The glass of water was warm. "I'll get you some fresh," he murmured, painfully aware Finn hadn't said anything. Was he regretting it? Guilt brought a flush to Talon's face. Finn was injured.

"Stop," Finn said, peering up at Talon. He clasped his hand and tugged to make Talon sit. "You're gonna give me a neck ache, staring up there," he grumbled, and Talon smiled cautiously. "I don't want this to be weird, Talon," Finn said urgently. "I really like you, but I know how to keep this separate. I don't want you worried I'm getting clingy." Finn's laugh was a little forced.

Clingy. The word rolled around in Talon's brain. He cupped Finn's cheek, and Finn sighed happily and leaned into his hand. Talon couldn't have replied if his life depended on it because he was too busy admitting to himself he wanted Finn to be clingy. In fact, a clingy Finn sounded perfect right about now.

Talon cursed as Charlie woofed from where she was curled up on the rug. She heard the door to his apartment open as soon as he did. They all had keys.

He looked at Finn. "The gang's here." He dropped a kiss on Finn's lips, enjoying the startled pleasure that warmed his green eyes. "I'll let them in and get them to start coffee. Then I'm gonna come back and see if you want a shower."

Finn picked at his grubby T-shirt in disdain. Talon grinned and took that for his answer.

He just had time to stand up when there was a knock on the bedroom door and the whole team barreled into the room. Charlie was ecstatic and immediately made a beeline for Eli and leaned in for some very satisfying ear scratches.

"Hey, kid." Vance sat on the bed while Talon stood to one side, and Finn clutched the sheets in alarm as it rocked violently with Vance's weight. "How's the head?"

Finn smiled at them. Talon watched as even Eli glanced down at him as if he wanted to know the answer. He didn't smile, but he didn't scowl either, which kind of amazed Talon. Finn put a hand up to his face. "The head feels okay at the moment. I just feel like someone broke my jaw."

"Nah," Sawyer said. "I did that once. You wouldn't be able to talk," he added comfortingly.

"Okay," Talon interrupted. "Finn's just woken up, so how about you all go make yourself useful with coffee and breakfast and let the kid shower?"

Gael turned to Finn slyly. "Need some help?"

"No." The protest was out of Talon's mouth before he could bite it back, stunning him along with the feeling of possessiveness that accompanied it.

Gael smirked, and Talon glowered. He knew the bastard had set him up.

"You really don't have to fight over me, you know."

The dry humor from Finn had Talon flushing, but even Gael took pity on him and shut up. He squeezed Finn's hand. "Good to see you're okay, kid." He never looked at Talon, just followed the others out of the room and closed the door behind him.

Finn laid his head back a little, and Talon noticed the movement. "I can tell them all to get lost, you know. They won't be offended. How's the head?"

"Not bad," Finn replied cautiously, and Talon sighed silently. It was okay a minute ago, so "not bad" was a deterioration.

He disappeared without a word, ignored the other guys, who were busying themselves with coffee, and walked back with a fresh glass of water. "Here," he said, passing Finn the water while he got two tablets out. Finn made no protest, and Talon decided to keep a close eye on him. If he thought the others were being too loud, he would throw them out himself. "Do you want a shower?"

Finn made a face. "Yes."

Talon went into the bathroom and started the spray to warm it up. He came back into the room as he pulled his T-shirt off.

Finn looked astonished. "What are you doing?"

Talon threw him an even look. "You're not going in there on your own."

Finn blinked, and Talon thought he was going to protest, but he sagged again a little. "Thank you."

"You don't have to get a shower now," Talon said, eyeing Finn. He was fading fast, and while he was bright thirty minutes ago, he looked exhausted now.

Finn screwed up his nose. "I feel dirty," he said plaintively. "I want to wash the hospital off me."

"Then I'm helping." Talon walked over to the bed and got Finn upright gently. He didn't seem dizzy, just tired, so Talon stripped him quickly and efficiently, helped him to the bathroom, and turned him around in the shower so his back was leaned against Talon's chest.

The shower took two minutes. Finn remained silent, and Talon was starting to get a little concerned. He sat Finn down on the stool with a big towel wrapped around him. Finn looked like he was struggling to keep his eyes open. Talon briskly rubbed himself dry and dragged his shorts and T-shirt on. He toweled Finn carefully, but by this time, Finn wasn't even pretending to stay awake. His head lolled on Talon's shoulder as he picked him up.

"Sorry," Finn sighed and yawned, snuggling into the crook of Talon's neck.

Talon swallowed. Fuck. Finn felt so right there. He was in so much trouble.

He tucked Finn back into bed, let himself out of his bedroom, and quietly closed the door. He walked into the kitchen, and Vance peered behind him as if he were hiding Finn back there. "He's asleep," Talon said shortly. He looked at Gael. "The shower completely wiped him out. Is that normal? He was fine thirty minutes ago."

Gael was the only one of them who had taken any sort of first-aid training. "Is he lucid?"

Talon nodded. "Yes, but his headache had started again." He looked around. There was no sign of Eli or his dog.

Gael pushed a plate of buttered toast and crispy bacon in front of him, but Talon wasn't very hungry. "Just keep a real close eye on him today. Any indication he doesn't know where he is, lack of coordination, call me or get him straight to the ER."

"Eli's taken Charlie out," Sawyer confirmed.

Talon sank into the chair, and Gael regarded him. "You like him," he said.

Talon didn't attempt to deny it. "We're not allowed relationships on the teams."

Gael seemed to ponder that. "Is that your only objection?"

He looked up. "What do you mean?"

Gael sighed. "I think you should give yourself a chance, Talon. If it comes looking for me, there's no way I'm looking the other way." Gael smiled, and the curve of his lips pulled the scarred skin out of shape.

Talon nodded in understanding. He never really noticed Gael's scar anymore. The humor shining from his eyes took the focus off the crisscrossed and puckered tight skin stretching from his cheekbone to his lips, but he knew Gael was convinced he was ugly and that no one would ever look twice at him.

He didn't bother offering platitudes. Gael knew Talon had his back.

The door opened, and Charlie came rushing in with Eli, delighted to have all of them here.

Vance stood. "We're going to make ourselves scarce. Go into the office to do those interviews you asked for on the missing kids."

Talon nodded. He knew agents were looking, but he felt guilty that other things had gotten in the way of the investigation.

"One of us will keep calling in, in case you need us for anything." Gael nudged Talon's shoulder, and Talon smiled. "I'm going to tell Gregory that Finn is making progress," he added with determination.

Talon stared at Gael. The same worry he had was reflected in Gael's eyes. They only had four weeks to prove the team was going to work. No one would take them on if Finn was laid up for at least one of the four, and from what he'd seen of him this morning, Finn didn't have the strength to remain upright, let alone rejoin the team in a few days.

Yep. They might not have to worry about hiding their relationship because the team might not exist anyway.

THE NEXT time Finn woke up, he felt the warm weight of Talon pressed comfortingly into his back. He blinked. The curtains were drawn; otherwise the room would be flooded with the Florida sun. His head felt a lot clearer even if his face felt just as sore. He reached out a hand for his water, and his belly grumbled at the same time.

"How are you feeling?" Talon propped himself up on one elbow and smiled lazily. He yawned.

Finn tried to cool the rush of blood to his dick by taking a few sips of water. *Horny.* The word echoed in his mind, but he didn't have the courage to repeat it this morning. He really thought the next move should come from Talon. He put the glass down. "Quite a bit better," Finn said. "A little hungry."

He tried not to gape in astonishment when Talon leaned over to brush his lips over his.

"How about I help you to the bathroom, and then we go get you settled on the couch? The team left tons of food."

Finn sat up slowly and peered around. "Where's your dog? Charlie?"

"Gone to the park with the kid next door," Talon said, smiling. Finn didn't say a word as Talon helped him stand and guided him to the bathroom. He only left him for a few minutes, even standing behind him protectively while Finn gleefully fished out his toothbrush from his own toiletry bag.

"The guys all left?" Finn asked as he brushed his teeth, thankful he felt cleaner.

"You've slept through another visit from Gael and Sawyer, and a separate one from Gael on his own. Gael is the only one on the team who's had any sort of first-aid training. I'm trying to get him more. I think it would be a good skill to have."

Finn blinked. "What time is it?"

"Just after four." Talon chuckled. "Gael woke you up, and you told him to fuck off, so we guessed you were feeling better."

Finn blushed. "I'm s—"

"No," interrupted Talon. "Don't even go there." He stood closer and cupped Finn's chin until Finn raised it under the gentle pressure. "You did an amazing job in there keeping it all together. None of the hostages were harmed except the old guy, and he's okay. All your team's proud of you. Especially me," he added.

"I didn't do much," Finn said. He sighed and stepped forward. Talon surrounded him with his arms as Finn hoped he would, and he leaned into Talon's strong body. He was sure he had something he thought Talon should know, but for the life of him, he couldn't think what it was. Trying to think brought his headache back. "I'm going in tomorrow," Finn said.

Talon chuckled and tightened his arms. "Mmm, well, we'll see if you can keep upright on your own first."

Finn froze, realizing how he was standing. He went to take a step back, but Talon held him still effortlessly. Finn's dick noticed, and he stifled a groan. He needed to put the brakes on a little. Apart from the fact that they weren't allowed relationships on the team, Finn wasn't dumb enough not to realize if he was kicked out, it would probably be the last time he saw Talon.

He knew Talon was watching him closely all evening. They'd gone into the living room, and Gael had come over once more to check on him. He managed one or two jokes with Gael, but his eyelids had been drooping since Talon came back from the dog park with Charlie. Finn needed to get to bed, but now he was wondering where Talon would put him. Talon had slept with him last night, but he had a feeling he would spend tonight on his own.

Finn waited until Talon came back from letting Charlie out. "Can I ask something?" Talon just looked at Finn and waited, so he said, "What happened to Gael's face?"

Talon dropped to the chair opposite Finn, and Charlie curled up at his feet.

Finn suddenly felt like he was intruding. "It doesn't matter."

"No," Talon interrupted. "It's not a secret, and Gael wouldn't mind me telling you. It was when he was twelve."

"Was it an accident?" Finn asked, standing up and deciding he would feel better getting back in bed.

Talon turned the TV off with the remote. "No. Gael's dad did it," he said flatly, following him into the bedroom.

Finn parted his lips in horror. *Gael's dad?*

"He'd transformed about a month previously. Gael lived with his dad, uncle, and younger brother just outside of Charlottesville. His mom had left with some other guy when Gael was around six and his brother was three. His dad was what I suppose would be termed a functioning alcoholic. He had an office job at a large insurance company, and he was up for promotion. I don't think it was the first time he'd knocked Gael about, but he lost it that day because instead of the promotion, he got fired.

"Gael had said he was an angry drunk, so he and his brother tended to make themselves scarce as much as they could, and his uncle worked shifts, so they didn't see him all that often. Gael had gotten thumped that day in the playground because of his scar, and he was standing in the bathroom on a stool, trying to cover his scar with some old makeup that must have been left by his mom. Gael had found it in a bathroom drawer."

Talon paused. "Did you know no one has ever been able to make anything to disguise the mark?"

Finn nodded his head. It was something the papers had a field day with around five years ago. He slid into bed wondering if Talon would follow him, but he just leaned casually against the dresser.

"Something about the mark burns through it. Stage makeup, the lot. Loads of companies have tried. It's also impossible to surgically remove, as it just reforms." Talon shrugged. "I suppose we should be grateful because the mark is the only thing that's stopping registration.

"Anyway," Talon continued. "Gael's dad saw what he was trying to do and completely lost it. He was drunk, very drunk, but that isn't any kind of excuse. They had a handheld gas lighter for the grill. He held Gael down while he pressed it to his face. Said it was likely Gael's fault he had gotten fired, and if Gael wanted to get rid of the mark, he would help him."

Finn's heart squeezed in his chest. Gael had been one of his supporters from day one. "What happened?"

"Gael got taken to hospital, obviously, when the neighbors heard the screams, but he told the police he'd done it to himself trying to get rid of the mark." Talon was quiet for a few seconds. "They believed him straight away." He gestured to his face. "I mean, who would want one of these?"

In an invitation, Finn lifted the comforter that was covering him. If Talon didn't come over, he would move himself.

Talon stared for a few seconds and then, unbelievably, he got up and crossed the room but lowered himself into the chair next to the bed. Not quite close enough to touch and obviously deliberate.

He settled on asking a question instead. "Didn't child protective services get involved?"

"His uncle wasn't interested in any father role, and Gael had heard all the rumors about enhanced kids getting locked up. He was worried for his brother and knew if they got taken into care, they would get split up. There were no foster homes for enhanced then."

Finn knew, and he wanted to cry for them both. One of the most heartbreaking stories he had read was of the government reopening St. Bartholomew's Hospital in Washington DC. It was a derelict insane asylum, and one of the first group foster homes for enhanced children whose families didn't want them. It was shut down about ten years ago when the government decided enhanced should only be kept separate if they were a danger to themselves or others. A small young-offenders unit had quickly been built and another converted.

"Anyway, Gael managed to keep it together even when his father passed out drunk and his cigarette set fire to the apartment with him in it. The insurance wouldn't pay out because an enhanced lived there, so Gael immediately dropped out of school and took three jobs to get a crappy studio apartment for him and Wyatt. Wyatt's due to graduate this year with honors from Georgetown. Full scholarship."

Finn was silent. He had no idea what to say. He wanted to ask about Sawyer and Eli as well, but he had a feeling it would be better to wait for another day. He stretched out a hand to touch Talon's arm cautiously. "Are you getting in bed?"

Talon gazed at Finn and hesitated.

"Separate," Finn said quietly. "Us and the job. I remember what you said."

Talon smiled and ran a finger along Finn's cheek. "Just let me go see to Charlie."

Finn's heart thudded. *Separate?* He was falling for Talon so fast, he was barely touching the sides as he went down, and he was awfully afraid there would be no one at the bottom to catch him.

Chapter Eighteen

FINN PUT his toothbrush down after he rinsed his mouth. He could hear Talon still puttering about with the dog and wondered if he was putting off coming to bed. He gazed at himself in the bathroom mirror. The swelling on the left side of his face looked a lot better, and the whole thing had settled to a dull ache. He had an awful black eye from the second time he was hit, and the eye itself was still bloodshot. Finn never thought he was particularly good-looking, but at that moment, he seriously wondered how Talon could bear to look at him.

He heard a noise behind him and glanced up. Talon was gazing at him and holding two tablets out. Finn sighed and took them, along with the water he was holding.

"How's your head?"

Finn grimaced. "It's not bad. The dizziness seems to be gone." He smiled shyly. "I don't think you're going to have to carry me into work tomorrow."

Talon frowned. "You do know there is absolutely no way any doctor will sign you off as fit, don't you?"

Finn dropped his gaze. "So what does that mean? I'm off the team?"

"Not if I have anything to do with it," Talon answered.

Finn smiled, loving that he said that. "You might not have any choice, Talon. Four weeks."

Talon drew a frustrated hand over his face, but Finn didn't hear an answer. It was so mixed up. Everything.

Finn slid into bed, noting Talon just sat on the edge and made no move to get in. He drew a breath. "Talon? Tell me something honestly."

Talon looked resigned and picked a thread from the sheet.

"What you said just now. About the team." The silence fell heavy in the room. "Have you genuinely changed your mind about enhanced partnering with regulars, or is it because I got hurt and you feel guilty?"

Talon's head shot up. Finn could see the denial on his lips, hear it in his head, feel it bounce around the room, but at the very second when he thought everything was going to be all right, the words never actually left Talon's lips, and the bottom Finn had been clinging to for a week finally fell out of his world.

At least I know he can't lie to me.

"Finn…," Talon started and went to take his hand.

Finn pulled it away, and Talon looked like Finn had hit him. "No. I understand," Finn said slowly. "I know how hard this must be for you."

Talon froze. "Do you? Do you really?"

Finn winced at the anger and the sarcasm that
bled into those few words. And the hurt. There was
so much hurt.

"Do you know what it's like for other kids to be
afraid of you? For them to run screaming because you
looked at them, or took your scarf off because you were
too hot, even though your mom tried to get you to keep
it on? Not because she was worried you would be embarrassed at showing your face, but because she was."

Finn didn't move. He knew this had been coming
for a long time.

Talon stood. "Do you know what it's like for the
other kids to call you a murderer?" He whirled around,
stalked to the window, and stared into the dark night.
His shoulders sagged. "The same kids you'd played
ball with every day after school? The same kids you
got into trouble with for talking in Sunday school?"
He turned and pointed to his face. "The same kids who
wouldn't even look at you because you woke up one
morning looking like a freak?"

Finn swallowed, but he didn't move.

"Do I frighten you?" Talon leaned his head to one
side. "I only have to think and your arms grow heavy.
Your lungs have suddenly got to work twice as hard to
pull in oxygen. Your legs become frozen. You can feel
your heart start to slow and your eyes burn because
you don't even have the strength to blink."

Finn's heart was pounding so fast, he thought
Talon would hear it. "You don't frighten me," he said
quietly.

Talon shook his head. "Then you're dumber than
I thought you were."

"Why?" Finn stood. "Because I don't read as well as some people? Or because I was stupid enough to think that loyalty meant something to you? We're supposed to be partners," he said bitterly.

"Partners?" Talon said incredulously. "Do you know why you're here? Because you're a poster boy for small-town America. Unthreatening. Pathetic." Talon curled his lips in disdain. "And because Agent Gregory's brother got a letter from your dad asking him to take pity on his son."

Finn sucked in a sharp breath and glanced at his chest. The pain was so immediate, he expected to see a blade sticking out. His dad? Gregory's brother was the agent he meant? Finn stared at Talon, bereft of anything to say that would ease the pain of what he had heard. He thought he was getting somewhere with him. He thought he was getting a chance because they thought he was worth it, not because of some stupid letter, and not because….

He closed his eyes. He'd nearly thrown himself at Talon. Talon must have been laughing at him. *I've never done this before.* He could hear the whispered admission. Would Talon have told the others? Were they all laughing at him?

He heard the door bang closed and opened his eyes to an empty room. He looked around and pulled his T-shirt on slowly. He couldn't stay, but he had no idea where he even was. Finn choked as a laugh turned into a sob. He had no one to call. He would rather walk than call Drew.

Gael? Gael was kind to him today. He was loyal to Talon, and if there were a choice, he knew which way Gael would go, but that was all right. That's how teams should be.

He remembered one of his dad's favorite stories from his time in 'Nam. The helicopter was downed. One of the team was injured, but they didn't leave him. They made a makeshift stretcher and trekked twenty miles through jungle and swamp to make their pickup point, and they all got out alive.

That time, anyway.

That's what Finn had wanted. The FBI meant belonging to him. Being part of a team. He never felt like he belonged to his family, and it wasn't because he was gay. It was because he didn't fit in with his brash mom and his even louder brother. His dad did his best, but he had his own demons to fight.

He picked up his phone from the bedside table and stared at it ruefully. It was completely dead, and his charger was back at his apartment.

TALON EASED himself up on his sofa a few hours later and stared at the closed bedroom door. He desperately wanted to go in there. He desperately wanted to gather Finn close and kiss him until he laughed and said it was okay. He would grovel if he had to. How could he have said those things to Finn? His mark, this job, his dad…. None of it was Finn's fault. Finn had done nothing since he got here but be incredibly cheerful and more than willing to accept every team member for exactly what they were. He put his trust in Talon, and Talon let him down time and time again. It was him who was the crappy partner, not Finn. Talon swung his legs off the couch. Somehow he had to make it right.

Talon took a step toward the bedroom and heard a knock on the door. He frowned when he looked through the peephole and saw Gael standing there. He didn't know Gael was going to come and check on Finn again. Talon swung the door open, a smile on his face.

Five seconds later Gael's fist connected with his jaw, and Talon went down.

"Aagh, fuck, Talon. Your face is like cement." Gael hopped and wrung his hand, then calmly stepped over Talon, who was still on the floor, wondering what the hell just happened.

Talon groaned pathetically and rolled to one side, holding his jaw in case it was broken or something. "What the...." Talon stopped speaking. He would just have to look indignantly at Gael because his jaw hurt like fuck.

Gael turned as he got to the kitchen and calmly started brewing coffee. He pointed to the bar stool as Talon staggered in. "Sit there and listen."

Talon winced because he forgot it would hurt his face to do so and nodded instead, which wasn't much better.

Gael sighed. "You're a fucking idiot."

Talon's eyebrows raised. Gael had called him that a few times, but he wasn't sure what exactly he'd done to deserve it this time.

Gael was silent for a minute while the coffee brewed, and Talon didn't prompt him for more insults. He knew Gael would tell him when he was ready. He glanced toward the closed bedroom door. He hoped Gael hadn't woken Finn up. He needed his sleep.

Gael pushed a mug of coffee across the counter to him and tracked his gaze. "You don't even know where Finn is, do you?"

Coldness washed over Talon, and he leaped to his feet. He yanked the bedroom door open and stared in disbelief at the empty bed. He stalked into the bathroom to make sure it was empty. "Where is he?" he snapped, ignoring the sudden pain in his jaw when he spoke.

Gael shook his head in disbelief. "He's your partner. He got injured, and you're so deep in your own pity party, you didn't even notice he left while you were off doing whatever instead of making sure he was okay. Anything could have happened to him. I'm just thankful he swallowed his pride and asked me, because he was ready to walk back to his apartment. Of course, he wouldn't know that it was over fifteen miles away because no one has even bothered to show him the area he lives in."

Talon winced as every word from Gael's mouth got louder and louder. "I went for a walk," he said. No justification. Talon picked up his keys. He would go get him.

"Don't bother. He doesn't want to see you. I had to promise I wouldn't let you go over."

Talon stood. "I have to. He can't be on his own." Talon firmed his jaw as Gael slow clapped him twice.

"Give that man a lollipop," Gael said sarcastically. "He's not on his own."

Talon bristled. "Drew?" he almost growled the name.

"Fuck no," Gael said. "When I left, Vance was making him a hot-water bottle."

Talon stared in confusion. "It's seventy degrees out there."

"Who the hell cares?" shouted Gael. "The point is, Vance is doing what you should be doing and making sure he's okay."

Talon sagged. He was right. He'd treated Finn like shit. "He called you?"

"He didn't, actually. I called your phone." Gael looked pointedly to where Talon had casually thrown it on the kitchen counter. "Finn answered because you'd left it in the bedroom when you stormed out. He admitted the phone was in his hand and he was just deciding whether to risk calling or to get a cab. Except he still hasn't got any fucking money."

Talon staggered to the stool and sat with his head in his hands. "I messed up."

"You think?" Gael drawled. He sat down. "Tell me."

"He tried to say he understood. I was cruel. I called him dumb."

"I'm sure he's heard worse," Gael said.

Talon looked up. Finn had, and it wasn't that. "He asked if I was looking after him because we're partners or because I felt guilty."

Gael blew a breath out. "Ouch. What did you say?"

Talon didn't say anything. He looked at Gael, and Gael's blue eyes softened.

He stood. "I'm going back. Gregory has called a briefing, and he's said if Finn is up to it, he'd like him there. That's why I was calling you in the first place. I was at Vance's when I got the call." Gael patted his flat belly, and Talon smiled. He knew Connie, Vance's mom, would have been feeding them until they could hardly move. The team spent more time at Vance's getting fed than they did in their own apartments.

"I know you want to go charging around there tonight, but to be honest, the kid still looks ill. He needs his sleep. I'm not 100 percent convinced he shouldn't still be in the hospital."

Talon curled his fingers, the nails stabbing his palms as if that could take away the how much his heart hurt.

"But, Talon, you need to decide. You know the team will follow you, but you also should know Vance especially likes Finn. If it had been him who had come here tonight and laid you out, you would still be on the floor." He punched him playfully in the arm. "Don't be a dick." Gael smiled and let himself out of the door.

Talon aimlessly walked back into his bedroom and stripped. He grabbed a pillow and drew it close. He wasn't stupid enough to think he could keep a working relationship separated from a personal one. He knew what Gael was saying. He had to decide. He had to decide if Finn was going to be just his partner or something else. Of course, the whole question could be moot, as Finn might not want anything to do with him after tonight.

What should he do? If Finn forgave him, could they work as partners in the team? They didn't have to be anything else.

Talon's short laugh echoed around the empty room, and he spent the next few hours until dawn trying to wrestle with a decision in his head he was frightened his heart had made over a week ago.

Chapter Nineteen

FINN SMILED as he heard the breaking cup from the direction of the kitchen and the muffled curse that followed it. His heart ached at the laugh that accompanied it because he knew it was Vance who had cursed and Gael who laughed, and he desperately wished it were someone else.

He looked up at the knock on the door, and Gael walked in. "Do you want a coffee? I think there might be one mug left that Vance hasn't broken."

"Hey," Vance protested. He followed Gael in. "Not my fault if they're fiddly little things." He held out one of his huge hands that resembled a dinner plate, and Finn's smile widened.

"How are you feeling?" Gael crossed the room, his professional demeanor firmly in place.

"No headache," Finn said. His head felt fine. It was his heart that currently felt like it was being ripped in two.

Gael grunted and peered at him. "No dizziness?"

Finn shook his head experimentally. "No."

"Okay." Gael smiled. "Vance is warming up breakfast."

Finn blinked. He had half a loaf of bread for toast, if that.

Gael chuckled. "You're gonna love Vance's mom, Connie. She's made it her life's mission to feed any-one she thinks might need it, which currently includes all the team. Vance left to go home last night so he could bring supplies back, and I slept on the couch."

"I'm s—"

Gael put his hand firmly over Finn's mouth and waved a finger admonishingly. "No. Not even going there." He walked back to the door. "You've got five minutes for a shower."

Finn yawned. He'd still been awake at something ridiculous like three o'clock, convinced any sec-ond Talon would march into his room. He didn't, of course. He knew he told Gael to tell him he wasn't to come, but he couldn't help thinking if Talon wanted to come, nothing would have stopped him.

Finn sat up cautiously. He'd exaggerated a little when he said he felt fine. He wasn't dizzy, but his face still hurt, and his tablets were at Talon's.

He blew out a sigh. Gael had told him they were all summoned for a briefing this morning, and his presence was requested if he felt up to it. It was possi-bly the last thing he wanted to do, and he had no idea what to say to Talon. He got out of bed and went to get a shower.

Two hours later Finn shuffled into the classroom behind Vance, incredibly grateful he could hide behind the big body. He knew the rest of the team was already sitting around the table. He didn't have the energy to get excited at Eli throwing him a nod in acknowledgment when he walked through the door.

"Finn?"

The low voice from behind him made him jump, even though he'd been hoping for it. He turned cautiously to see Talon raking his eyes over his face. He knew he was inspecting the bruises like he had every morning for the past two days.

"Finn?" Talon caught his arm. "Please, we need to talk."

Finn stared absently at Talon's hand on his arm until Talon dropped it. *We need to talk.* The four most ominous words in the English language.

"Gentlemen." Agent Gregory hurried in. He looked up at Finn but there was no smile forthcoming. "Finn, nice to see you up and about," he said quietly.

Finn's heart dropped and started beating in his boots. Something was wrong. He collapsed onto the nearest chair.

"Deputy Director Cohen was invited by Channel Seven news this morning to talk about the successful resolution of the bank hostage situation. Apparently the media has been hailing it as another win for the team, and our input to discuss the team was invited. It was exactly the sort of coverage the director was hoping for, and we were eager to participate. What we didn't know was that Isaac Dakota would find out." Gregory pointed to the TV showing the live security camera footage from outside as the deputy director arrived. "The interview started live fifteen minutes ago." Placards were waving the same as before, but there was no Monsters scrawled in red paint. The word everyone was shouting was HEROs.

Finn blinked slowly, his muddled brain trying to work out why Gregory didn't look pleased. Surely this was what he wanted? Deputy Director Cohen should be doing cartwheels.

Isaac Dakota's face flashed on the screen as a reporter shoved a microphone at him. "You must be thrilled with the support," the reporter said.

"Absolutely," Dakota confirmed. "This bears out what we have been saying for years. That America would be a safer and more powerful country if the enhanced were in charge."

Vance groaned.

The reporter picked up on Dakota's phrase straight away. "In charge? You think the enhanced should be running the country?"

"I think we have a group of individuals who are especially suited to this task, yes."

"Why?" Gael asked in complete disbelief. "We get good press and the idiot has to go and tell people we're going to take over the world again."

Gregory sighed but didn't respond.

Finn gazed at him. The tired eyes, the firmly pressed lips. There was something else....

He stared, completely frozen, at the man who was speaking. It was the guy who was held hostage with them at the bank. The CEO of Swann Industries, Alan Swann.

The interviewer leaned forward. "So what exactly are you accusing the FBI of, Mr. Swann?"

Alan Swann smiled congenially. "I'm not accusing the FBI of anything, per se. I'm just saying that in this day and age, when terrorist threats are at an all-time high, their screening procedures should be higher, that is all."

The screen flashed to the film of Talon raising his hands and walking to the bank door to gather up the hysterical female employee. He barely glanced at the murdered guard lying on the floor. Finn hadn't seen any of this, but he could hear the sound of the shots in his head as if they were in the room.

"What exactly do you feel is the problem, Mr. Swann? I can assure you our training and selection process is among the tightest in the world." Everyone in the room stared as the deputy director joined in.

"Is that true, Deputy Director?" Alan Swann picked an imaginary piece of lint off his trousers. "Then perhaps you can explain why a specialized unit of enhanced humans has been set up with trainees who have barely completed one week of training?" Alan Swann waved his arm at the screen. "The hostage resolution is being hailed as a success for the team, but I was there. The fact that your trainee was inexperienced could have easily been the reason one of the hostages was harmed."

Finn closed his eyes in despair. That was so unfair.

"The trainee concerned was present as a bank customer and was responsible for keeping everyone calm and for none of the hostages being killed," Cohen replied. "We are very proud of him and his ultimate handling of the situation."

Finn held his breath. He knew from the satisfied smirk on Swann's face there was something else coming. He didn't dare look at anyone else, but then, they were all staring in disbelief at the TV.

"What worries the general public, Deputy Director, is that you are ultimately arming individuals who are likely to lose control over their abilities at any given minute," Swann continued. "And what is worse is that the FBI seems to be in such a desperate rush to let this happen, they are ignoring their own screening protocols."

Cohen frowned. "I can assure you no protocols are being sacrificed with regard to this initiative. Tighter restrictions, if any, apply."

"Is that so?" Swann asked. "Then can you explain to me how it is that your trainee, one Finlay Mayer, has been accepted even though he is the childhood best friend of one of the bank robbers who was involved in the hostage situation?"

The silence was so absolute in the room Finn knew no one had even taken a breath. He just heard Swann say Adam also had enhanced abilities before Gregory sighed and paused the TV.

He looked at Finn. "I have to admit that I only found this out a few minutes ago myself. We actually called the briefing expecting Alan Swann to praise the unit. The man is very influential, and that is the only way he got the deputy director to agree to appear."

"Is this true?"

Finn looked up at the bewilderment in Talon's voice.

"You know him," he stated flatly. "Why didn't you say? We could have stopped this happening."

"I doubt if you would have been able to stop Swann, Talon," Gael said.

Gregory sighed. "Yes, but we would have been able to stop the deputy director sharing air space and ultimately making the FBI look foolish."

He raised saddened eyes to Finn, and Finn knew exactly what he was going to say.

"I have been given no choice," Gregory said. "The unit is disbanded with immediate effect. You are all required to hand in your official service weapons and IDs before you leave the building. I'm sorry, but I also have to instruct you that agents are to accompany you to the lockers so you can retrieve your personal belongings only." Gregory's voice lowered, and he looked at Vance, who was in uniform. "Your uniform must remain here as the property of the US government. Finn, you have until the end of the week to find alternative accommodation."

Finn jumped as Talon shot to his feet, his chair skidding across the room. He flung his gun and his badge onto the table and turned to stalk out.

"Talon," Finn whispered, his voice breaking. For a second Talon paused, but then without even looking at Finn, he strode out of the room.

Finn sat in a complete daze as Sawyer and Eli both charged after Talon. Gregory looked like he wanted to say something else but just walked out. Vance and Gael were staring at each other in shock.

"I forgot," Finn whispered. "I knew there was something I was supposed to tell him." He rubbed his pounding head and looked up at Gael. "This is all my fault." He choked on the last word as his voice broke, and he covered his face in his shaking hands.

"No, it isn't." Gael drew Finn's hands down gently. "You shouldn't even be here. You suffered a severe head injury doing your job."

Vance sat and stared at Finn. "Did you do it on purpose?"

"No!" Finn said in horror. "Of course not."

Vance laid a huge hand on Finn's, and Finn looked at it helplessly. Vance would have covered three of his handspans completely. "Exactly. I know you didn't, kid," Vance replied, his voice softening. He looked at Gael. "I think we should get him home."

Gael peered at Finn, who desperately wanted to close his eyes and sleep. Gael looked worried, and Finn closed his lids under Gael's intense scrutiny. "I'm not completely sure he shouldn't be back in the hospital."

Finn forced his eyes open. "No, please, I just need to sleep."

Gael shot a troubled glance at Vance. "Help me get him back."

Finn barely remembered the journey home and Gael tucking him into bed. To be honest he didn't remember much of the next day either. He knew the doctor turned up once and said that he needed rest, and if he didn't stay in bed, he would readmit him immediately. He was just aware enough to hear the doctor asking where his partner was, and was able to wait until everyone left the room until he couldn't hold it in any longer and he sobbed quietly. He had ruined everything. The team was disbanded. Talon had disappeared, and even Vance and Gael told Finn they couldn't get ahold of him.

He hadn't felt this wretched since his dad died.

He opened his eyes to bright Florida sunshine the next day. He blearily reached over and picked up his cell phone and squinted at the time; he'd slept for nearly thirty-six hours. He downed the full glass of water next to his bed.

Finn took a breath and cataloged his injuries. His face was sore only if he poked it. His headache was completely gone. He sat up cautiously and was relieved when the room didn't sway as it did whenever Vance or Gael helped him to the bathroom yesterday. He could hear the muted sound of the television from his living room and decided to get a shower before he went to see who was there. He knew who wouldn't be there, and the thought made him want to disappear under the covers and never come out.

It was over. Whatever had tentatively started between them surely ended the second Talon looked at him in anger and disgust yesterday. Whatever his excuse, he knew he would never be forgiven.

He stood and walked to the shower. It was only the thought of wondering how Adam was that made him put one foot in front of the other. He would get showered, get dressed, go visit the hospital, and then somehow... somehow he had to start the rest of his life.

TALON OPENED his eyes blearily and squinted at the nearly empty bottle of Dutch vodka that was staring at him reproachfully. He heaved himself to his feet and went in search of a glass of water, thanking whoever was listening that the same ability that caused broken bones to heal quicker also burned through alcohol just as fast. Talon walked straight to the fridge and shoved the glass that was on the counter under the water dispenser.

As soon as he had drunk the second glass, his head cleared and the memories of yesterday that he had been trying to drown out last night resurfaced.

Apart from stopping to buy the vodka when he left the field office, he'd done nothing yesterday but wallow in his misery.

He spied his cell on the counter and picked it up. Seven missed calls from Gael and two from Vance. He wasn't surprised to have heard nothing from Eli or Sawyer. They would have each disappeared to lick their wounds, the same as him, and misery definitely needed no company in this instance.

Talon leaned on his counter and rubbed his eyes. He needed a shower.

No. No, that wasn't what he needed—or not just, anyway. What he really needed was a certain man with green eyes and freckles back in his bed. It wasn't Finn's fault. They hadn't had a chance to talk about the bank robbery, and Finn wasn't exactly firing on all cylinders yesterday. It came under the general heading of *shit happens*, which kind of described most of his life.

Now that he'd had a chance to think about what was said yesterday, he wasn't completely convinced the knee-jerk reaction from Cohen would be the end of things. The public seemed to be supportive. Hell, Gregory even said the Vice President was making noise about wanting to meet them. He honestly didn't think the whole thing was as dead and buried as Cohen seemed to want it to be.

Talon put his glass down and headed to the shower, and, of course, as soon as he stepped in, the image of the last time Finn was in here was the only thing he could think of. He ignored his suddenly interested dick and scrubbed himself quickly. Now that he had calmed down, he knew he owed Finn a big-ass apology. Maybe he could get the team together at Betty's? Treat them all to breakfast and plan what they were going to do and who they needed to talk to.

His cell phone was bouncing around the kitchen worktop when he walked back in fully dressed. He saw it was Gael, who was calling him again as he snatched it up. "Yeah," he answered.

"Talon, what the fuck, man? I've been trying to call you for hours."

Talon grimaced as he registered how angry Gael sounded. He interrupted him as Gael took a breath. "I know. I'm an ass," he admitted. "I think we should get everyone together and go to Betty's." He paused and clutched the phone a little tighter. "How's the kid this morning?"

He heard the sigh on the other end of the line, and his heart thudded hard.

"Gael?" Talon ground out.

"I don't know," Gael replied. "He was completely out of it yesterday, and I got the doctor from the hospital that Vance's mom knows to come and look at him. To be honest it was touch and go whether the kid should be back in the hospital."

A cold, hard fist clutched at Talon's heart. "What about this morning?" Talon's feet unglued, and he reached for his car keys.

"He's not here," Gael said.

Talon froze. "What do you mean?"

"I mean, he's not here. He was in bed asleep when I looked in around two hours ago. I fell asleep with the TV on, and when I got up, he had gone."

Talon was out of the door before Gael finished his sentence. "His car?"

"Back at the bureau. Someone collected it from where it was still parked outside the bank yesterday."

"Then how the fuck has he gone anywhere? Cell?" Talon ran straight past the elevator and started down the stairs two at a time.

"His cell was destroyed at the bank. I guess he has a personal cell, but I have no idea what the number is."

Talon clutched his phone tighter. "And it's not there?"

Gael sighed. "Talon, nothing's here. He took his bag and clothes." There was a beat of silence. "He left a note. It's addressed to us all."

Talon rammed the door open and jogged to his car. "What does it say?"

"Just that he's sorry he let us all down and he's clearing out because he hopes with him out of the way, Cohen might give us another chance."

But that was the thing. Finn hadn't let anyone down. Talon had. And in a spectacularly cruel way. "I'll be there in ten minutes. Call everyone in." Talon threw his phone on the front seat as he got in the truck. He needed to find Finn. Then he'd work out what he would do to sort everything else out, but he needed to find Finn first.

Chapter Twenty

FINN STOOD with his bag and watched Drew drive away. It had been awkward, and neither of them really knew what to say to each other, but Finn was fortunate to spy Drew going to his car as he stepped outside his building.

When he'd finally dressed after his shower, he walked into his living room to find Gael stretched out asleep on his couch, the TV on low, and kids' cartoons playing. He'd been wondering what the hell to say to Gael and almost got giddy in relief when he realized he didn't have to. He couldn't just walk out, though, so he had taken the coward's way and left a brief note apologizing once more.

He had gathered up his few clothes and his dead cell phone and asked Drew to drop him at the hospital. He wanted to see Adam before he tried to visit the bank again, and if he didn't see him now, he didn't know when the next time would be. The only bright spot in his morning was that Drew made a quick phone call to confirm all his travel expenses had been reimbursed into his bank yesterday, so he had enough cash to find some cheap accommodation while he looked for a job. Agent Gregory must have been listening after all.

Finn walked in the door, and in a complete stroke of luck, spotted the nurse who had looked after him coming out of the elevator, pushing a lady in a wheelchair. Finn stepped up. "Hi, sorry. I don't know if you remember me, but—"

The nurse grinned. "Of course I remember you. It's not often I get to look after celebrities. How are you feeling?" The guy raked his assessing brown eyes over Finn's still-bruised face.

Finn waved off the question. "I'm fine. I was hoping to ask for a favor."

The nurse raised his eyebrows and bent down to the lady. "Ooh, do you hear that, Alice? Intrigue." The woman he was pushing took no notice, just grunted unsympathetically. "Just wait there. I'm just delivering Alice to X-ray, and then I'm on break."

Finn nodded in relief, and in two minutes, the nurse was back.

He grinned and put out his hand. "Jeremy."

"Finn," Finn replied and shook hands, then felt really silly as the nurse knew who he was.

"Come on. I need a coffee, and the surgery staff's break room will be completely empty, as they are halfway down this morning's list."

Finn smiled and followed Jeremy down a corridor, into a small room, and to the coffee machine in the corner.

"Want one?" Jeremy waved a cup.

"Yeah, please." Finn put his bag down and glanced around. A few easy chairs and coffee tables. A small microwave sat next to the coffee machine. Some old magazines were flung in the corner.

"So I saw the TV. Shit really hit the fan, huh?"

Finn glanced at Jeremy warily, but Jeremy looked like he was trying not to laugh. Finn relaxed. "Yeah."

"So what can I do for you?" Jeremy sat and hugged his coffee mug.

"There's a patient...," Finn started.

"Let me guess: Your friend from school?"

Finn gaped, but Jeremy shrugged. "It was all over the news, and my girlfriend's obsessed with it. I'm not too sure I shouldn't be asking for your autograph or something. My girlfriend's older brother's got a mark." Jeremy tapped his face. "We haven't seen anything mind-blowing, but he's incredibly strong. He works construction with his dad and their other brother."

Finn smiled. He sounded like Vance. "I need to get in to see my friend."

Jeremy frowned. "So what's the problem? I mean, can't you flash your badge or something? Cops would let you straight in."

"I don't have a badge," Finn said. "They disbanded the unit after the interview, and I'm currently out of a job."

Jeremy leaned back and whistled. "Well, that sucks. Your friend is awake. He came to a few hours ago, but the doc has refused all interviews until later on, after the surgeon's seen him when he's finished in surgery. About an hour, I think." Jeremy suddenly jumped up. "I know just what to do."

Ten minutes later Finn was dressed in identical blue scrubs to Jeremy and clutching an empty bedpan covered in a disposable sheet. Jeremy had assured him the cops would have no interest in challenging anyone who carried one of those, and he was right because they both walked straight past them and into Adam's room with the cops barely glancing their way.

Jeremy took a quick look at Adam's monitor and whispered, "You've got five minutes." Finn squeezed Jeremy's shoulder in gratitude, and Jeremy said, "I still think my girlfriend wants an autograph." He chuckled and let himself out of the room.

Finn stared somberly at Adam. He was propped up, bare-chested, with wires and small suction pads attached at different points, and hooked up to a monitor that beeped quietly every few seconds. A huge gauze pad was taped to his chest, presumably covering where the bullets had hit him. Adam had gotten shot protecting him.

He was seven the first time he got on the school bus and met the new boy who was sitting on his own. "*I'm Adam.*" Finn had just been made the class buddy, and it was his responsibility to make sure any new kids made friends. He had serious responsibilities, like making sure no one touched the frozen strawberry jelly because everyone knew it was made from blood because their school cook was a vampire, and never sitting behind Rolly Jameson in class after lunch. Well, not without a mask and goggles. In fact, Annie Tollinson had boasted her brother was a diver in the Navy and could get them all proper oxygen tanks next time Rolly ate pizza rolls.

Adam had looked at him in awe that any kid was talking to him, maybe being nice, and they hadn't been apart on the school bus ever again. Until that last day, when Finn had to travel alone.

Adam's eyes were closed, and he was breathing slowly. He looked asleep, but Finn didn't think he was.

"Adam," Finn said.

Adam's eyes shot open, and they stared at each other in silence. "You look good, Finn," he said quietly. "Well…." He gestured to Finn's face.

Finn's face broke into a huge smile, and he hurried forward. "I can't believe it. Do you know how often I tried to find you? How many hours I spent on the computer at college, searching?" When Adam blinked a few times, Finn bit his lip. "I missed you."

Adam swallowed. "So… FBI, huh? Look at you." He grinned. "You in disguise?"

"I don't know where to start," Finn admitted. "But I'm not FBI anymore." He told Adam what happened.

"But that's nuts, Finn. We haven't seen each other in more than ten years."

"I know, but…." Finn took a breath. "How can I help?"

Adam shook his head. "You can't, Finn. You need to stay away from me. I've caused you enough trouble already."

Finn put his hand on Adam's. "This isn't you, Adam. You wouldn't even steal one of my fries at school."

Adam gripped Finn's hand tightly. "That's because you'd have given me every last one anyway." He sagged a little. "Everything's messed up. I made some bad decisions. I think they'll lock me up and throw away the key."

Finn shook his head. "No, they won't, and I'll speak for you. You were trying to protect me when you got shot, and you never used your gun."

Adam opened his mouth to answer, but at that second, they heard a shout from outside and loud foot-steps. "Shit, Finn. Get outta here. I don't want you getting in trouble."

Finn turned and then ducked automatically as rapid gunfire and shouting was heard from the corri-dor. He didn't have time to reply, shout, or anything as the door burst open and two huge guys ran in. Finn froze and raised his hands slowly, staring straight at the identical scars on both their faces. *Enhanced.*

One of them lifted their gun, and in that split sec-ond, Finn knew he was going to get shot.

"No," yelled Adam. "He's a friend."

Finn cringed, but then the accompanying silence made him look up, straight into a pair of luminous gray eyes. Finn was caught, staring into the swirling depths.

"Friend, huh?"

Finn heard the voice as if it were far away and tried to pry his eyes from that powerful gaze.

"Sleep, then," the voice said again, no threat to it at all, and Finn felt himself relax as a wave of tired-ness rolled over him. The man stepped closer. "Sleep."

Finn stumbled and put a hand out to be caught by another strong one. His eyelids were closing, and he forced them open, but the effort was too much, and they slid closed. He vaguely heard the word "sleep" whispered once more, and Finn relaxed completely. He didn't fall; he felt arms seem to cradle him as he floated quietly away.

TALON DROVE through the gate at Finn's apartment complex and spotted Vance's truck. Gael opened the door to the apartment block, followed by Vance, as he drew up. They jogged up to Talon's car.

"So what's the plan, boss?" Vance grinned, and Talon shook his head in amazement. Vance humbled him. He never had any doubt their abilities were a good thing, that he would get to be part of the law enforcement community he'd wanted to be a part of for so long. Talon wished he had his confidence.

"Let's eat first," Gael suggested. "We need to meet up and form a plan."

Talon frowned. They needed to find Finn, but equally, they couldn't turn up at an office they were escorted out of yesterday.

"We can kill two birds with one stone," Vance said and walked to his truck. "Daniel's home."

Gael grunted in satisfaction. "I'll tell the others to meet us there."

That isn't a bad idea, Talon thought as he got in his truck and followed the other two out.

Vance's mom would feed them all with pleasure, and Daniel was a senior intelligence officer in DC. He'd never been an agent; his skill set was all about information technology, and last Talon heard on the quiet was he was wrapping up a huge mortgage fraud investigation that would cause a lot of financial ripples on Wall Street. He was desperate to recruit Gael with his language skills, and he didn't mean talking Swahili or any shit like that. It was weird what he'd seen Gael get computers to do, as if Gael understood their language as well... which was nuts and made Talon's head hurt in all sorts of ways.

Of course, Cohen was a superior to Daniel, but Daniel had a lot of friends and was influential in his own right, even if he was technically a civilian.

Talon sighed and thought about Finn. He knew at least two of Vance's brothers could get Finn's other cell phone number. He was pretty sure Jacob, who was a sergeant in the TPD, might be able to unofficially look for him as well.

Talon swallowed his worry down and pulled up to join the line of cars that was spilling out of Vance's driveway. What he was most afraid of was Finn still being sick and Talon not being there to make sure he was okay. He shouldn't have let Finn come into the office two days ago, and if he'd been with him instead of throwing his own pity party, he would have been able to make sure.

"Hey, little brother!"

Talon couldn't help the grin that accompanied all five feet eleven inches of Daniel unsuccessfully trying to wrap his arms around Vance, who was bigger than most people Talon had ever met. In fact, now that he came to think of it, he was pretty sure he didn't know anyone to top Vance's size.

Talon shook hands with Vance's younger brother Tim, who was also seated at the table, and got enveloped in a hug from Connie. Talon was ashamed to say he stood a little quieter and a little longer in her embrace than he usually did. Connie took a step back and gazed at him. He didn't bother hiding his anguish. His defenses had been useless against her for the last year since the first time Vance brought him and Gael home to meet his folks.

He heard the door open and shut, and the kitchen was suddenly full with Eli and Sawyer as well. Connie understood not to touch Eli. It was enough of a win getting him seated around her table. Eli didn't do families. He used to say his own experience of them cured him for life, and even Talon didn't think he knew the whole story.

Talon inhaled and his gut rumbled as Connie put a basket of homemade biscuits on the table. Vance stopped her from bending to the oven and sat her down while he got out the cooked bacon and sausage patties.

Connie smiled indulgently and patted Vance. "I'm going to sort out my rooms upstairs. You all give me a shout when you're done talking shop."

Talon looked apologetically at Vance, but Vance shook his head. "It's okay. She ate already." That wasn't what Talon meant, and Vance knew it. Evicting Connie out of her own kitchen felt wrong.

"Okay," Daniel said with a small smile as he helped himself to more coffee. "I saw the news. Someone want to tell me what shitstorm you've all been brewing, now?"

Talon barely joined in the laughter and listened as Gael brought Daniel up to speed on what was happening, but he gave up picking at his breakfast, even with the looks the rest of the team kept throwing him.

"So you need me to find out what support you have? See if there's anyone who can influence Cohen?" Daniel asked finally.

"No," blurted Talon. He rubbed a hand across his tired eyes. "Yes, yes, we do."

"But we gotta find Finn first," Gael finished for him.

The room was silent for a few seconds, then Eli's chair scraped a little. "Do we, boss? Is that what you want us to do?"

Talon looked at the faces in the room. He knew what Eli was really asking him, and he knew he would have to be careful what he said in front of Daniel and Tim.

"I think he's good for the team," Talon said slowly.

"So do we," Gael said firmly, as if the matter were decided.

Talon stared at Eli. Eli didn't smile, but he didn't frown either, and after a few seconds, he just nodded to indicate his agreement. Talon felt like he'd just won a huge battle.

Daniel stood. "Let me get his cell phone number first." They all watched as Daniel dialed the number for the Tampa field office. He could have found out via his laptop, as he had a much higher clearance than even Agent Gregory, but Talon had a feeling he wanted to make his interest officially known.

They all listened while he exchanged pleasantries with the operator, but Daniel's smile vanished as he listened to whomever he was just put through to. He looked around the room and was silent for quite a few minutes as he listened intently. "I'll tell them all to report immediately."

Talon's heart started pounding.

"That was your A-SAC, Tony Gregory. He was just going to dial all your personal cells, seeing as your company ones are still there. The team is recalled as of immediately."

"What?" Talon exclaimed as he lurched to his feet.

"Finn Mayer was dropped off by an Agent Fielding at Tampa General over an hour ago. His intention was to visit the prisoner from the attempted bank robbery. Thirty minutes later armed enhanced broke through security. Shots were fired but no fatalities. The enhanced left with the prisoner, but they also took Agent Mayer. The press has gotten hold of the whole story and is out for the FBI's blood. Apparently the poster-boy image you were all trying to create has worked. In particular the elderly mother of Senator Julio has been vocal on News Seven. She was one of the hostages in the robbery and is definitely part of Finn's cheerleading section, and by association, all of you," Daniel added dryly, but Talon hadn't heard anything since Daniel said they took Finn.

Talon tried to swallow the fear that tightened his throat. He'd let Finn down again.

Chapter Twenty-One

"GAEL, YOU and Eli go to the field office and get everyone's IDs and service weapons. We need to go to Tampa General, and it's in the opposite direction," Talon ordered.

Vance opened one of the bottom cupboards in the kitchen to reveal a safe. He keyed in the code and withdrew two guns. "They're both registered to me already."

"Vance?" They all turned at Connie's question. She was staring at the guns.

"The unit has been recalled, Mom," Vance replied as if that explained everything.

She turned to gaze at Talon, resignation written on her features. She'd been a cop's wife a long time. "Bring them home safe."

"Yes, ma'am." Talon brushed a kiss on her cheek, as did Vance and Gael. Sawyer gave her a pat on the shoulder, and Eli even smiled.

They ran outside, and Vance and Sawyer climbed into Talon's truck with him. When they had Finn back safe, he would personally make sure they got whatever armored vehicle was the biggest and baddest and keep Finn locked up in there, or something, at all times.

Talon shook his head. He had a feeling half his life would involve keeping his partner out of trouble. And he would keep him out of it. He just needed the chance to be able to.

They pulled up at the hospital, and Talon nearly said a prayer of thanks when he saw Lieutenant Dobbs from the hostage crisis, who strode over as soon as he spied him and stuck out his hand. Talon returned the handshake immediately. He liked Dobbs, a no-nonsense sort, and after the bank robbery, he felt comfortable working with him.

"I've just been given the news that your team is taking point. If you want to follow me, the video surveillance shows a reasonable image of the assailants entering the corridor. No cameras in the rooms, obviously."

They followed Dobbs into a small ground-floor office. "I reckon we're going to be seeing much more of each other," he added with a wry smile.

They all crowded around the monitor where a guard had the image of the gunmen entering the hospital.

"They're making no attempt to hide their enhanced status or their appearance," Sawyer noted as the two big guys breezed down the corridor. The screen blurred to the next image of the cop at the entrance to the corridor where Adam Mackenzie was being treated, facedown and cuffed with his arms behind him.

Dobbs gaped. "Is there something wrong with the tape?"

"Rewind and play it back in slow motion," Talon ordered, hoping his suspicions wouldn't be correct.

"Well, shit," Dobbs said as the tape showed one of the enhanced moving so fast, it didn't look like the other enhanced and the guard even took a step. He knocked the guard out with his own gun he had snatched out of the man's holster before the guard knew what was happening. By the time the other enhanced reached the guard at about a distance of six feet, the guard was unconscious and cuffed. They both stepped over him, and the last image before they disappeared down the corridor was the other enhanced pulling out a gun and shooting at the ceiling.

"That was just to cause fear and panic," Talon confirmed. "Was the guard the only one who was injured?"

"I'm afraid not," Dobbs answered and fast-forwarded the tape as both enhanced appeared again.

One was carrying Adam Mackenzie carefully, presumably not to cause further injury, but it was the second guy's appearance that caused the heavy silence in the room. The second enhanced was walking with a body casually slung over his shoulder. A clearly unconscious body. Anger and pain warred for dominance in Talon's gut. It was Finn.

The guard stopped the tape at the point where they got into a truck and drove away.

"He hasn't had a good week, really," Dobbs said in the silence.

Talon couldn't respond but was saved by Gael and Eli arriving with their things.

"Gregory says we have to wear these." Gael handed out their uniform shirts.

Talon closed his hands around one of them. He knew what it would say on the back, and he didn't want to put it on. He threw it onto the chair. He wasn't going to wear something that proclaimed him for something he wasn't. He'd never felt less like a hero in his life.

"The helicopter has been circling for fifteen minutes. The plates have been confirmed as false, but there's been no sighting of the car since it left the hospital. It should have been picked up pretty much straightaway on street cams, but it seems to have vanished," Dobbs added.

"Talon, do you think it's an ability?" Gael said slowly, and Talon narrowed his eyes.

"To hide a whole car and its occupants?" he said skeptically. "It's unlikely, and it's certainly not something we've ever come across." As far as they knew, Sawyer was the only one who came close, and it wasn't the same, anyhow. Sawyer changed his body's composition, almost; he didn't hide anything.

"Is that even possible?" Dobbs asked in astonishment.

Talon shook his head and stared at the screen. "How about we start simpler? Do you have any maps of the surrounding area?"

"Yeah," the guard piped up. "They're talking about expanding. We just got a bunch." He stood and went to the filing cabinet in the corner. The guard spread the map out, confirming what Talon was just working through in his head. The hospital was surrounded by water on all three sides.

"They didn't go over the causeway to Bayshore. Street cams would have picked them up," Sawyer said.

"What about north to that industrial area? Are there any street cams up there?" Eli pointed at the map.

Dobbs shook his head. "No, and there's a chance if they went into a garage or something fairly quickly, the helicopter completely missed them." Dobbs suddenly got dispatch on his radio, and he stepped out of the small office.

"Are all these medical buildings full?" Talon pointed out the pediatric and the dentist facility.

"Yeah," said the guard. "Actually no." He pointed to a building on the edge of the large parking lot. "That's empty and hasn't been rented. The master plan is that they build a multilevel parking lot and free some ground space for a new therapy department. This building would be demolished, as it's in the way for the new parking lot if they decide to go that route."

"Sawyer?" Talon looked at him. "We'll get you as close as we can, but there's nothing surrounding it for any type of cover. I need you to go see if there's anyone in there."

Vance piped up. "Surely the helicopter has thermal imaging. That would tell us straight away."

Dobbs stepped back inside and shook his head. "We've actually got two, but the one with thermal imaging is on a hunt for a gunman from a reported ATM grab as of thirty minutes ago. This one generally does traffic snarl-ups—no infrared." Dobbs paused. "We have handheld I can get down here."

Talon nodded, but he had no intention of waiting that long, and Dobbs disappeared out of the door again to call. Talon was also unsure of the distance the hand-held infrared would work at, and the problem was the building was set apart. He didn't want to warn anyone.

He pulled Sawyer to one side. "I hate to ask," Talon said.

"Why?" Sawyer replied bluntly. "Don't think I don't know you wouldn't do exactly the same for any of us, Talon. It's obvious you like the kid, but"—he shrugged—"this isn't what this is. This is just doing my job."

"This is doing a damn sight more than your job," Talon growled.

Sawyer put a hand on Talon's arm. "No, it isn't. Finn isn't the only one who needed something extra to get in the FBI. My ability is what I am, Talon. I never even graduated high school. Let's not kid ourselves that I'd be here if I couldn't do any of this."

Talon sighed. He was right. This was what they all signed up for. "Okay—I'm gonna drive to the edge of the parking lot but no farther than the cars already there. Too suspicious to suddenly park away from that. I'll get out and pretend to hunt for something in the trunk. You follow me unseen out of my door, and I'll wait for you to come back. No heroics," Talon added. "We just want to know if they're in there."

Talon's phone rang in his pocket, and he absently took it out. It was probably Gregory wanting an update….

"Talon?"

Talon's knees nearly buckled when he recognized the thready voice. He gripped his phone and raised a hand. Everyone immediately fell silent. "Finn?" he echoed in disbelief.

"Agent Valdez." The cool voice came on the phone almost immediately. "As you heard, we are holding your partner, but we just want to talk to you."

"Then let him go."

"I don't think so. There is a blue sedan waiting outside the fire exit nearest to where you are sitting watching security tapes. You have sixty seconds to get in it, or we will just shoot your partner. We have no interest in regulars." He ended the call almost immediately at the other end.

Talon took a step and was blocked by Gael. Talon looked at him, agonized. "I have no choice. Just do whatever you can."

Gael stepped to the side, and Talon was out of the door in ten seconds. He walked quickly to the car, and the back door opened as he got close. The same enhanced he saw on the tape cuffing the guard got out and gestured for Talon to get in.

"You'll have seen how fast I am already," he said. "Don't bother trying anything."

Talon nodded and got in. The man reached over before Talon could even blink and removed Vance's gun from his waistband. If Talon hadn't felt the touch on his back, he would never have known what he was doing. He didn't acknowledge the sardonic smile the other guy gave.

The car wove in and out of traffic, speeding north, and eventually entered the warehouse area they'd looked at on the map. The car shot around a corner after the first warehouse and straight up a ramp at the side. The whole journey took a little over five or six minutes, and Talon understood how they missed them. The enhanced got out, pulled Talon from the back, and the shutter door rolled down behind. The black truck they saw on the vid was parked to one side. The other enhanced on the hospital tape started walking through some doors, and the first one waved the gun to show he wanted Talon to follow him.

Talon walked through an archway and came to a stop in surprise. Finn was tied up and gagged, sitting on the floor. A third enhanced he had never seen was pointing a gun at him casually. Adam Mackenzie sat propped up on the floor next to him, awake but looking like shit. His hand was pressed tightly to the gauze covering his chest, which was now covered in red stains. Talon took a step toward Finn, but a hand dug into his shoulder.

"No reunions yet," the enhanced who was following him ordered.

Talon stared at Finn, who apart from being tied up and gagged, looked okay. In fact, as the green eyes glittered at him, he looked downright pissed.

That's when Talon noticed the third person who was seated on the floor next to Finn and blinked in surprise. Oliver Martinez, the eight-year-old missing child they were supposed to be finding.

Talon heard footsteps and looked up at the man who had walked in. He recognized the enhanced who was walking toward him as Isaac Dakota, the enhanced who spent more time on television than the fucking news anchors.

"Talon Valdez." Isaac held his hand out. Talon ignored him, and Isaac dropped it in amusement.

"What the hell are you doing, Dakota?" Talon ground out.

"I'm doing what we should all have done twenty years ago," Dakota snapped. "Enhanced are superior to regular humans in every way. They keep us belittled or locked up because they are frightened of us, and with good reason. Most of us are treated like common criminals."

"Yeah," drawled Talon, "because kidnapping is illegal in all fifty states."

Anger darkened Dakota's features, but it quickly fled when he laughed shortly. "You may have a point," Dakota conceded, "but I wasn't the one to start holding perfectly law-abiding citizens against their will. I didn't make it impossible for law-abiding citizens to get health care. I didn't make it impossible for us to get something as simple as a car loan or a mortgage, or ban some children from school. I didn't even make it impossible for certain kids not to be allowed in a fucking movie theater." He pointed to Oliver, who was trying his best to huddle next to Finn. "I didn't ruin so many kids' childhoods just because one morning they woke up with a mark on their face!" He stabbed wildly at the mark on his own cheek.

Talon grudgingly admitted most of the points, but whatever Dakota was doing wasn't going to improve those childhoods. He was going to make a lot of them ten times worse. "Just what do you think is going to happen here?" Talon asked, trying not to look at Finn's green eyes, which seemed to be boring into him.

"I have a proposition," Dakota answered immediately. "Join us. You and your team. We will fight for enhanced to get equal if not better rights than the rest of the US. Our skills can be used to make America the great country it once was. The enhanced shouldn't be just allowed to serve in the military. They should be running it. Imagine"—Dakota threw his arms back wide—"the next third-world dictator who wants to blow up Americans will think twice when he realizes who's in charge."

Talon blinked. The man was certifiable. No, he amended. The man was egotistical and ambitious and *very, very dangerous*. He glanced at Oliver, and everything suddenly clicked. "You're responsible for the enhanced kids going missing, aren't you?"

Dakota smiled. "I wondered if you'd worked that out. The gifted children are wasted in the paltry foster homes that are being hurriedly put together. They should be trained, their gifts explored, molded."

"How about you let them be kids?" Talon said incredulously. "Toss a football. Go to school."

"I am merely taking what the state has already thrown away," Dakota argued.

"Well, Oliver's mom hasn't thrown him away. She wants him back." Talon saw Oliver raising his head and, unbelievably, Finn bumping shoulders with him a little.

"For how long?" Dakota snapped. "Until the next time he loses control?" He paused and heaved a huge sigh. "Join me—join us." He glanced around.

Talon thought quickly. He had to try to convince Dakota he was interested. "Let Finn and Oliver go, and I'll stay."

Dakota shrugged. "I'm afraid not. I have a use for both of them, and the child is valuable."

"He's eight years old," Talon said in disgust. "He's a child, not a commodity."

"Don't be naïve," snapped Dakota. "Everything's a commodity. It's the world we live in."

Talon suddenly twigged. "You're behind the bank robberies?"

Dakota looked furious. "Of course not," he spat. "They were only brought to my attention when I realized they had the help of an enhanced, and I am not interested in a couple of lowlifes who can do paltry smash-and-grab when I have access to people with the ability to control the world's finances." He shot Talon a calculating look. "I'm pretty sure your team's value would increase if they knew exactly what you can all do."

Talon stiffened at the implied threat. Just how much did Dakota know? "Let them go and we'll talk," he insisted.

Dakota smiled and turned to the enhanced behind him. They both seemed to share a joke. "I'm sorry. I know full well you have no intention of joining us. I just wanted to see how far you would take it to convince us."

Talon frowned. *What?*

"I have no need of someone with your ability, Talon." Dakota inspected a nail casually. "So you can kill people? Big deal. I can go to a dozen street corners in this city and pay someone less than the cost of my dry cleaning bill to do the same."

Talon blinked.

"What I really want is Gael, Sawyer, and Eli," Dakota continued, and Talon's heart thudded. "I know they have much more interesting talents, but while you are here, while there is a chance of your team succeeding, I know I would be unable to recruit them. Your vision of a normal life may be degrading and beneath their talents, but I suppose it must have its charms.

"And unfortunately killing you may have the opposite effect. I don't want them continuing in some disgusting obligation to your memory. So I have a quandary. I need to humiliate you. I need the world to dislike you, and I need your pathetic little team disbanding so I can add them and their talents to mine."

He gestured to Finn. "Untie the regular and the child, and bring them here."

The enhanced calmly walked forward, bringing Oliver.

Talon's heart bounced hard in his chest and seemed to drop. He had an awful feeling about this.

"You have to choose one of them to be the test subject."

"What?" Talon said in horror.

Dakota laughed. "Choose one of them to demonstrate your ability on." He lowered his voice and gestured to Oliver. "Pick one."

"Are you insane?" Talon said, thinking furiously, his heart pounding in his ears.

Finn was dragged in front of Talon, and the gag dropped from his mouth. The other guy Talon hadn't seen do anything took Oliver's hand and led him quietly next to Dakota. Oliver was sniffing softly, and the lights started flickering.

Dakota looked at the ceiling and glanced at Oliver, smiling reassuringly, and the lights returned to normal. "Interesting," he murmured.

"Now this is Raoul." Dakota gestured to the enhanced standing beside him. "Raoul has got quite a unique ability with energy. He can heat a room. He can also heat a body." Dakota nodded as if he were talking to himself. "Over seven thousand people die of heat stroke in America every year, did you know that? It's fascinating, really."

Dakota carried on almost conversationally. "The first thing that happens is that blood is diverted away from the major organs to the skin's surface." He stroked a finger idly down Finn's cheek, and Finn tried to pull away. Raoul just held him firm. "Your sweat glands try to release water to cool your skin, and that's when the real problems of dehydration begin. Of course, the sweat glands can't cool the skin fast enough, so that causes your heart to pump even more blood from your vital organs. Once your core temperature gets above a hundred and four degrees, you're in serious danger. Blood flow stops to the brain, and your brain begins to swell. Hallucinations and seizures may occur, followed by a loss of consciousness. People actually stop sweating because their bodies simply run out of fluid to do so."

Talon always knew he was strong, but right at that moment, he didn't know how he was still standing and not holding that sick son of a bitch's throat in his hands and squeezing the life out of him.

"I am aware of what you can do," Dakota continued. "You haven't kept it secret in the department, and money loosens tongues anyway. So I'm going to ask you again. Pick a victim."

Talon took a slow breath, trying to remain calm.

Dakota beckoned to the other enhanced behind him, who stepped up with a video camera, and Talon suddenly understood. He was going to have to murder on film and have it shown to the world. That was how Dakota would get the team disbanded.

"No one will fall for it," he said derisively, but inside, sick panic was clutching at his gut.

"Oh, the tape will be judiciously altered. I have another of our team who can alter any recording and make it undetectable. All the world will see is you losing your temper at me and your partner begging you to let me go before you kill me. Of course, your lack of control is well documented, and when you unleash your ability on your partner and kill him, no one will be surprised."

Talon fisted his hands, and Dakota sneered. "Keep going." He nodded to the camera. "We're getting some lovely shots of you losing your temper. I wonder if your father was scared of you, his own son, before you killed him as well."

Talon let out an agonized cry and leaped for Dakota. Instantly both enhanced from the car had guns pointing at Finn. Talon forced himself to stop.

Dakota raised an eyebrow. "Lovely control, but I think we'll edit that part out." He turned to Oliver and smiled at him. Oliver glanced at Talon in fear, but Talon had no idea how to reassure him. "Whichever you choose, Raoul will demonstrate on the other. I want to see who is the fastest, until someone's heart stops. Oliver's or Finn's.

"I should add, to be sporting, we will give you a head start. If you succeed with Finn, Raoul won't need to start on Oliver at all. Which is just as well," Dakota whispered as he covered Oliver's ears with his large hands. "I'm afraid Raoul's talent is very painful. I have heard the brain can literally boil in the skull." Dakota smiled and cuffed Oliver on the cheek, and Oliver looked confused and took a step away.

"So which do you pick? I'd go for Finn, really. I mean, you don't have any choice, I suppose. You're not going to kill a child, and if you don't kill your partner, then I will let Raoul loose on the boy."

FINN HEARD every word Dakota said. He came around slowly a few minutes before a phone was shoved in his face and Talon was being led into the warehouse. He had no idea where he was or how long he'd been out. He vaguely remembered the enhanced appearing in Adam's room and had no idea what he'd done to him. Whatever it was, it put him out quickly.

Finn glanced back at Adam. He looked like crap, to be honest. His worried gray eyes bored into Finn, but Finn wasn't sure what, if anything, anyone could do. Adam was tied up, so presumably they weren't sure of his loyalty yet. He hadn't seen Adam demonstrate any ability apart from bending the metal safe door, and whatever the other enhanced guy did, he put Finn out nearly instantly, so he guessed he could do the same to anyone.

He could feel Talon's panic. He knew Talon was trying to look and sound calm, but the rapid pulse point in his neck kind of gave it away. Well, to him, anyway. He wasn't sure the others either noticed or cared. He vaguely acknowledged it was odd he wasn't panicking himself. Dakota had just given Talon an impossible choice, and one that, unless the team found them, would mean he was going to die.

His breath hitched in the silence that weighed heavily in the room, and Talon swung his eyes away from Dakota and fixed them unerringly on Finn. There. Those gorgeous fucking blue eyes that saw everything, shining straight at him, carrying helplessness, anger, an apology almost? Was that what it was? It wasn't that Talon was being given an impossible choice—he had no choice at all, really.

Finn tried to smile. He tried to tell Talon that it was okay, that he understood Dakota made it impossible. He wanted to be brave, to be the big man. To tell him he was forgiven... but what he really wanted was to cry and be told it wasn't hopeless and it wasn't going to really fucking hurt. He didn't want to die, but most of all, if he were completely honest, he didn't want Talon to be the one to have to kill him.

"I don't have all day," Dakota said, sounding bored.

Talon wrenched his gaze back to Dakota. "My team is on its way. There is no way you can get away with this."

Dakota smiled. "My family owns this warehouse. Disused for the moment, but we keep security cameras trained on the perimeter in case of a break-in. So there is no team outside. There are no cops. There is no cavalry, and no one is going to ride to the rescue." He glanced at Oliver and sighed. The boy was wearing a thin T-shirt and a small jacket. It was fairly cool in the warehouse. "Oliver, you may want to take off your jacket. It's going to get a little warm in here." He looked at Raoul. "Raoul, if you please."

"Stop," Talon ground out. "You can't do this."

"Oh, yes, before I forget," he continued. "If any of us feel like you are trying anything, Raoul will kill the child immediately. For the few seconds he can't breathe, he will retain his ability to kill both you and the child. So don't even think about trying anything.

Raoul has also demonstrated his abilities on more than one victim at a time. I doubt if you have."

Raoul now had a firm hand on Oliver, who was crying. The lights started flickering alarmingly.

Dakota followed Talon's gaze to where he glanced at Adam. "No, no help there either. Some abilities are useful but not deadly. Adam can merely open locked doors, and while that would have been incredibly useful in the early days financially, Adam has decided he doesn't want to join us, so we're just going to let him bleed out here on the floor."

Adam's face was gray and his eyes were closed. The gauze was now completely covered in blood, and Finn didn't know what to do to help, but somehow, knowing his best friend was still his best friend made the day a little less shitty.

"Bring Finn a little closer, if you please."

The enhanced holding Finn dragged him nearer to Talon.

Raoul caught hold of Oliver's shoulders and pulled him to stand in front of him. He took off the boy's jacket and then turned him back around to look at Talon.

"Talon." Dakota's voice carried a warning this time. "I am running out of patience." He nodded at Raoul, and Raoul looked at Oliver closely. Everyone saw the boy lift a shaky hand to his head to wipe the sweat that had suddenly bloomed there.

Finn had seen enough. "Talon. It's okay."

Talon looked at him, incredulity and agony etched on his face. "I can't," he whispered.

Everyone heard the tiny whimper from Oliver as the boy's body sagged against Raoul, the flush stark on his previously pale face.

"Talon, you have to," Finn said, glancing once more at Oliver as his eyes rolled up in his head and he slid to the floor. Raoul made no move to catch him.

"Stop," Talon ordered and looked at Dakota. "There will be nowhere—nowhere you can hide that I can't find you, nowhere you can run that I can't catch you. You will regret this day every second for what remains of your miserable life."

Dakota just raised his eyebrows and looked pointedly at Finn. "Last chance." He looked at Raoul. "Raoul?"

"No," Finn shouted. "Talon, look at me. Do this for me. You're not killing me. You're saving a child's life."

Dakota lifted his hand to Raoul to indicate he should continue, but at the second everyone saw him do so, Talon took a step toward Finn and stared at him, the blue eyes Finn loved so much brittle with the agony of what was being forced upon him. Finn wanted to tell him it was okay. More than anything he wanted to tell him he loved him, and as he opened his mouth to speak, Finn's breath caught just as he was going to take the last one. For a second it seemed time stood still, and then his lungs tried to expand and nothing happened. His arms grew heavy and his feet wouldn't move. The heart that had been pounding in his chest slowed down.

No pain. Even as he felt himself toppling over, the arms he longed to feel caught him and held him. Finn heard a whispered apology and felt wet cheeks. No burn. No lungs screaming for oxygen. It was almost like falling asleep. Something brushed his cheek, but it was getting too dark to see. It could have been a kiss. He almost imagined it a kiss.

Chapter Twenty-Two

TALON'S ARMS shook as he watched the life go out of Finn's eyes. The life he was draining. He choked back a cry and pulled the still body to him tightly. He couldn't survive this. He was done.

He looked up, anger flooding his body. He didn't care anymore.

"Talon." Dakota stepped back as he issued the warning, and Talon smiled, satisfied Dakota had seen in him his future and he knew his life was forfeit.

For a second the silence was ominous, and then an explosion rocked the building and Talon fell back, still clutching Finn.

Smoke, panic, sirens. People—it seemed hundreds of people—none of whom mattered to Talon except the one he held in his arms. He barely registered the guns firing and the bodies flying. He took no satisfaction in seeing Raoul take three bullets before he could kill anyone else.

"Talon." Gael shook his arm. "Talon, let us see to Finn."

Talon was helpless as they ripped Finn from his arms. The noises fell away. The sounds. The smoke. None of it registered. Not even the paramedics desperately trying to restart Finn's heart—the heart Talon stopped.

Talon watched as the paramedics cleared everyone from Finn's lifeless body. The jolt as the electricity flooded it. The second attempt… and the third. He wanted to scream when the paramedics sadly shook their heads.

"No. No, let me."

Talon raised his eyes as Adam, who was awake, struggled against the paramedics who were trying to help him. "Talon," he cried desperately. "Let me. I can save him."

Talon bolted upright and grabbed Adam, oblivious to the freshly gauzed wound on his chest. "Let him try," he ordered and practically thrust Adam down next to Finn.

"My ability isn't just opening doors." Adam grunted in pain. "It's—well, look." Adam hovered a shaky hand over Finn's chest, and sparks began to crackle and fire from the ends of his fingers.

"Stand back," Gael shouted, pulling Talon out of the way.

A second bang and Finn's body seemed to jump from the floor. Adam was flung three feet away, and the paramedics swarmed once more.

"We've got a pulse!" one of them shouted in excitement.

Talon let Gael hold him because he wasn't sure
his own legs would. He didn't realize he was crying
until Vance dragged him from Gael and hugged him
and he wondered why Vance's shirt was wet.

FINN OPENED his eyes to familiar white walls
and closed them again almost immediately. He was
getting really, really sick of waking up in the hospital.

"Look at you."

Finn cracked a shaky smile as he recognized Jeremy's voice and opened bleary eyes. He heard a snore
to his right and saw Gael stretched out asleep between
two chairs. His heart plummeted. Gael opened his
eyes and sat up in a hurry, then started to smile and
stopped when he saw Finn's eyes fill with tears. It was
stupid, and he closed them.

A big hand covered his. "Ah, kid," Gael said
apologetically, but Finn wasn't listening. He was too
busy hearing the sound of his heart breaking.

He must have gotten himself worked up with the
crying because a doctor appeared, glanced in concern
at the monitor, and added something to his IV that
made him go back to sleep.

The next time he woke up, he blinked as Vance's
face came into focus. Vance shot to his feet. "Shall I
call someone?"

Finn almost smiled at the faint panic in the big
guy's voice. Almost. "I won't have another melt-
down." He tried to swallow and sipped gratefully at
the water Vance held to his lips. He wanted to ask
where everyone was, but he knew Vance would see
straight through his question and know he wanted to

know where Talon was. And he wasn't sure he was ready for the answer.

"The team's in the waiting room. Jeremy says he's trying to get the hospital to designate a special one for us, seeing as you seem to be making a habit of it."

Finn looked up. It was no use. He had to ask. "The whole team?"

Vance sighed. "I'll go get Gael."

Which told Finn everything he needed to know. He didn't bother trying to stay awake for Gael to have to tell him Talon wasn't there.

THE NEXT time he opened his eyes, Finn was astonished to see Agent Gregory quietly sitting in the chair, reading a report. "Sir?" Finn said.

Gregory beamed and closed his file. "Agent Mayer. Good to see you awake." Gregory patted Finn's hand awkwardly. "My boy, the FBI is very proud of you. Deputy Director Cohen himself sends his thanks."

Finn parted his lips soundlessly and then he remembered. "Adam?"

"Adam Mackenzie is recovering nicely, and with a little help, has got himself a good attorney. Isaac Dakota is completely lawyered up, unfortunately. Raoul Esperanza, Mark Allen, and Thomas Kent were all shot and killed at the scene."

"Oliver?"

"Oliver Martinez is at home with his mom, who has apparently kicked Oliver's dad out. Isaac Dakota has been incredibly clever and is simply blaming his dead colleagues. He is insisting Raoul Esperanza threatened him into using his family's money and contacts. He has only a low-grade telekinetic ability documented, so the lawyers are working through all that now. We are still no nearer to finding out where the other enhanced children are, but that will be the number-one priority for your team when you rejoin them." Gregory smiled. "I actually have a letter sent from the new classmates of the boy you helped in the bank. He's started at a new school, and his mom has had a T-shirt made with the HERO logo. Totally against regulations, I might add, but what can I do?"

Finn's heart shrank a little even as he was pleased to hear the good news about Bobby. He was being offered everything he ever wanted.

"Agent Gregory? Please accept this as my official notice of resignation," Finn said quietly.

"Resignation?" Gregory repeated as if he hadn't heard properly. "What do you mean?"

Finn looked him in the eye. "I am resigning from the team."

"You don't have to worry about the four weeks anymore," Gregory quickly countered. "You will receive training along with your regular duties from now on. In fact, I have another candidate in mind to partner either Gael or Vance."

Finn wanted to cry again. But this time he didn't. He couldn't work with Talon. Talon clearly couldn't bear to be in the same room as Finn, which made it impossible for the team. And he loved Talon. He was sure of it. And Talon needed the team more than Finn did. He would do this for Talon and walk away.

"Talon is temporarily suspended until he gets a psych clearance, but I expect that to be a formality," Gregory added.

Because he killed me. "I'm sorry, Agent Gregory. I know you took a chance on me, and I will always be grateful, but my decision is final." Finn lay back and closed his eyes. He knew it was rude, but he couldn't bear to see the condemnation on Gregory's face.

THE NEXT day Finn got dressed slowly. He was fine. A little shaky but fine. He was sure, despite Gregory being pissed at him, he would give him a reference. He had a job to get, an apartment to find, and a car to rent. He had the rest of his life to sort out, and wallowing in pity in a hospital bed wasn't getting him anywhere.

Gael had left him his wallet and bank cards they got back from the bank, and he was going to come back for him this afternoon. But Finn wasn't going to wait for him. He liked Gael, but Gael's loyalty should be for his team leader, not for him. He wasn't sure he was ready to admit he couldn't be in Gael's company without being constantly reminded of Talon.

Jeremy walked back into his room to find Finn dressed. "I didn't realize you were going this early. I thought it was this afternoon. Isn't Superman coming back for you?" Jeremy picked up his charts.

Finn smiled. Jeremy called everyone on the team "Superman." He knew it was a term of affection. "I'd appreciate if you'd call me a cab."

Jeremy sighed. "Really?"

Finn nodded.

"Okay, but you'll have to give me fifteen minutes to get your discharge paperwork ready," Jeremy replied, and Finn settled back down to wait.

A pleasant lady came in to ask Finn to sign some insurance forms about ten minutes later, and Jeremy returned with a wheelchair a few minutes after that.

Finn screwed up his nose.

"Hospital policy," Jeremy said and grinned. "Park your butt."

Finn sat and tried not to grumble while he was pushed out to the entrance.

Jeremy stopped by the doors. "Your cab's just outside." He smiled. "I don't want to see you back here anytime soon," he scolded.

Finn smiled, picked up his bag, and headed out of the doors. Then he came to a complete stop as he took in the huge black armored vehicle currently blocking all the cars behind it. He blinked in shock as he read the white letters on the side of the BearCat.

Human.

Enhanced.

Rescue.

Organization.

Shit. Finn's eyes filled. He was going to cry again, but not at the stupid car or the silly name. It was at the man who had jumped down and was solemnly holding the door open for him.

Talon.

"Someone told me you wanted a ride?"

Finn stared at Talon, who wasn't just holding the door. Those big hands were cradling Finn's heart. He cleared his throat and ignored the honks of the cars that couldn't get past the BearCat. "That depends entirely on where we're going," Finn said, ashamed at the wobble in his voice.

"With me," Talon answered. "I don't care wherever it is you want to go, but you have to take me with you."

Finn, aware of the crowd gathering to stare, let Talon help him up into the front seat. Talon ran around and climbed in. Within seconds the powerful engine had rumbled to life, and Talon pulled away from the hospital.

"Where do you want to go?" Talon asked cautiously, as if he were afraid of the answer.

"Why, Talon? Why did you come and get me? Don't you think it makes it harder?"

Talon swore quietly, pulled the BearCat into the parking lot, and killed the engine. He didn't speak for a few seconds.

"I killed you." Talon ground out every pain-filled word. He stared unseeing in front of him. "I held you in my arms and took the life from you. I couldn't come, because how could you even bear to look at me when I can't even bear to look at myself?"

Finn clamped his lips and swallowed. He put a hand gently on the shaking shoulders. "You don't think I blame you, do you? Talon. You had no choice. Neither of us did. There was no way you could let Oliver be hurt."

Talon made a pained sound in the back of his throat, and suddenly Finn was dragged into his embrace. "I killed you." Talon's muffled voice came from where his head was buried in Finn's chest. "I had to watch you die. I came to the hospital, but as soon as they said you were okay, I ran." He lifted his tear-soaked eyes. "I couldn't watch you blame me. I couldn't watch you realize I am the monster they've all been calling us for years."

Finn dragged his own arms around Talon and held him tighter.

"I had my phone turned off, but then Gregory turned up. He told me you had resigned from the team. Gael was going to collect you and bring you to my place so we could talk. Then your nurse called and said you were leaving."

Finn squeezed Talon tighter. *Jeremy.* He should have known.

Talon loosened Finn's arms and gazed down at him. "Talk to me, please. I know I don't deserve you, but—"

Finn silenced Talon the only way he knew how: with his lips.

Talon took over the kiss nearly immediately, and Finn melted. Talon broke the kiss and pulled back a little, their foreheads resting together. "You still haven't said anything," Talon urged.

Finn grinned happily. "I kind of thought actions spoke louder than words."

Talon chuckled and dipped his head for another kiss that Finn felt down to his toes.

"Just so I understand," Finn said. "You want me as your partner *and* as your boyfriend?"

Talon clutched him tighter, and Finn took that as a yes also.

"But what about the team? About Gregory?"

"The team knows. Vance and Gael were pretty vocal about me finding a quick way to get my head out of my ass. Sawyer's cool with whatever, and Eli actually suggested I come in this." Talon patted the dashboard with pride. "Gregory won't care so long as we're discreet. To be honest he's so desperate to have you back, I'm pretty sure he would agree to anything."

Finn sighed happily, but then another thought quickly wiped the smile from his face.

"What?" Talon said.

Finn was getting everything he ever wanted, wasn't he? "This isn't because you're feeling guilty, is it? I mean, I'm a big boy, Talon. I can just be your work partner." Finn flushed. Crap. That sounded like he was assuming Talon wanted to be another sort of partner. "I—"

Talon silenced him in exactly the same way Finn had just done, then broke off reluctantly. "Let me spell this out. I want you in my life. I want you to partner me at work, and I want you in my bed. I can't promise forever because…." He shrugged and fell silent for a few seconds. "I'm dangerous, Finn. Whatever else this is, I still killed you." He pulled away a little. "Why do I not terrify you?" he asked, bewildered.

Finn tilted his head to one side. "So it's not that you don't like the sound of forever, it's that you don't believe you deserve it?"

He watched in fascination as a slight flush stained Talon's cheeks and he didn't answer. Finn was entranced. For all his bluster, all his confidence, Talon simply didn't think it was possible anyone could love him.

Finn smiled and took a steadying breath. "Looks like I've got a lot of convincing to do. How about you take me home so we can start?"

Talon grazed a finger down Finn's cheek and nodded.

"Oh, I forgot. I brought you something. Have you seen what the papers are calling you?"

Finn blinked at the change of subject as Talon handed him a copy of this morning's *Daily Post*. He stared at the obvious likeness of him wearing a Superman T-shirt, arm extended and flying through the air. The caption "Superman joins the FBI" was blazoned underneath.

"I'm pretty sure Cohen would give you his first-born right about now." Talon chuckled. "The team's all at my house, waiting for us to come back. They swore once they said hello, they would all make themselves scarce. Eli can take this back for us. Pretty sure I'm not gonna be able to fit it in the parking garage." Talon started the BearCat, and it roared throatily to life. He looked lovingly at Finn.

Finn beamed back. "One question, then."

Talon raised his eyebrows.

"Can I drive?"

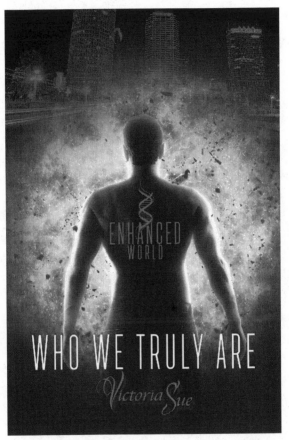

Chapter One

FINN GRIPPED his Glock 19, trying not to let his hand shake. Heart pounding so loud he thought the perp would hear it, he crept behind Sawyer along the hallway of the house he had just entered. Two, possibly three guys and multiple hostages. He glanced at the small kitchen as he walked past and silently checked no one was hiding out of sight behind the door. He gave the tiny room one last look and moved down the corridor. Sawyer paused to the left of the door, with Finn behind. He knew the drill for clearing a room—he could do it in his sleep. SWAT teams never operated with less than two, and Sawyer had waited until Finn got in place. He gripped his gun tighter, willing his sweaty fingers not to cramp.

The ominous click behind him made him freeze. *Shit.*

"Bang. You're dead."

"Drew?" Finn blurted out indignantly as he swung around. "What are you doing here?"

"Shooting your sorry ass" came the familiar drawl from behind Finn, accompanied by Vance's chuckle.

"But...," Finn started protesting as Vance took the training gun from him.

"You didn't check under the kitchen sink," Talon said with a sigh, coming to stand beside Drew.

"That's because all you bastards are too huge to fit under there!" Finn argued. "I didn't know you'd planted Drew here. That's chea—" He clamped his lips together one second too late.

"Cheating?" Talon repeated incredulously. "*Cheating?* This isn't a fucking game, Finn." Talon threw his hands in the air and stormed out as Finn winced. Drew sent him an apologetic look as he followed their team leader out of the empty mock-up house they used for training.

Shit. Finn closed his eyes in despair. He'd screwed up royally. He'd made assumptions that Sawyer had already checked, and because Drew wasn't in the car when they'd arrived, he'd taken it for granted no one was there. Drew wasn't even one of the team, but he did join them for training sometimes. Finn knew he was supposed to check anywhere someone on two legs could hide. He kicked the baseboard in temper before walking out.

Vance chuckled again, and his huge hand settled on Finn's shoulder. "Don't get bent up about it, kid. We all make mistakes."

"Some of us more than others," Sawyer added.

Finn kept his mouth shut this time. Didn't even protest at the "kid" moniker they all used. He deserved it. He'd already screwed up with the target practice because he was too worried about tomorrow. The team was doing this as a favor for him so he wouldn't be completely out of his depth when he drove up to the FLETC in Georgia. He'd been so excited when their boss, A-SAC Gregory, got him a place on the active shooter threat training program. The Federal Law Enforcement Training Center in Glynco was in high demand, and he was sure Gregory had probably pulled some strings to get him in so soon. Then he'd been told there might be some written simulations, and his newfound confidence had taken a dive. His team knew about Finn's dyslexia. It wasn't an issue, and because they were relaxed, he was relaxed and it hadn't posed any problems. But Gregory had excitedly told him yesterday how everyone would know he was from the new team and how he was sure Finn would make them all proud. Which, of course, was absolutely the wrong thing to say, because suddenly there was a real possibility that he would let them all down.

Finn silently followed Sawyer and Vance into the back of Talon's truck. Talon sat in the driver's seat, and Finn blinked in astonishment as Drew hopped up beside him. They usually left that seat for Vance, to give the huge guy room to stretch his legs. Finn pretended not to listen as Drew started asking Talon's advice about a task force he had applied for.

"Are you hoping you might get to see your parents a little more often if you get transferred up there, or is this something you're interested in?" Talon asked as he exited the training area.

"To be honest, I don't think I'm using my talents here. Wiretaps may be important, but I am not planning on spending the next three years listening to them. I'm fascinated with the BAU, and I need to get to a space where I have a good chance of being considered," Drew replied eagerly.

Talon shrugged. "I have an older brother who has his forensic behavioral science degree. He lectures some now. I can give you his email."

Finn seethed. Drew Fielding was a regular agent who often joined in with Finn's training, but Talon didn't especially like the guy since he'd caught Drew trying to get into Finn's pants. Talon had said that Drew would make a good agent if he spent less time on manicures, and they'd all had a good laugh. Finn often sparred with Drew and had only been able to get the jump on him once, even with Vance giving him tips at hand-to-hand. And what was the sudden objection to wiretaps? He'd told Finn it was easy money for sitting and doing nothing strenuous.

Talon waved his ID at the security barrier as they pulled into the parking lot behind the Tampa FBI field office that was their base. The *only* field office that had a security barrier. Talon had told him it was just for them, but that was plain-ass stupid. No flimsy barrier was going to stop any of his team—well, apart from him. Because, and despite Agent Gregory saying he had found one or two candidates to join them, Finn was still the only regular human on a team of enhanced humans.

H.E.R.O. Human Enhanced Rescue Organization. *Heroes?* The press seemed to think so—well, at the minute anyway—but of course, that could turn on a dime.

Everyone got out. "Finn, wait up," Talon said, and Drew, Sawyer, and Vance immediately made themselves scarce without any comments.

Finn let out a long breath while he waited for the earbashing he was about to get. Then, without warning, Talon curled a hand around the back of Finn's neck and drew him in so fast he nearly fell against the lips that touched his. Finn melted instantly against the hard body, then stumbled as Talon let go just as fast, glancing around to make sure no one had seen, but the lot was empty.

"I need you safe," Talon ground out, and Finn's heart turned to mush, along with his muscles.

"I know." And he did. Talon was struggling with being his team leader and his... *boyfriend*? Was that what Talon was? They'd hardly been out of each other's sight for six weeks. If he didn't stay over at Talon's, then Talon stayed at his apartment. Not often, though, as Drew had a place in the same complex as Finn, and Talon's monster truck was very visible. Their boss knew about their relationship and was choosing to ignore it, but that didn't mean they had to wave it in anyone's face.

Today marked the official start of his eighth week in the FBI, and he still wanted to pinch himself daily. Finn let out a slow breath as he turned to follow Talon toward the field office. *Eight weeks.* Eight weeks since he'd gotten the letter saying his application for the FBI had been rejected and then, an hour later, got the cryptic phone call from A-SAC Gregory saying he had been selected for a secret specialized training program in the FBI, to tell no one, and to report, not at Quantico, but at the Tampa field office in Florida.

That had been the strangest day of his life. He'd never forget meeting his new partner, Talon. All six foot five inches of him, with the gorgeous, blond-haired, blue-eyed Greek-god thing he had going on. Then he'd seen Talon's face and nearly had a heart attack. The mark. All enhanced had a scar under their left eye shaped a bit like a lightning bolt. It was completely impervious to any type of makeup or even plastic surgery. There was something about it that burned through makeup, and it reformed just as quickly if it was surgically removed.

Talon stopped as they rounded the corner. "I know you got a little bent up 'cause of what Gregory said."

Finn rubbed his chin against Talon's shirt. "I don't want to let you all down." He didn't look up until he felt Talon's finger tilt his chin.

"It's my fault. We shouldn't be doing this rushed. The whole thing isn't fair to you. You should be getting proper training."

Finn stared into the deep blue he loved so much. "And we both know I would never have made the *proper* training. It is what it is, T." Which was true; the FBI had wanted to fill an extra eight hundred and fifty agent posts last year. In the space of six weeks, they had gotten over two hundred and seventy thousand applications. Finn's grades would normally never have made the cut.

"It still doesn't mean I'm about to put the team, *including* you, in danger over something I should have sorted out."

"And you will," Finn soothed. It wasn't Talon's fault either. In the last four weeks, they had gone from persona non grata with the Tampa PD to having nearly every sergeant calling them, wanting their input on various cases. And because the team was doing their best to get enhanced accepted with the general public, Talon was struggling not to turn down any request for help.

Finn's belly rumbled as he stood in the elevator. The others had been holding it for them when Talon and Finn caught up to them, which was a shame, but he didn't want to go into the locker rooms with a hard-on, and he would have if Talon had kissed him anymore. Finn smirked—who was he kidding?—and tried to adjust his pants unobtrusively. He risked a quick glance at Talon and knew by the flare of his bright blue eyes that he'd failed miserably. His belly rumbled again.

Vance chuckled. "You hungry?"

"He's always hungry," drawled Talon.

Finn lifted his T-shirt and patted his flat stomach lightly. "Maybe I've got a worm."

Sawyer spluttered, trying not to laugh. Vance just grinned.

"A worm? What the hell?"

"That's what my granddad used to say when I ate a lot." Finn grinned. "Did you know the longest tapeworm ever taken out of a human was one hundred and eight feet?"

Everyone groaned, and Sawyer made gagging noises. "Talon, please, for the love of God, shut him up, or he's not gonna need any more training. I'm just gonna shoot him in the elevator."

Talon chuckled, and Finn smiled, relieved. He didn't know how he retained all the useless facts he did, but if it lightened the mood, he was all for it.

The elevator dinged at their floor. They had their own corridor—a *whole* corridor. Two huge classroom spaces, a locker room, and a gym. Gregory's office and the clinic were on the floor above. The gym was new, though. There was a large one downstairs, but all the agents had access to it, and Gregory had successfully requisitioned one for their team. Gregory said he was sick of the complaints after Vance broke another piece of equipment down there.

Vance—all three hundred pounds of him—was easily the strongest guy, and possibly one of the largest, Finn had ever met. Strength was one of his abilities, and the phrase *bench-pressed trucks* wasn't just a descriptor used on Vance. He had actually lifted the beast Talon drove.

Drew sidled up to Finn as they walked down the corridor. "Sorry about that."

Finn glanced at Drew. His usual tanned skin looked a little pale and his brown eyes tired. *He needs a few tanning sessions*, Finn thought waspishly, then immediately felt guilty. Finn had resented Drew from the beginning because Drew was everything he had always wanted to be. He was a regular human FBI agent and had bested Finn physically, even though it was to be expected. Drew had tried to make friends, and Finn suddenly felt ashamed.

"My fault. I shouldn't make assumptions."

"I couldn't say no when Talon asked after all the help he's giving me." Drew smiled and turned to walk off down the corridor, leaving Finn with a million questions. Help? What help? Drew and Talon had chatted so easily in the car, and Talon never did that.

It was stupid. Stupid, and he was jealous. The trouble was, he had no confidence in their relationship. It wasn't like he was some catch. He might look okay, but Talon, of all people, wouldn't go for someone based on looks.

They all trooped into the locker room and headed toward the miserable-looking vending machines. There was a canteen on-site, but they all hated it, since it was shared with the other agents and the cops who came in sometimes. They were sick of the whispered comments and sly nudges. The sad fact was that even though a lot of the cops were being swayed over the advantage of being able to call an enhanced team out when needed, a lot of regular agents still resented them.

Gael and Eli followed them in. They'd been absent for the training because they'd both had their monthly medicals.

"Gregory wants us now," Gael said.

Vance groaned, just reaching the vending machines, and Finn sighed sympathetically, ignoring his empty belly. He would go and try to fill it with coffee.

"ABSOLUTELY NO fucking way." Talon nearly overturned the desk he sat behind in his hurry to get to his feet.

Here we go.... Finn ignored Gael's and Vance's smirks at Talon's reaction to the news Gregory had just delivered, and tried to concentrate, since he'd been too distracted by the real possibility he would starve to death.

"Talon—" Gregory started.

"He's been here *two fucking months*—and half of that time, in the damn hospital. He's just successfully demonstrated the perp would have to be fucking standing still for him to get a shot off—"

Finn closed his eyes and slid down his chair, desperately willing the heat he could feel climbing up his neck not to reach his cheeks. The hospital had been a complete exaggeration. Two weeks in total, tops. Well, okay, twice he'd been in for concussions. And there had been the black eye when Vance got a little enthusiastic on the mats, and then there was the broken nose last week when the perp had swung at him and Finn hadn't gotten out of the way in time, but he hadn't been admitted for either of those.

This morning was the first time he'd had to try for a moving target. He practiced at the outside shooting facility they called "the Farm" most days, and he thought he was getting quite good. Then they'd set the fake hostage situation up, expecting Finn to do better, and it had gone worse than the target practice.

Fucking enhanced. They thought they were so damned perfect.

"He's perfect," Gregory yelled back at Talon, and Finn started, shocked his boss agreed with him. He wasn't about to miss any compliments. "He can absolutely pass for seventeen," Gregory added, and Finn gaped in horror.

Seventeen? What had he missed?

"I-I'm twenty-four," he stuttered out, wondering how he'd managed to lose the entire thread of the conversation.

"And you're still the only one on the team who can go undercover in one of the new group homes."

Finn's jaw dropped as he stared at his boss. He was going undercover? Like real, honest to God... *undercover*? Finn's gaze dropped to the floor, and he breathed out slowly. He didn't think he would earn any respect by jumping to his feet, fist pumping and shouting his excitement, which he desperately wanted to do. This was his chance to be an active member of the team and earn some respect. He glanced cautiously at Talon, who was still arguing with Gregory.

"You obviously won't be going to Glynco tomorrow, but I will rearrange that when this op is done," Gregory continued, ignoring the outburst from Talon.

His team leader—*his boyfriend*—wasn't exactly showing a lot of faith in his abilities, and as the only regular human on the team, he had a lot to prove. Finn half smiled at his own words. *Regular.* An ordinary human being, unlike the rest of his teammates, who were all *enhanced*. Humans who had changed suddenly around adolescence and got kickass abilities, such as speaking every known language without ever having to learn them like Gael, or setting things on fire just because he thought about it like Eli.

"And there is one obvious problem," Sawyer piped up.

Oh good, Finn thought. *Only one?*

"He doesn't have a mark?" Gregory guessed correctly, and Sawyer shrugged.

Finn stared at Gregory and gave Sawyer grudging points for stating the obvious. The US had originally panicked when the first kids were born with superabilities because, while some of the abilities were quite cool, like the Superman strength Vance had, a lot of them were downright deadly, like Talon's. The public had calmed down mainly because the enhanced were so easily identifiable. They all had the mark Gregory mentioned, and despite various attempts, none of them could get rid of it.

"We know that marks cannot be covered successfully for more than a matter of minutes, but we can very easily add one."

"Add one?" Finn blurted out. "I didn't know that." He ignored the dark look Talon sent him.

"It's only something that's just occurred to us that might be useful," Gregory admitted.

"Yeah," drawled Eli, "because who the fuck would want one of these?"

Finn didn't know what to be more shocked at: that he was getting the chance to contribute, or that the normally silent Eli had spoken.

"We have a makeup artist who has been working with us," Gregory said, "and Finn is the only one on the team who can do this."

Finn nodded eagerly. He was desperate for the chance to actually do some work. "What would I be doing?"

"Not a damn thing," Talon snapped.

"Sit down, Talon, and let me explain," Gregory huffed out. Talon glowered at Finn as if daring him to reply, and Finn pointedly focused on Agent Gregory. "Let me go back a little. There are still no genetic markers that tell us if kids are likely to transform."

Finn knew this. If ever an older sibling transformed and the families agreed, the younger ones would be subject to a barrage of tests until after adolescence. There had been a few cases where a younger brother had transformed, but so far there was still no scientific reason for it.

"We actually know very few definites," Gregory said. "All enhanced children ever born are male, and the incidents are restricted to the US."

"And there's never going to be any baby Gaels running around," Gael interrupted, his scarred face twisting as the skin pulled awkwardly in humor.

"So there are benefits, then." Vance chuckled as Gael flipped him off, though he smiled at the teasing.

All enhanced were sterile, something the papers had made a meal of about fifteen years ago when the news headlined. Many people thought the knowledge that the enhanced couldn't reproduce made the rest of the population breathe a little easier because they weren't suddenly going to be outnumbered.

Gregory had made them go talk at a couple of high schools since they'd become celebrities after Gael saved a judge from being shot. Of all of them, Gael had been the most enthusiastic about going to the schools. It had to hurt that he would never have kids of his own.

Gael had been all over the news because he'd put his life on the line to protect a guy who was vocal in his dislike of the enhanced and thought they were a threat. The papers had loved it and eaten it up. Finn hadn't been to either school visit, since the first time he had been in the emergency room when Vance nearly flattened him, and the second had been because of his nose.

He winced. Maybe Talon had a point. His timing sucked anyway.

"What about Drew?" Talon asked.

Finn gaped. *Drew?* Talon thought Drew would do a better job than him? The knowledge settled heavily in his gut.

"Drew would never pass for seventeen," Gregory argued.

"That's true, boss," Vance agreed. Talon glowered. "How many other recruits get sent undercover after being given eight weeks training?"

Gregory sighed. "Do you remember one of the foster kids who disappeared last year—Dale Smith?"

Sawyer frowned. "Yes. We've never been able to find any trace. He has an older brother who turned eighteen in December and aged out of the system, but he hasn't had any contact either."

Gregory opened a file on his desk and passed around some photographs. Finn paled when he saw what they were. Tattered clothes lay in shreds on top of a skeleton. "The remains of what has been identified as Dale Smith's body were found last month buried in a shallow grave on the Westside Trail on the Atlanta BeltLine when they were clearing old tracks. We have been unable to identify a cause of death as of yet. This has been brought to our attention finally because yesterday police were called to a boarded-up house in old Port Tampa. The house was empty and showed no sign of being lived in, with the exception of the storeroom. That's where they found the body of another enhanced."

"Did we know him?" Talon asked.

Gregory shook his head. "We haven't been able to identify him. ME says a young adult and showed signs of physical abuse. He was emaciated, and the ME says he was basically starved to death. None of the previously registered occupants of the house are alive." He paused. "The cops have found signs of access, but the whole place is derelict. This is where we come in and how it may be related to Dale Smith." Gregory passed another photograph around.

Finn stared at the picture. It was Dale Smith, taken before he developed the mark, likely a school photograph.

"If you remember, Dale Smith was being attacked and beaten by his stepfather when the cops were called. His mom was a crack addict, and the so-called stepfather her pimp. Dale was removed for his own safety, but the car the cops were driving crashed. Both cops were knocked unconscious and Dale ran off. The cops had no memory of anything after leaving the house. No one has been able to locate Dale Smith."

"And apart from their enhanced status, how are they related?" Gael asked.

"Because the photograph of Dale was found in the storeroom with the other dead male."

Everyone was silent.

"Our focus right now is on the foster home and the missing kids. The past murders are being investigated separately. I want you to make sure no other kids vanish. You have complete access to any and all information on both victims, and you will be kept up-to-date with any new information." Finn risked a look at Talon, who had stopped objecting when Gregory passed the photographs around.

"You should know that the powers that be, who wanted the enhanced children taken away from their parents for the parents' safety, are now talking about removing the kids for *their* own safety."

"Very clever," Gael said sardonically.

"And as of this morning, we have another problem," Gregory said. "Two more kids have disappeared."

The room was silent again.

"Where from?" Talon ground out.

Gregory looked pointedly at Finn, and suddenly Finn didn't need telling. The home. They had disappeared from the foster home. Finn swallowed. It was shit, complete shit. One of the things they were all hoping for was that kids with the mark didn't get treated like baggage. They were only removed from the parents if the parents couldn't cope. And that was why they were all here. It wasn't as simple as just a specialized crime-fighting team. It was all about perception. The school visits were all about hope. Hope that the enhanced kids would be accepted and that they had a future.

Finn remembered Vance telling him about the day he'd woken up with the mark. *"And just like that, my life was over."*

Except it wasn't, and for all the kids, it was up to their team to make sure of that.

Chapter Two

FINN LOOKED around at the somber faces, and his eyes finally rested on Talon. Nolan Dakota wanted to take the enhanced children and had been prepared to kill to make his vision of enhanced dominating the world a reality. Finn still struggled with his memories of Dakota. Finn had woken more than once in a complete panic that he was being suffocated. The doc had said kindly it was to be expected after what he had gone through, when he had confided in her. And the whole incident in the warehouse had changed Talon. He had always been protective of Finn, but it was nearing the smothering point and Finn had no idea what to do.

The sad fact was that despite all the threats to the team and to Finn in particular, the greatest one to Finn had been Talon himself. Humans had let the kids down in a spectacularly cruel way. Enhanced kids were only taken from their parents if the parents didn't want them, and Finn had seen that personally. When he was eleven, his best friend, Adam, had transformed, and his parents had called the cops to take him away, even though the only thing Adam had done was wake up with the mark on his face.

"Who?" Finn asked, dragging himself back to the present.

"Jason and Samuel Harker. Jason's eleven and transformed a year ago. Samuel's seven and regular at the moment, as far as we know."

"How is this place not shut down?" Talon asked, exasperated.

"Because these are the first two children to disappear who were living there since the new manager started, and they weren't in the home when they vanished. They disappeared on a day's outing to the beach, and apart from these two going missing, the home has a good reputation."

"What about the kid Dakota took—Oliver Martinez?"

"Oliver was taken in the night by an enhanced who put out the external security cameras. The home had no way of securing against this, and if we make a fuss, then the authorities will simply lock away all the enhanced children and argue it is for their own safety. Oliver was persuaded to go with the man by being told he was going to his mom's, but it was a secret so his dad wouldn't know. It is a fine line between safety and freedom," Gregory added.

"Why has Samuel been taken?" Gael asked. "Surely kidnapping nonenhanced is pointless?"

"There are three possibilities. First, that it was an accident. Sam saw or heard something that he shouldn't.

All the kids had been accompanied by three staff members. Sam needed to go use the bathroom, and Jason took him. The public restrooms were barely a hundred yards behind them, and there was no reason to think Jason couldn't cope with Sam. Second, that Sam had been taken to force Jason's cooperation."

"And the third?" Sawyer asked.

Gregory glanced down, and Finn felt the reaction in his belly. This was gonna be bad. "That it was deliberate. That the perps are hoping Sam will transform because of his brother and are keeping him because of that."

"But where?" Sawyer exclaimed. "If that's true, then they're a lot better organized than we've been giving them credit for. Dakota kidnapping kids for some secret army was bad enough, but having the resources to take ones on the off chance they will transform?" He shook his head. "That takes money. A lot of money."

"Are we still watching Dakota?" Finn asked, proud of the way he sounded so matter-of-fact.

"Yes," Gregory said. "He's out on bail, and he has fancy lawyers who are dragging their feet, but he hasn't made any attempt to contact anyone."

"You know," Finn said. "We assumed that taking him out would stop this, but there are at least three kids who haven't been found, and now two more have been taken. What if Dakota was never in charge in the first place? What if he was just a figurehead, and we never stopped anything?"

The room was silent for a third time.

"I hate to say it, but the kid's right," Vance mumbled. He shot a look at Finn. "I mean, I didn't hate to say you were right… just that you are, er, right."

Finn offered a weak smile. He knew. Vance had been one of his supporters. Him and Gael. He narrowed his eyes at Talon, and Talon's bright blue gaze settled on him defiantly. Finn's gaze dropped to the tick in Talon's jaw. He was angry.

"This is particularly bad timing, as the papers have been full of the latest statement from Swann Industries."

Finn's ears pricked up immediately. He'd met Alan Swann, the CEO of Swann Industries, just over a month ago when they were both hostages during a bank robbery. Finn had just been there to see if he could get an advance on his wages, and Swann apparently was meeting the vice president of the bank since his company was expanding in the area. Swann had been a dick on TV afterward. Found out Finn had known Adam, who had gotten involved in helping the robbers until he'd done the right thing and ended up saving Finn's life. Swann had nearly been responsible for disbanding their team.

"What's he saying now?"

"He's offering to set up a boarding school for enhanced children. Completely free."

"Because he wants to get his hands on them," Vance said in disgust.

"Yes, but he has a lot of friends, and he's making a good argument. If he can convince enough people, it would empty the foster homes of enhanced children. With the current inadequate funding, his offer is being given serious consideration."

Sawyer gave Eli a bleak look.

"If he does everything by the book, it's unlikely anyone would stop him." Gregory heaved a sigh. "You should all know that Deputy Director Cohen is no longer in charge of the unit."

Gael inhaled sharply. "I didn't know Deputy Director Cohen *was* in charge of the unit," he said bluntly.

"Then you're more naive than I gave you credit for," Gregory snapped.

Finn didn't dare move. No one said a word. In eight weeks, he'd never seen Gregory be anything other than pleasant and totally unflappable. He shot a look at Talon, whose eyes were narrowed and staring at their boss. Something had gotten Gregory spooked.

"Talon, you are required to meet Assistant Director Devan Manning with me. It might not be until tomorrow."

"I've never heard of him," Vance said.

"*She* has just been given the new position after successfully leading a joint US-European terrorist task force." Gregory paused. "The good thing is, this unit is attracting a lot of attention. There is talk about setting up something similar in New York and San Diego." He smiled wryly. "You're blazing a trail, boys."

Finn stared. For the first time, he wondered just how many enhanced there actually were. It hadn't been something he'd ever wondered about, and without registration, he guessed it would be impossible to tell accurately.

"Do we have any idea how many enhanced there actually are?" Gael asked, as if he plucked the question from Finn's brain.

"School records are showing a little over three hundred at the moment, but that may be hopelessly inaccurate."

"Actually," Finn said, "there's a study going on trying to link geographical and climate factors. There is a high incidence in the Southeast."

Gael chuckled. "Something in the water?"

"There are also arguments suggesting that the presence of our team might be a cause." Finn smiled. He'd actually discussed it with Dr. Natalie, their team doctor, at his last physical. "Doc said it's likely that the popularity of the team is making more enhanced either move to what they consider a safer place or declare themselves more quickly."

"Well, that didn't help the boy in Tampa," Eli said flatly.

Gregory turned his attention back to Finn. "Finn, the makeup artist is going to meet you at a tattoo parlor called Inked on East Seventh Avenue. Ask for Maggie and be there at five. The team is going to spend the rest of the afternoon helping Finn with background. Familiarize yourselves with the content of these envelopes. It gives names and descriptions of all the kids and staff in the home. I need you back here at seven." Gregory passed a larger envelope to Finn. "Drew and Sawyer are going to escort you to the home. All your information is in there, including how to contact Sawyer."

Finn's gaze shot from the brown envelope Gregory had just given him, to Sawyer, then to Talon. Sawyer? Why was Sawyer his contact? Talon's mouth clamped firmly shut. He knew something.

"Sir?" Finn said as he glanced at Gregory.

"It's lunchtime," Gregory said, glancing at his watch and then pointedly at Finn as if he knew what Finn was going to ask. "Go through the packages together. Sawyer?"

Sawyer's cool green eyes glinted at Gregory.

"Explain to Finn why you are his contact. Your cover is in there as well." Gregory took one last look at all of them and headed for the door, but paused as Talon spoke.

"If these kids are in real danger, they need to be moved, or they need more than one agent in place protecting them."

More than Finn. Finn knew what Talon had meant. He didn't need to spell it out.

"There is no reason to suppose the kids are in any danger while they are actually in the home. This is merely a way of collecting information. Kids are much more likely to talk to other kids, and even as enhanced, you are still law enforcement, and that, as we know, makes a difference. Any more inside and we lose the chance to catch them," Gregory reminded him. "And we're not expecting Finn to have to go into combat, just keep his eyes and ears open."

Sawyer sniggered, and Finn nearly groaned as he felt the heat rise in his face.

"I'll leave you all to discuss it. I'll be in my office if you need me." He looked at Gael. "We will have your latest test results back by tomorrow. Call in first thing."

Gael nodded briefly and stood, picking up his mug, then wandered over for a refill.

Finn met Talon's worried look. Gael had to go for regular checks. Well, all the team, him included, had to have monthly physicals, but the flip side of Gael's ability was that the gene that caused his skin to become impenetrable was also responsible for skin cancer. All the docs were keeping a close eye on him.

Gregory paused with his hand on the door. "Finn, the case information has been sent as an encrypted file to your phone."

Finn nodded his thanks. They were all trying to make life a little easier for him, so he needn't worry about missing any details. He would just listen to it on audio.

"Oh, and I am asking Drew to be involved in this. We have no reason to suppose Sawyer will have any problems with his cover, but he is enhanced and as you know…." Gregory trailed off. "He has taken some personal time this afternoon, but I will make sure he is briefed and present later." The implication that Sawyer might not be treated with respect as his case worker because he was enhanced was obvious.

"I vote Betty's," Vance said in the silence after Gregory left, and Gael chuckled. Vance was still hung up on the thought of eating. Even though Finn's head was spinning in a million different directions, it was a good suggestion. He was starving, and the diner was one of his favorite places to eat. In fact, his belly rumbled again just thinking about it.

"Okay," Talon sighed, standing at the same time as there was a knock on the door. Everyone looked up as Harry, Betty's brother from the diner, put his head around the door and grinned.

"Someone rang for takeout?"

Vance practically vaulted to his feet, rubbing his hands in glee. "Awesome."

Harry walked into the room, carrying two huge coolers. "We got the order from a Tony Gregory. Must admit, it's the first time I've been escorted on a delivery by guys carrying. When we get an order from the cops on the Boulevard, we only get to see the front desk."

Vance took a cooler off him. "You're not missing anything down there." He chuckled. "Trust me." Of course, he would know. His whole family were cops.

Talon stood and got his cash out, but Harry waved him off. "Nah, Tony's taken care of it. I'll be by to get the coolers later."

Everyone looked in astonishment as Harry disappeared out the door.

Vance turned from the cooler and threw Finn two wrapped packets, and Finn groaned in appreciation. Still warm, and as he saw Talon unwrapping his pulled pork, he knew what was going to be in his—Betty's meatloaf melt, which he loved. It looked like Betty had sent their favorites since, with the team eating there at least two times a week, she knew what they all liked. Even Eli smiled in appreciation as he took a bite of his chicken parm.

Finn made short work of the sandwich. He loved that the escape from his home meant an escape from their boring food. Fries with whatever was usual for the day of the week.

"Ya know," Talon drawled, eyeing Finn licking his fingers and the speed in which he had polished it off. "Sawyer isn't gonna need to shoot you. You're just gonna die of a diabetic coma."

Finn grinned even as the others laughed. *As if Talon isn't always trying to feed me.* He was getting used to Talon's dry humor, and while he was always on the receiving end of whatever joke from the team, he would rather have Talon cracking jokes than shouting, or silence... which was when he knew the shit had really hit the fan. He shrugged and reached for his envelope.

"So, Sawyer... why you?" Finn was curious, and he'd been given carte blanche to ask questions, which was one of his favorite things to do. He still didn't know much about Sawyer, and nothing about Eli, even though he knew the rest of the team had seen his whole file.

Sawyer opened his own envelope and pulled out some papers. An ID badge fell out. "I'm gonna be a social worker's assistant," he said evenly.

"I guess they're thinking you can come and go without being seen?" Finn replied. Sawyer—as incredible as it sounded—could make himself invisible. Finn looked up when Sawyer didn't reply, and he swallowed. Sawyer was fingering the ID, his face pained. No one said a word.

"No, that's not why they want me," Sawyer said at last and looked at Finn. "It's my experience."

"With social work?" Finn asked, puzzled.

"No. Because I spent twelve years in and out of seven foster homes."

"Twelve years?" Finn echoed, hurting for the guy. "But—" He clamped his mouth shut. He knew Sawyer was twenty-four, the same age he was. He would've had to leave the system at eighteen, so that meant he was six when he entered. Too young to have developed a mark.

Sawyer smiled, but there was no humor in it. "Yeah, I was six when I got taken off the old man. I changed at ten." He stared unseeing out the window. "Funny thing was, I'd gotten a good placement. Lady was even talking about adoption. Then this happened." Sawyer gestured to his face. To the mark. "She freaked, and I went back into the group home that afternoon."

Finn didn't know what to say. No platitude would help and would be insulting.

VICTORIA SUE...

Victoria Sue fell in love with love stories as a child when she would hide away with her mom's library books and dream of the dashing hero coming to rescue her from math homework. She never mastered math but when she ran out of library books she decided to write her own. Loves reading and writing about gorgeous boys loving each other the best—especially with a paranormal twist—but always with a happy ending. Is an English northern lass currently serving twenty to life in Florida—unfortunately, she spends more time chained to her computer than on a beach.

Loves to hear from her readers and can be found most days lurking on Facebook where she doesn't need factor 1000 sun-cream to hide her freckles.

Facebook: www.facebook.com/victoriasueauthor
Twitter: @Vickysuewrites
Website: victoriasue.com

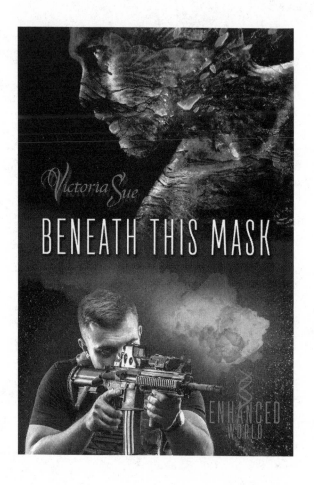

Enhanced World: Book Three

Gael Peterson has spent years hiding behind the enhanced abilities he wears like a mask, even though he is an important, confident member of the FBI's exclusive H.E.R.O. team. The hurt and betrayal of his mom's abandonment and his father's fists are secrets buried deep beneath the ugly scars on his face, and he doesn't trust Jake, his new regular human partner, with any of them. In a world where those with special abilities like Gael's are regarded as freaks and monsters, it won't be easy for him to rely on Jake to have his back, especially when the abilities of a vulnerable nonspeaking enhanced child make that child a murder suspect.

Tempers rise and loyalties are challenged, and when the serial killer targeting the enhanced finally sets his sights on Gael, not only will Gael have to trust Jake with his secrets, he might have to trust him to save his life.

www. dreamspinnerpress.com